Copyright Page

Self Published Authors Network

1369 n. Hampton rd #60

Desoto Texas 75115

Tel: 1-469-537-8905

Ordering information

Quantity Sales. Special discounts are available in quantity purchases by corporations, associations, networking groups. For details contact www.SelfPublishedAuthorsNetwork.com at the address above

Individual Sales. Self Publishing Investment Network publications are available online www.SelfPublishedAuthorsNetwork.com
as both a paperback and an ebook.

Includes biographical references and index

Contents

COOL NIGHTS

Introduction

I started writing Cool Nights as a hobby that grew into an obsession. Seven years ago while living in Denver, Colorado I was sitting in my living room writing lyrics to a song I planned on recording, when I got a rush of emotional creativity. Literally the movie and all its scenes rushed through my head as if I had seen it already. I instantly put my pen down and rushed to my computer to begin the creative process. I have never been trained on writing, none-the-less a script, but I embarked on this journey anyway.

First, let's get this understood. Cool Nights is not in any way shape, form or fashion a description of my life or anyone else from a nonfiction life. Desmond Coolwater is a character who can be defined by a great night in Denver. A great job where you're getting paid and living the life of one of the city's elite and well known.

Denver, Colorado is a metropolitan melting pot of diversity, fashion, food and entertainment. The skyline if viewed while driving into the city has been the backdrop for many artists and photographers pictures / portraits. The entrepreneurs in this city have ideas, dreams and visions like no others. They also have an uncanny knack for making it all happen here.

Every location in this fictional tale is real and I would highly recommend that you visit them when you come to Denver, Colorado. I love Denver and that love for the city moved me to write this romantic comedy. Let Cool Nights be your tourist map around the city. I hope that this funny, dramatic and sexy story moves you to come here and walk the 16th St. Mall. Go have dinner at Earls or tune into our famous trio at the radio station K.S. 107.5 because their morning show is the most hilarious show you'll hear!

Check out a Nuggets game or a Broncos game or a Rockies game. GO party in Lodo or in the Denver Tech area if you're looking for a more mature crowd.

In any case Denver, Colorado is the bomb and I've had a great time, anytime I've planned a night or day in the city!!

I SUCCEED WHERE YOU EXPECT ME TO FAIL,
BECAUSE I DON'T TAKE YOUR "no" SERIOUSLY...

-Keylend Wright-

A Cool Thank You

To my mother Cora Bristol who loves me unconditionally every day. Thank you for fostering my ever growing base of creativity. I can't imagine the amount of hair-brained schemes and ideas I've had over the years that you've had to listen too. I appreciate you for everything. I appreciate you never allowing me to give up. Even when I've failed horribly you manage to make a ribbon in the sky appear and I love you dearly for every time you directed me to take a nap when I was frustrated, hurt, feeling down on myself and throwing a pity party. Thank you.

R.I.H Cora Lee Mitchell…. My grandmother, my Big Mamma and my heart!! I miss you EVERY DAY and I mean that. There is not a day that goes past without you in my thoughts in some shape form or fashion. Thank you for all the undying love, the lessons, the guidance, the unconditional love, the food, the STRENGTH and my identity. You taught me so many things that ring true today that it would take a whole other book just to list those lessons in detail. I love you with all my heart and I hope you know that. I hope you see me down here being the man that you helped my mother raise me to be. I pray I make you proud!!

Thank you to my Grandfather Leroy Bristol, Sr. I'm a hustler. I'm creative with my thought processes on how to make money. I'm resourceful and I know I get that from you naturally. I'm an Entrepreneur and I know you would be proud of me…. R.I. H.

Thank you to my Grandfather Ronnie Mitchell. You were stern and loving in your own way. You seemed grouchy most days, but I know that is because you worked hard EVERY DAY and you took care of our family of women EVERY DAY. I love and appreciate you. I work hard EVERY DAY because of the lessons I learned from you by example. You were a man's man with the weight of responsibility and the world on your shoulders and you carried every pound of it on those shoulders like the GIANT you were. I hope to be the same kind of giant as you. Thank you and I love you from the bottom of my heart. Your Grandson.

To my dearest Aunt Natalie whom I love with all my heart. You invested in me on a venture some time ago and I lost the money due to inexperience. I write this with tears and laughter in my eyes because I thank you so so much. You don't know how much that meant to me. Thank you for believing in me my whole life. Instead of asking me to pay you back the amount you loaned me, all you asked for was the $14 it took to overnight it to me. My God… This is for you!

Thank you Aunt Scoobie for constantly and consistently seeking out the right connections for your nephew to reach out to in my never ending journey for success! Thank you with all my heart. Thank you Aunt Linda, Aunt Sandy and Aunt Ronnette for being my guardian angels and leading this little boy through the wild. I appreciate and love you. Thank you Aunt Renee…. thank you for the love, the knowledge and wisdom. I understand the difference between the two. Having knowledge of something doesn't mean that you are smart. It just means that you should know better. Being wise means you've learned a valuable lesson which you apply every day. Wisdom is always the goal… always. Work smarter and not harder. Thank you for the big red dictionary you supplied me with in order to turn my knowledge into wisdom. I'm listening even when you think I'm not. Thank you Uncle Leroy for being a father figure to me and showing me what a man could be when he follows God. I love you for all the guidance. Thank you.

Thank you to my sister Donna for taking this little boy in with you and the 5 children you already had and showing me endless and unconditional love every day. You have been a symbol of strength and toughness for me. I am forever your little brother, that little boy who said "You won't whoop me" lol and you did in order to make me understand that I will follow the rules and behave. I love you and thank you. Thank you to the entire Mease family for being my family and having my back no matter what. Ride or die, sink or swim.

Dad… it took us a while to get started as father and son, but we are full fledged partners. I know who I am and what kind of man I am. I understand where my cool, calm demeanor comes from. I know and understand my abilities better as a man now because of you. I thank you for all that you now are to me and you have my undying love forever. Your son.

R.I.H. Uncle Squeaky, Uncle Big Boy and Uncle Benny Boy. You 3 fellas showed me what cool is and what it looked like throughout my life. Some of the coolest and smoothest men I know. A Wright can be wrong sometimes, but a Wright is always a Wright all of the time. I understand that. I will always love you guys and my memories of you never fade.

Thank you to Susan Horn and In Harmony for the outstanding photo shoot she made happen. The photos of the ladies and Mr. Shannon Mosley was flawless. You made sure that every aspect of the shoot was on point and I am so appreciative of your friendship and professionalism. Thank you!

R.I.H. To Mr. Leo Frohman although you are gone now, I have not forgotten you for everything you did to make my dreams materialize back in 2006. I will never forget you! Thank you.

Thank you to my Godbrother Javon Howard …..aka…….Mr. Jaize Van Crump. I love you bro and know that. No matter what in life happens and the distance doesn't matter. It's still H.O.O.D.M.A.D.E. for life. **H**ustling **O**ver **O**bstacles **D**aily **M**aking **A**ll **D**ollars **E**qual.

Mr. Johnny Mack from S.P.Y.O.B. thank you! Thank you. Thank you. You're more than just my publisher. You are my life coach and I'm riding with you my friend. Big things to come!!

To all my family and friends that have helped me throughout my life… thank you. There is just too many of you crazy people to name, so I just want to say I love you and when I say I love you know that, believe that I appreciate each and every one of you for what you have done for me throughout my life and words cannot express my deepest hearts lack of words.

To Louise. Thank you for all of your love, understanding and support. I know it has not been easy dealing with me and our kids at the same time, but I just want you to know, I want everyone else who reads this book to know that I appreciate you and love you! Thank you.

To my babies... Dad loves you with all my heart... all of it. I want you to reach for the stars, reach for another galaxy, reach for whatever you set your eyes on. It can be achieved if you just try. And hell... if you just land on the moon then at least you still have a better view than the rest of the people who never tried or put forth the effort to explore successful possibilities. Daddy loves you!!

SHANNON MOSLEY.... My brother words cannot explain how deeply humbled and thankful I am to you for accepting my request to be Desmond Coolwater. I came out to L.A. trying to shop this as a script and you allowed me into your home for a few days as well as drove me around Los Angeles on your own gas and didn't ask me for a dime. I know that may sound small to you but to me... that was the whole trip bro. I thank you for everything that you have done to make this book happen and I promise to push this thing until somebody hear me. Please don't ever give up your dreams and ambitions. I don't think people understand how hard you work for everything that you get the opportunity to do. You are the symbol and definition of grind and perseverance. You've got a friend, a brother, a supporter and fan from me. You're a big deal and the world will know it..... soon!!

Thank you Madame Q you are exquisite and I appreciate you being here to help make this project look fabulous. Made my cover look grown and sophisticated!! I appreciate it from the bottom of my heart. Thank you. Big shout out and thank you to Mr. Markeane Smith also for giving me direction, motivation and being a constant source of inspiration. You and I are about to move mountains my brother..... Nightwatch Entertainment is in the building.

Thank you Kymara Woolbright for gracing the cover of my book and making it look young, sexy and fun! The element I was looking for you took and ran with it. Thank you for being open to my vision and for that I will forever appreciate you. You can always call upon me. I got you. Thank you!!!

I would also like to say thank you to everyone that supports Cool Nights. The mere fact that I could write this and get away with selling it blows me away. I am blessed to have a strong support system with my family and friends. I have been blessed to be around some true go getters, hustlers, and people who transcend the average level of understanding. I am truly inspired daily by the people in my life in some shape, form or fashion and I thank God for everyone of you out there that I'm talking about.

There is only one thing that makes a dream impossible
to achieve.... The fear of failure!
-Keylend Wright

Dedication

This cool story is dedicated to everyone who supports me or has supported me in the past. I hope you enjoy!

COOL NIGHTS

Chapter 1 GOOD MORNING

The atmosphere is hot, humid and busy with men and women mingling. Some patrons are laughing and some are sipping their drinks. The whole crowd's body language gives off heat exuding the very essence of grown and sexy. Between the crowd of dancers and couples grinding you see a V.I.P. table occupied by two men, three women flirting, joking, and smiling promiscuously, while pouring drinks. The streets are empty. It's after 3:00 a.m. with the occasional couples still walking to their cars.

A gentleman and a beautiful young lady are kissing vigorously, fondling each other and laughing as they shove themselves into a taxicab, yelling out the address as they continue the sex charades in the back of the taxi down the street to their destination. Outside the sun is coming up and the couple exits the cab and walk up the stairs to the door of a residence, where the gentleman pulls out his keys while swerving back and forth with the female in the other arm still kissing on his neck.

Once inside the apartment the couple proceeds to grabbing and ravaging at each other while getting undressed. The woman gets undressed quicker and taunts him as she seductively runs towards the stairs and up to the bedroom. He gives chase as he fights to get undressed. There are screams and giggles coming from the room as the two bring an amazing end to a fantastic night.

My name is Desmond Coolwater and most of my nights normally start and end like this. Five star restaurants, V.I.P. treatment, bottles, models, sex and prestige. I am a woman's wet dream. There's nothing like doing what you want, how you want and when you want. Now… the dictionary defines SUCCESS as: The achievement of something desired, planned, or attempted or the gaining of fame or prosperity, but I define it by being able to write a check that your ass can really cash. This is the life…!!!

A perfect view of the mountains peer over the interstates

southbound lanes in Denver, Colorado as the morning radio show narrates the flow of traffic and everyone's preparation for the day. The alarm goes off and Desmond opens his eyes to find the beautiful fair skinned woman that he had brought home had left and the loud sounds of the radio on the nightstand is getting on his nerves. He smacks the clock's off button and rolls out of bed to the bathroom and begins his grooming process. Desmond is suited and booted in his tailor made suit heading out the door when his phone rings and he answers it.

"This is Des...what's up?"

A very smooth and professional voice on the other end speaks. It's his boss, William Dean Elmhurst. William Dean Elmhurst is the CEO and OWNER of FLY MAGAZINE where Desmond works as the head entertainment and advertising editor. A job he landed right out of college.

"This is your boss and I sure hope you got good news from our clients at last nights business meeting?"

Desmond starts to recall how his night went with the sexy representatives from Coors Light. "Mr. Elmhurst, the meeting went fantastic. I had the reps eating out of my hands by the time we got to the end of the meeting!" Desmond started to have flashbacks of the wild time he and the beautiful Coor's reps had after the meeting was over. Mr. Elmhurst chuckles... "I bet you did. I expect the full story when you get into the office young man." Desmond replies, "Yes sir, will do... see ya when I get to the office."

"Oh and Desmond?" Desmond replies "Yes sir?"

"Good job!" Mr. Elmhurst says.

"Thank you, Mr. Elmhurst." Desmond hangs up with Mr. Elmhurst and continues his journey to the light rail station with his bag in tow headed to meet his friend Henry at the gym for their morning workout. Desmond reaches the light rail just in time before it leaves the station. He is sitting on the light rail riding to his stop when he looks down the aisle to see this beautiful, fair skinned woman sitting on the other end. He stares at her for what seems to be five minutes, but was only a moment's time. The beautiful stranger meets Desmond's eye contact with a contagious smile and then turns her head back towards the window. With only two stops left before he needs to exit the train Desmond decides to go introduce himself. "Hello!" he says to the beautiful woman.

"Hi! she says as she smiles." Desmond points to the open seat and says "Do you mind if I sit here?"

"Not at all… it's a free country." replies Sincere Desmond and the young lady exchange smiles as he sits down and introduces himself. "My name is Desmond. What is your name?"

"My name is Sincere… Sincere Bouvea!"

"Well Ms. Bouvea, it's my pleasure…I was sitting down there as you could see and could not help, but notice that you were the most beautiful woman on this train! I had to come say hello to you! I mean your look is amazing! Are you a model?" Sincere smiles.... "Uh? No, I'm not a model. Does every beautiful woman you see have to be a model or some object of a man's carnal pleasure because of her physical features? Or will you Mr. Desmond shock me and tell me that you are actually here talking to me because you are interested in my intellectual thoughts and frame of mind?"

Desmond laughs sarcastically…"Well seeing as how I approached you hoping for more than just a beautiful smile, I must say that I am rather intrigued by your rhetoric and over abundance of confident tone. I'd like to take you out to dinner or coffee so I can hear more?" Desmond asks…

Sincere replies "I suppose since you seem to be quite the gentleman that it would be alright to have a martini with you at least." Desmond smiles. "Here is my business card. Give me a call and we will work out the details." Sincere hands Desmond her business card. Desmond takes the card says "Sounds great! This is my stop and I'm headed to the gym before work, but how about I give you a call this evening?" "Well I'll be at work late, but sure give me a call. I'll probably need a break by then." Sincere says.

"Great! It was a pleasure to meet you and I look forward to dinner." Desmond says in an excited tone. "I can't wait! Call me! Bye!" Desmond goes to shake her hand and she extends her hand in true lady-like fashion. Desmond takes the opportunity to kiss her hand and make one of the smoothest exits written in the player's handbook of exits! He waves goodbye to Ms. Sincere Bouvea as he steps off the train and heads towards the steps to the exit.

CHAPTER 2 AT THE GYM WITH HENRY

The sounds of weight room equipment are slamming back and forth against each other and the constant running sound of treadmills are grinding in the background. Desmond is spotting his friend Henry with his bench press repetitions, while telling Henry what transpired at his business meeting. Henry is in the middle of doing his repetition on the bench and speaking to Desmond.

"Your job has got to be the best forms of employment that I know of! I mean how many single, young men have a job that involves them meeting beautiful, powerful, intelligent, and sophisticated women and taking them out on the company's dime?"

Henry finishes his rep and Desmond takes his place on the bench press. "You're starting to sound a tad bit bitter about that Mr. Henry?" Desmond said. Henry replies with a sarcastic laugh. "Ha ha ha ha… no! Bitter? Not at all! I just find it weird how only a few of you lucky bastards exist! While the rest of us male gendered HOMO-SAPIENS seem to be stuck in a perpetual frigid winter season of females telling us NO! HOW DO YOU DO IT?" Desmond Answers "It's not the job that makes the ladies love me man. It's my class A swagger that keeps them interested. Coolwater is a sexy brand! That the ladies love!"

"Yeah right! You need to get out of that King Dez mind frame. One day you are going to meet your match and she is going to have you feeling real "SENSITIVE" like RALPH TRESVANT." Desmond is doing his rep on the bench press while he delivers his reply.

"Uh? No, I don't think so... my salty friend." Desmond responds in an overly confident tone. "I am unsinkable, undefeatable, unmovable and the ultimate authority in women affairs. They love me and I can't wipe it off me man. Give me some love?" Desmond completes his repetitions, sits up and reaches his hand out to get some dap, but Charles leaves him hanging and walks away. Desmond says: “Oh...that’s cold man...real cold!”

Desmond gets to work, enters the doors to Fly Magazine where there are framed pictures of each magazine cover since the companies inception into the paper media world. The hallway is busy like I-25 traffic during lunch time and Desmond swerves and maneuvers thru them with a Ferrari like swagger, as the above hallway speakers are tuned into 107.5 Denver’s premier radio station. Desmond is stopped by Stacey, the office administrative assistant right before he goes into the main doors.

“Hey Desmond! I hear you landed the Coors deal last night...or should I say landed on the Coors DEAL last night!?” Stacey asks inquisitively.

“Ha ha ha” he laughs sarcastically “Yes, I did actually and brought home the whole account!”
“I bet you did young man.” Implies Stacey. Stacey smiles at Desmond as she passes and pats him on the back with a good job gesture as she heads out to lunch. Desmond has a look of disbelief as he watches the beautiful older woman walk away smiling and he walks into the entrance.

Desmond makes it to his desk and is just about to sit down when he is interrupted abruptly by Cindy McMann, the office intern who has a secret crush on Desmond, but is too young and not the style of woman that Desmond would pursue. Cindy is the hyperactive cheerleader type kind of female with very high energy that talks very fast.
Just as Desmond sits down is when Cindy approaches him and startles him “Hey Dessie!”

Desmond jumps a little when Cindy calls his name. “Hello Cindy and the name is Desmond…”

Desmond corrects her abbreviation of his name but she ignores his correction and continues to speak as if he didn't say anything.

“Yeah so...I heard that you landed the Coors deal?”

“Uh… yeah I did and it was…” She interrupts him as if she didn’t hear a word he said and continues talking at the speed of light! “Oh Good! I just knew you would land that deal! You are so persuasive and smooth Desmond and I just think you are the…”

Desmond swirling stuck dead in the middle of Cindy’s whirlwind of speed talking and right as he is about to interrupt, Mr. Elmhurst walks up and instructs Cindy to take the papers from his hand and go make copies. “Excuse me? Cindy can I have you make copies of these and sit them on my desk please?

“Yes, sir… Mr. Elmhurst.” Cindy says. “Thank you young lady.” Cindy walks away in a burst of energy. Just as quick as she appeared! Mr. Elmhurst giggles…"She’s a firecracker, isn’t she?”

“Uh… yeah” Desmond nods sarcastically. “Real firecracker! If you hadn’t walked up, she would have hit warp speed on me!” Mr. Elmhurst agrees and then tells Desmond “Come to my office son so we can go over last night.” Mr. Elmhurst leads and Desmond follows him into his office where Mr. Elmhurst takes his jacket off, goes behind the desk, pulls out a cigar and cuts the end off. He then leans back into his seat and gives Desmond the green light to inform him of his night.

“Okay Dez lay the story on me...?” Desmond begins to explain how the night transpired. “So first I have them meet me at THE LOFT WINE BAR over in the DENVER TECH AREA for wine tasting and orderves.” Mr. Elmhurst asks inquisitively. “The Loft Wine Bar?” Desmond reads Mr. Elmhurst's curiosity about the wine bar and finishes his inquiry. “...is a moderately small yet classy new establishment! I promise! Come on boss!? It’s me, Desmond!” Mr. Elmhurst agrees and continues to follow the story.

“Yeah-yeah…. okay! Okay! You're right… what was I thinking!? Carry on with the story?”

Desmond continues… "So it was the head of marketing who was this fox with green eyes dressed to impress! She also brought 2 other reps with her who were your typical office babes who just wanted to get out for the night."

Mr. Elmhurst sits in his seat with a skeptical look on his face, but continues to listen intently. "Mmm Hmm… so what did you spend from the expense account?" Desmond replies "Well…!"

Mr. Elmhurst is starting to get impatient. "Well what Desmond? How much?" Desmond answers "I only spent $385 for the VIP bottle of wine and appetizers."

Mr. Elmhurst sits up in his seat after Desmonds answer and says… "You spent $400 for a damn bottle of wine and some freaking finger food DESMOND!?" Desmond comebacks at Mr. Elmhurst with the most important part of the recent nights events.
"Yes! But I also got them to commit to a years worth of promo material, model participation at all events hosted by us and last, but not least a whopping $15,000 plus dollars in addition to the $50,000 they are already committing to!"

"Why are they committing an additional $15,000?" Mr. Elmhurst asks. "For the exclusive services of Desmond Coolwater…" Mr. Elmhurst sits back in his chair and calmly takes a puff of his cigar. "What services is that pray tell?"

Desmond starts to smile as he explains everything that Coors has agreed too. "Well they want me to personally oversee all of their company promotional parties, events and also use me as a liaison to their advertising department in conjunction with Fly Mag's promotional seasons so they can stay on top of every change in trend." "Hmmmm… well you've really outdone yourself this time Mr. Coolwater!"

Desmond smiles as is if he knew Mr. Elmhurst would approve of his business moves.

"I suppose you think you should have a raise or something huh?" Desmond replies "Well actually?"

Desmond sits up in his chair and looks Mr. Elmhurst in the eye while he straightens his blazer and positions himself to deliver the proposal "I'm thinking I could get your desk and say… maybe a seat on the Fly Magazine partner mothership?"

Mr. Elmhurst sits back in his seat with a thought provoking smile while Desmond tries to play it cool watching Mr. Elmhurst's expressions and reply. "Well Desmond you know there is no one under 40 years of age on that board young man. However, we have spoken about it and we all admire your drive, motivation and ambition. I can tell you that this particular discussion has taken place many times."

Desmond looks at Mr. Elmhurst with the enthusiasm of a five year old boy on Christmas and says...

"Yes!? And what? What? What?"

Mr. Elmhurst laughs. "Whoa, whoa, whoa… slow down son let's get you in this seat first and then talk partnership from there young buck!" Mr. Elmhurst extends his hand to Desmond and Desmond shakes it firmly and says "That's a Deal!" Mr. Elmhurst sits back in his seat once more. "Now… Get out of here and go make me some more money!"

Desmond smiles like $100 bucks, stands up, salutes like a soldier and walks out the office.

COOL NIGHTS

CHAPTER 3 MEETING AT THE NIGHTCLUB

Outside Market 21 nightclub the view of Denver is picturesque as ever today and the KS 107.5 lunch radio show is blaring in the taxi ride. Desmond is riding with his co-worker/assistant James Wright to a lunch meeting with local rap artist Innerstate Ike / Elite Ent. at Market 21 night club. Ike is the hottest artist representing the state and has a body of work like no other from mixtapes and albums to energy drinks and clothing without a major record deal. Desmond is meeting with him to get him to open up and give a story to his reporter for the month.

Inside Market 21 during the day, lunch is being served and the meeting is taking place. Desmond walks in. Ike is sitting at the table surrounded by a few other artists and crew from Elite Ent. Desmond is speaking to James as they walk in "Damn they look mean than a mutha fucka... right?!" James pumps his chest up as he walks with Desmond and says… "I ain't scared of they ass. Open up a can "Whassssaaaaa-whoop ass."

James makes a loud karate noise and does a kung-fu kick as they walk up and then Desmond grabs him after he does that and gives a sarcastic laugh and then the smile fades away as he whispers close to James ear in a serious tone…"it doesn't matter if YOU ain't scared of them James! Do you see the look on there face?! Does it really look like they care what you think? They will rape you and shoot me!?"

James stops Desmond with his arm across his chest for a moment. He is shocked that Desmond would imply that he would get molested instead of getting shot. "Wait a minute? Why I gotta get raped? Why can't I get shot?" He says with a frustrated tone.

Desmond begins to walk again as he talks with James. "Because you look more girly and I refuse to get raped!" James replies with: "Man that's some bull SHHhhhhhh…" Desmond interrupts James as he is speaking because they are at the table. "Aaaahhh… Ike what's up my man! I've been hearing alot about you! It's a pleasure to finally meet the man, versus just hearing ya music!" Desmond reaches his hand out to shake his hand, but he doesn't move a muscle or crack a smile. "Okay!? Well… lets get down to business then."

Desmond takes a seat at the table and James goes to grab a seat, but Ike nods his head towards him and two of the biggest dudes stand up, grab James and drag him out of the club kicking and yelling. They stand in front of the door after throwing him out with their arms crossed staring down at James as he talks shit. "Get yo...(tussling)... get ya'll...(tussling)... Get ya'll hands off of me!

Ya'll dont scare me, big overgrown Florida Evans looking mutha fuckas… Ya momma's Yeti and ya grandma-ma's a pigmy!" James then tries to run past them and they grab him and throw him in the dumpster across the alley. You can hear him cursing them out and still talking shit as they walk away...

Meanwhile, back inside Market 21 the look on Desmond's face is utter-disbelief as he watched James get carried out the backdoor. He then turns back around in the chair and begins to talk. Ike and his partners don't crack a smile or even blink. "Sooooo?! Ike… like I was saying it's a pleasure to meet you my man. The Hood/the streets are talking and FLY MAG is listening. We want your story?!" Ike replies…"No!"

Desmond repeats what Ike said. "NO?" Ike replies… "Nah, what's in it for me? What do I really have to gain by being in your wack-ass mag huh? I got the streets, I got shows, I got my own vitamin water! All of this without a deal...so you tell me? What can you do for me?" Desmond is stumped momentarily and then it hits him...(inner thought "**PERFECT**")

"Uh...EXPOSURE! Exposure is what you get. Exposure for you, exposure for the hood, for your company and sports drink! Exposure to the rest of the city! See this interview isn't really for YOU...(pause)...nah?!" Desmond gets excited and stands up, but one of Ike's people standing behind him puts his hand on his shoulder and calmly pushes him back down in the seat as if saying calm down and sit down.

Desmond continues pitching his idea to Ike as he sits there watching him. "This interview is for the city! It's for the people that call this place home and are proud of it! It's for the people that see you and never feel like they get to know the man behind the music!? Behind all the hype from the clubs and sports drink biz! This interview is for the people my man… Not you! For the people!

Desmond finishes his acceptance speech with his punchline, takes a deep breath and looks across the table at Ike like a criminal in front of a judge pleading his case? "Hmph!? Indeed… you make a good case. Maybe you aren't so spongebob squarepants like I thought you were at first. Let me think about it?" Ikes bodyguard gives Desmond the nod to beat it!

"Well...!? Ok...... then? I guess I'll just leave now… and uhhh!? Wait for you to call… me?" Desmond gets up and starts to walk away and Ike says "A Coolwater?" Desmond responds…"Yeah what's up...?" Desmond turns around. "I'll do the interview, but on one condition?" Desmond listens intently and then says "What's that?" Ike responds with..."You do the interview!" Desmond cracks a devious smile, walks back over to the table and attempts to shake Ike's hand and this time he shakes his hand!

Meanwhile, outside the club James is pissed off still talking shit about being thrown out of the meeting, while Desmond is laughing and trying to hail a cab. "Desmond that was fucked up! Why'd you let them kick me out like that?" Desmond is standing there smiling without a conscious and says "You were the one that came in there with all that noise remember? Whasaaaaaaa…"

Desmond mimics what James was saying as they walked into the meeting. "That's probably why they did that to you. Who do you think you are BRUCE LEROY!? Whaaassaaa...catches bullets with his teeth? Catches bullets with his teeth? Nigga please!" Desmond laughs as he quotes a line from the famous Berry Gordy movie..."**The Last Dragon**" James looks over at Desmond and says "Whatever man! I still would have kicked their ass! They weren't all that tough. I'm from the hood!"

Desmond glances over at James with a curious sarcastic look and says "What hood?" James replies with "I'm from 42nd and whoop a niggz ass avenue and that's right around the corner from spank ya momma and slap yo daddy blvd. 21st and leave ya granny in the middle of the street instead of walking her all the way across! That's Where I'm from! You can Google me sucka! A big picture of me socking a nigga in the jaw will be right under the definition! You can check my dental record!"

Desmond bursts out into an hysterical laugh "Shut up man! You stupid!" They both laugh and continue cracking jokes while they stand there patiently waiting on a taxi.

Chapter 4 BACK AT FLY MAGAZINE OFFICES

Desmond is at his desk listening to his ipod and typing up his meeting notes from the Coors meeting and some ideas for helping them advertise/promote in the magazine when Stacey comes up to his desk with a stunning tall Caramel skin colored woman named Lyriq Moore.

Stacey kicks his desk and says "DESMOND?? Desmond answers back with a startled "Hey! What the...?" Stacey interrupts Desmond before he can get out the rest of his sentence.

"DESMOND... I would like to introduce you too Lyriq Moore." Desmond extends his hand out to shake Lyriq's. "Well hello…" Desmond says in a mesmerized tone. Desmond stands to meet this stunning lady.

Lyriq reaches her hand out and shakes Desmonds hand while responding with "Hello Desmond! I've heard a lot about you sir." Desmond is taken back by what she said. "You've heard about me? Hmmm… I'm sure it was good!" Lyriq smiles with a very sexy, yet sarcastic expression on her face and says "Define good and where and what situation to apply the meaning of… good?"

Stacey interrupts the conversation politely finishing the introduction. "Lyriq was hired by the board as your counterpart to oversee and make sure that the feminine side of each issue was addressed from here on out."

Desmond is put off by this revelation and says "What? What do you mean as my counterpart? Can I speak with you for a moment? Excuse us Lyriq."

Desmond takes Stacey to the side and says "What do you mean the board hired her? I just spoke with Mr. Elmhurst this morning and he didn't say anything about this?"

Stacey answers Desmond "Mr. Elmhurst didn't have to say anything about this to you. He is but one person of many on that board and they voted her in to help you with keeping the magazine gender balanced. What? You afraid of a little friendly competition Mr. Coolwater?" Desmond smirks and says "Competition? What competition? I'm Desmond Coolwater… I got this!"

They both walk back over to Lyriq and Desmond extends his hand to shake hers. "Welcome to Fly Magazine! I look forward to working with you!"

Lyriq gives fake smile and says… I'm sure." Stacey looks at Lyriq. "Okay Lyriq, lets go see where we'll be sitting you. Bye Desmond." Desmond nods his head and says "Adios ladies!" Both women walk away. Desmond sits down on his desk top, but is zeroed in on Ms. Moore's walk with an irritated yet, curious sexy stare on her walk. Just at that time she looks back and smiles with a devilish grin back at him.

Desmond shakes his head, then decides to continue with his work in the conference room, so he grabs his bag and heads there. He is making some calls, closing up some business proposals for Coors, and a few other advertising loose ends. As he paces back and forth with his headset on looking out the window at the view of the mountains from Fly offices.

Desmond is speaking with Vanessa the Coors representative and still walking back and forth. "Okay, Vanessa so what I'm thinking for your ad is a photo shoot in the mountains next week, say Tuesday? Is that too soon? Vanessa replies intently with "No, no, no, not at all. What else do you have for me?"

Desmond continues "Well what I was wanting to do is take some shots near some hot springs. Have some young adult men and women relaxing in the spring, while a few are standing outside of the spring with just a white robe on or maybe even a white fir?" Vanessa adds in her thoughts as well…"If we can add some Coors products in there we are Golden!" Desmond responds "But of course! What would be a Coors shoot without the Coors product? Right?!" Vanessa pauses for a moment and then says "I like it! I think that-that would be very sexy and somewhat sophisticated. Soft yet very firm in the point we are trying to get across. You ARE GOOD Desmond!"

Desmond replies in a confident yet flirtatious tone "You have no idea!" He smiles a boyish grin and then continues with "But you'll see…" As Desmond says that he turns towards the glass windows of the hallway only to find that Lyriq is seductively staring him down as she makes her way past the glass windows with some board members towards the exit.

They both smile at each other and Desmond does the presidential wave while she continues her catwalk down to the exit. As Lyriq walks past he whispers to himself, but loud enough for Vanessa to hear him: "Kiss Ass!" Vanessa hears him and says "Excuse me Desmond" Desmond puts his thoughts back together and apologizes to Vanessa. "Nothing! I was speaking to a coworker of mine." Vanessa laughs and says "Well geez!"

Desmond covers his blunder up well with a smooth explanation and apology. "I'm Sorry about that. So I will have my assistant James get back to you Thursday with the rest of the plan and to finalize the photo shoot. Sound good?" Vanessa responds happily. "Sounds good Desmond, I look forward to working with you again!" Desmond replies with a very smooth "The pleasure is all mine." Vanessa giggles and says "Actually the pleasure was all mine. We will have to get together again sometime!"

"Agreed! You have a great evening!" Desmond says. Vanessa says goodbye "Chow!" Desmond stares off into the mountain scenic view, he decides to call Ms. Sincere Bouvea for evening martinis. He pulls her business card out and dials the number. The phone rings 4 times… Sincere's voicemail comes on "Hello! You have reached Sincere Bouvea and I'm not available at the moment, but if you leave a detailed message with your name, number and reason for calling I will gladly call you back at my earliest convenience… Thank you!.. Beep!"

Desmond leaves his voicemail. "Hello Ms. Bouvea, this is Desmond Coolwater and I just wanted to call and maybe invite you to The Mint tonight for a drink. Maybe a glass of wine or two? The Mint is located downtown by…" Sincere's automated voicemail cuts Desmond off before he can complete his message: "Beeeeeeepppppppp! If you are hearing this then your message is too long...bye!" Desmond looks at the phone and says "Shit! Oh well…"

He hangs up the phone, picks up his coat and heads out of the office for the evening. Outside the sun is setting on downtown Denver and as it goes over the mountains you're able to see a crystal clear view. All the business lights are visible from the interstate.

The traffic is jam packed heading north and south this evening and Desmond is taking a taxi to THE MINT to have a few drinks before he goes home to call it a night. The taxi pulls in front of Mint and Desmond pays the driver and exits the taxi curbside right in front of Mint. He enters MINT...

Chapter 5 MINT NIGHTCLUB

Inside Mint is calm, with the sounds of smooth jazz playing through the bar speakers. He walks up to the bar where Vincent an older gentleman with a full head of white hair, a freshly shaved face and suave smile is serving drinks. Desmond and the bartender greet each other. "Vince! Hows it going sir?" Vincent the owner is behind the bar stocking the bar says "Hey Dessi, what's going on my friend?"

"Not much. Had a long interesting day!" Desmond said. "Yeah, well nobody said it was easy being an Alpha male." Vincent replies as he continues to restock the bar area and moves glasses to their proper places. Desmond agrees with Vincent as he sets his bag down, takes his coat off and sits it around the back of his chair. "Ain't that the truth... Hey let me get a Heineken and a shot of Grey Goose Vodka please!"

Vincent reaches into the mini-fridge to grab the bottle of Heineken as he walks towards Desmond. He pulls out a glass to pour the beer into and then asks Desmond: "Want a glass or keep it in the bottle??

"Keep it in the bottle. It's all in glass anyway right?" Desmond said. Vincent opens the bottle and places it on a napkin by Desmond. "A bit of German sophistication with a splash of Russian octane huh?! What a way to fuel your engine Desmond." Vincent pokes fun at Desmond and smiles. "Yeah, well I need something to help me relax and go to sleep. I can never sleep." Desmond replies. Vincent is still moving back and forth behind the bar while speaking to Desmond. "Gotta stop burning so much midnight oil Dessie. Give the love oven a rest for a while."

"Maybe you're right?!" Desmond responds. They both look at each other, smile, and say in unison
"NAAaaaaaaaaaaaahhh!"

They both chuckle a bit and share a shot of vodka as the evening pursues and talk more. The background music takes the place of conversation as Desmond and Vincent talk over drinks. Time passes away as Desmond and Vincent talk. Everyone else in the bar are moving about having a good time. It's a mid week day so there are not very many people around at the moment. The conversation continues with Desmond deciding to call it night.

"Well Vince, I've had enough of you for tonight my friend. I was supposed to have some better looking company, but I couldn't get in touch with her. Left half a message on her VM so I don't really think she'll be showing up!" Desmond said.

Just as Desmond tells Vincent about his day and the company he expected to have for drinks, a tall caramel, fair skinned, beautiful woman enters the door. Ms. Sincere Bouvea walks in the front door of Mint towards Desmond at the bar as Desmond is stopped by her stunning entrance and rendered speechless. Desmond and Vincent are both stunned by her beautiful cameo-esq interruption.

"Well I guess I made it just in time then Mr. Coolwater! Huh? Looks like I missed happy hour so how about dinner instead?" she said. Desmond is taken back by her offer "Uhhh? Umm…" Sincere gives Desmond a seductive, breath taking, full-toothed grin as she stands there in all her sexual glory.

"Well… I'll take that as a yes then?" she said. Desmond looks at Vincent. He and Vincent smile and then Vincent nods his head towards the door urging him to go. "Well how can I refuse an invite like that?" Desmond asks.

"You shouldn't, so lets go…" Sincere responds. Desmond looks over to Vincent "Hey Vince how much do I…" Vincent interrupts Desmond already knowing what he was going to say "...on the house kid. Get out of here!"

"Thanks Vince! I'll see ya later this week." Desmond tells him.

“Think nothing of it. Your Lodo royalty around here kiddo…” Both Desmond and Sincere walk out the door with Desmond holding the door for her in true chivalrous fashion. They are outside of Mint trying to decide exactly what to do and where to go. “So where too Mr. Coolwater?” Sincere asks. “Ahhh.... you sound so formal! Call me Desmond please! This is an informal occasion right? Lets relax, have some dinner and nice conversation.” Sincere nods her head and says “Deal!”

“So with that being said.... I know this nice place we can go eat at right in the 16th street mall area called EARLS. The food is great, the atmosphere will be relaxing and I know the owner.” Sincere agrees with his choice. “Hmmm......... Sounds fantastic!! Lets go! I am starving!!” She said.

COOL NIGHTS

Chapter 6 EARLS RESTAURANT

Desmond and Sincere are at Earls eating, enjoying some great food and laughs over some glasses of wine in a candle lit section of the restaurant. Music by Tyrese Gibson is playing in the background.

Sincere breaks the silence and the tension by starting a conversation. "So Desmond what do you do? What is your profession?" Desmond wipes his mouth as he finishes chewing his steak. He then takes a sip of his drink, sits his napkin on the table and smiles before he answers her question intently. "Well I'm the head of the Marketing/advertising/promotions department for Fly magazine."

"Are you serious? I love that magazine!! I have a subscription!" Sincere replies in an interested tone.

Desmond sits up in a surprised posture. "Is that right?" Sincere smiles… "Yes, thats right. I read it religiously along with my Jet, Ebony, and Cosmo!!" Desmond takes a sip of his drink and responds. "Really!?!? So what do you like most about Fly mag? Is it informative, do you use the events guide in the middle pages to find out where to go for entertainment or what? I mean what draws you to the mag?"

Sincere is taken back by his modesty and boyish humbleness. She smiles as she begins to speak. " Well I enjoy the articles. I don't go out much due to my ever busy schedule, but if I did I would definitely use it. I would say that I think the look of the magazine as well as its colorful ways of advertising is certainly interesting and a definite attention grabber."

Desmond shakes his head in acceptance of her explanation. "Yes Indeed….." Sincere begins to realize the passion Desmond has for his job as they continued to converse. "...of course it helps to have a handsome exec like yourself attached to it. So I bet you take a lot of girls here seeing as how you are a hot single guy with no strings pulling on you?!?!" Desmond smiles "Contrary to what you assume I don't date a lot. I don't have the time. I am a work-a-holic and I have goals that I have to meet."

Sincere replies sarcastically. "Mmm Hmm...Is that right? What would those goals be? Dessie." She says seductively.

"Well................" Desmond is about to answer her question and he is interrupted by a group of young college girls passing by just to say hi. The Group of ladies all say "Hi Desmond!" in unison. Desmond looks over at Sincere, smiles and then replies to the ladies. "Hello ladies!" Sincere looks at Desmond with a sarcastic smile. Desmond looks back at Sincere and chuckles. "It's not what it looks like"

"Uh-huh" Sincere says. Desmond begins to try and explain. "I know what you're thinking and that ain't it Sincere" Sincere notices Desmond is looking a bit uncomfortable and so she keeps playfully poking fun and asking questions. "Now how would you know what I'm thinking?"

Desmond realizes his lack of cool and leans back into his seat as he continues to explain how he became acquainted with the group of ladies. "They are all models for an agency that we did a story on and they were used for the stories photo shoot."

"Uh-huh.... so how come there were no guys in that photo shoot Mr. Coolwater?" Sincere asks.

"Valid question..... to which I have an answer" Desmond replies. Sincere looks at Desmond with a very inquisitive expression. "Ookkay...... and.... why?" Desmond replies simply with "Simple... it's an all female modeling and acting agency." He smiles and takes a sip of his drink while maintaining his eye contact with Sincere.

Sincere looks back at the group of girls and then back at Desmond. "I get the feeling that there is more to you than we have time to talk about Desmond."

Desmond smiles and says “Well I’m in no rush.” Sincere takes one last sip of her drink before she speaks.

“I really have to go Desmond. I have an early meeting in the morning and I need some time before I go to sleep to prepare, but I really enjoyed our time together tonight getting to know you.” Desmond makes a sad face at her to make her feel guilty about leaving so early. “Awe come on the nights early! I know this really cool place we can go to and they have a live band, poetry and the whole nine.”

Sincere touches Desmonds hand while she declines his invitation. “I seriously can't Dessie.” Desmond gives in reluctantly and eases up on his advances for the night. “Alright alright...... I guess all good things must come to an end sometime or another.” Sincere stares at him with those sexy hypnotic eyes and gives him the prettiest and most seductive smile he has ever seen and then says “Just for now anyway. Come walk me out so I can catch a taxi please!?”

“But of course. I’m a gentleman Ms. Bouvea.” Desmond replies.

Desmond looks at the bill and pulls out cash. He pays for dinner, then gets up from the table and goes to help Sincere out of her seat. They both make their way through Earls outside where they wait to hail a cab. Sincere begins to speak to Desmond while they wait. “So Desmond I really enjoyed my time with you this evening.” Desmond responds in a monotonous tone “Ditto” Sincere looks at him and says “Thats it...? Just Ditto?”

Desmond looks at her with a sad puppy dog face. “No, I had a great time! A great time with you. Dinner, wine.... the whole thing. Just didn't want it to end so soon.” Sincere looks at Desmond and walks over to him to hug him and thank him for Dinner. Desmond embraces her and leans for a kiss and she pulls away, but pulls back in and kisses him on the cheek and the neck right by the collar to leave lipstick on his shirt!

Sincere backs up and says ”There! I don’t kiss on the first date, but I loved your cologne so much that I had to get close enough to smell you."

"Hmmmm…" Desmond smiles. A taxi pulls up and she jumps in it, but before it pulls off she says to Desmond thru the window. "Later Tiger" Desmond blows a kiss at her and she says "Oh yeah I accidentally left my lips on your collar......... sorry!" Desmond touches his collar and replies "Expensive shirt" Sincere smiles as the taxi pulls away and yells..."Bill me later!" Desmond smiles and watches the taxi drive off. He looks at his watch and its only 9:15 so he decides to go back into Earls and have a few drinks while mingling with the group of ladies from earlier.

Chapter 7 THE GYM

Desmond and Charles are working up a sweat running on the treadmill. Desmond is bickering about how he got blindsided by the board hiring Ms. Lyriq Moore for the feminine wing of the magazine. "So let me get this straight? You have been working for Fly mag for what? Three or Four years now, bringing in the biggest accounts, high profile stories, breaking in the newest fashion trends for men AND women and you think that they should make you partner after all that.... right?"

Desmond doesn't miss a beat while he keeps running. "Yep!"

Charles working hard to keep running while speaking with Desmond. "And by them bringing in this Ms. Lyriq Moore to just head the feminine side of things you feel disrespected?" Desmond gets irritated and answers with a scowl on his face. "Hell yeah!! How would you feel? I've been working hard for Fly for sometime now and then the board goes and does something like this? I should quit and go to Image Magazine!"

Charles pokes fun at Desmonds so-called adolescent tantrum. "Oh you Poor baby!! See your problem is that you have been spoiled this whole time!?"

Desmond presses the stop button on the treadmill to stop running and look over at Charles, perplexed by his statement. "What!?"

Charles reiterates what he said with no problem or worry of how Desmond was feeling. "Yeah I said it... Damn Right! You ARE spoiled!! Since I have known you going all the way back to our freshman year in highschool you haven't had to work hard at being great as you are already. You have always been successful at getting your way and what you want. Don't get me wrong? You deserve everything you got because you have worked your ass off for it, BUT....... you have no idea what we in the regular world call FAIR COMPETITION."

Desmond is still irritated by his statement. "Bullshit...!" he starts up his treadmill again and begins to jog.

Charles continues to explain in detail how Desmond needs to grow from this experience and not shut down in the midst of some healthy competition.

"Ah ah ah....... no I'm being serious Desmond and you need to listen and look at what I'm saying objectively, not personally. Taking constructive criticism is not your strong point. All I'm trying to say is that sometimes in life things are put in your way to learn how to overcome them and become a stronger and smarter person.... I'm just saying!"

Desmond speeds up and begins running harder as he listens to Charles lecture. He continues to run and look forward as they both breathe heavily. He then looks over at Charles, jumps off the treadmill and presses the stop button on Charles treadmill causing Charles to stumble.

Chapter 8 FLY MAGAZINE OFFICES

Desmond is at work getting ready for a meeting with the K.S.107.5 morning show when Lyriq comes over and sits on the edge of his desk to speak with him. “Hello Desmond” Desmond looks up at Lyriq. “Good morning Ms. Moore....what can I do for you?” He continues to type on his computer after acknowledging her. “Well I thought I would come by and just speak with you seeing as how we are going to be working close together. Do you have a problem with me being inquisitive?”

Desmond smiles and responds sarcastically while still typing. “Nope! Not at all. I’m glad you're here. I think that competition is healthy!” Lyriq is taken back by Desmonds thoughts. She stands up and continues to engage the conversation with him in a sassy, yet agitated demeanor. “Competition?? Desmond I think you may have this all wrong, see I am here to take over the women’s interest of this magazine, not take your job.”

Desmond stops working and smoothly sits back in his chair to continue speaking with Lyriq.
“Funny thing is that up until yesterday I was the pick to take over all of promotions and marketing operations. Then all of a sudden surprise-surprise here you come?” Desmond then sits up and rubs his chin while looking at Lyriq with an inquisitive stare, as if indirectly asking how she even got the position.

Lyriq smirks at Desmond and says “Desmond look?! Lets try and work together on this. I mean we are
co-workers now and nothing can change that so lets make the best out of it and be successful! We barely know each other. You never know we may just make a great team? Truce??” Lyriq holds her hand out to shake Desmonds hand and just as he decides to shake her hand, his assistant James comes to his desk furious and trying to confirm the rumor about Ms. Lyriq Moore being hired on to take on the feminine side of marketing for Fly Magazine instead of Desmond being named head executive over all of the department.

"Excuse me! Desmond!? James steps right in front of Lyriq like she's not even standing there. "What the hell is this I hear about some chick being hired for the feminine operations of Fly Magazine? I thought you were a shoe in bro?? Who is this hoochie and how can we get her out of here?" James interrupts the conversation rudely and waits for Desmond to answer. Desmond stands up and turns James around to face Lyriq who he cut in front of and then introduces him.

"James let me introduce you to Ms. Lyriq Moore. She is our new Fly magazine rep overseeing the feminine side of things." James extends his hand out to Lyriq to shake her hand and Lyriq says "Yes...hello James. I am Lyriq the new chick slash hoochie." She smirks devilishly and shakes his hand. James Smiles back and says "My pleasure" Lyriq decides to leave after meeting James. "Well....this has been a productive conversation. Desmond catch ya later. James? It's been a pleasure!"

Lyriq walks away with a cat like strut that only runway models walk with. Desmond and James watch intentionally. James then says "I don't like her!" Desmond agrees as they both watch her walk away. "Yeah but she has a mean walk doesn't she?? James agrees as well. "Yeah....that she does!"

They both are staring at her walk away she stares back at them as if she knew they were watching. Just then Cindy the hyperactive office intern breaks up their trance like state to inform Desmond that Mr. Elmhurst wanted to speak to him. "Hey Dezzie!"

Desmond looks at Cindy and says ".......Desmond!" Cindy has a bewildered look on her face as as she asks Desmond "What?"

"I prefer to be called Desmond. Nobody calls me Dezzie!!" Desmond explains. Cindy totally ignores Desmond and continues delivering the message that she came to deliver. "Ok........so........Mr. Elmhurst wants to see you in his office."

"Thank you Cindy" Desmond replies. Desmond walks off towards Mr. Elmhurst's office.

James looks at Cindy as Desmond walks away and asks her out for dinner. “Hey Cindy…..so how about me and you go to the steakhouse, get a couple of medium well steaks. Go back to my place and watch the Nuggets game tonight??” Cindy looks at James and says “I don't eat meat James. I’m a vegetarian......sorry.” and then walks away.

James stands there looking at her as she is walking away with his ego bruised.
“What?!” He yells out in shock. “No wonder yo ass is so damn skinny!! Looking like a ex-runway model on a summer diet. Need to eat every minute of the day, walking around here looking like a toothpick with a boob job.........crazy bitch.”

James is talking bad and cracking jokes to himself about Cindy as she walks away from him.

COOL NIGHTS

Chapter 9 MR. ELMHURST'S OFFICE

Desmond walks over to Mr. Elmhurst office to meet with him and Mr. Elmhurst meets him at the door and invites him to lunch to talk about the recent developments at FLY mag. "I just got the message that you wanted to see me Mr. Elmhurst."

Mr. Elmhurst is sitting in his seat looking at Desmond as he comes into the office. "Yes, Desmond I wanted to talk to you about the recent events going on with the mag......i.e interviews, shows and the recent acquisition of Ms. Lyriq Moore. So meet me out front in about 45 minutes alright young man?"

Desmond replies "Yessir" Desmond gets up and heads out of the office so he can gather his things for the lunch meeting with Mr. Elmhurst. Desmond and Mr. Elmhurst are sitting in a quiet part of Maggio's Italian grille located in the 16th st shopping mall, where they are discussing recent events and the boards decision to bring in some friendly competition to put Desmond on his toes. "So Desmond I wanted to get away from the office and address the recent events. I know you probably have some questions and concerns?"

Desmond asks "Can I be honest and open with you Mr. Elmhurst? I have an issue with this!! I mean how can they go and hire someone for a part of the company that I have been running successfully for 4 almost 5 years with no mishaps or shorts. I'm on time all the time, I get the big accounts with ease, I get the top models for all photo shoots, etc., etc., etc!!! I mean.........How can the board do this to me?"

"Desmond calm down son. I know how you are feeling and that is why I brought you out here today, so we could talk. The boards actions are very sporadic, which is not unusual in my mind, but for someone like you I can see how and why you feel the way you are feeling." Mr. Elmhurst explains.

"How am I supposed to react to this? I feel betrayed, stepped on and used!! I deserved that position Mr. Elmhurst I really did.

I've worked hard for it. Desmond says "And you will have it Desmond, but the board is testing you." Desmond responds in a shocked tone. "Testing?? Testing me for what? Haven't I proved enough?"

"Of course you have. More than enough, but they want to see you rise above the competition before they approve of my recommendation." Desmond stares off out of the window towards the street as he ponders what Mr. Elmhurst is saying. "Desmond they are going to test your metal, they are going to push you to the limits that you may not like and you have to shine above it all." Desmond accepts the challenge and says "I will take this opportunity to show them what I'm made of and I won't let you down!!"

Mr. Elmhurst pulls out a cigar and gets ready to light up, when a waiter walks past him and tells him that this is a non-smoking establishment. Just then Desmonds phone rings and its his mother. "Mr. Elmhurst I have to take this call, but I will meet you back at the office later after the meeting with the KS 107.5 morning show." Mr. Elmhurst gets excited that Desmond decides to keep it business as usual and says "Now that's the Desmond that I know!!!! That's the young man that I hired right out of college talking right there. Good Luck and remember what I told you!"

Desmond is getting his blazer and briefcase together. As he heads towards the door about to answer his phone he runs back to Mr. Elmhurst shakes his hand and says "Yes sir!" They shake hands and Desmond is off into the city again, back to business as usual!!

Desmond is outside waiting on a cab and his mother, Mrs. Janis Coolwater is calling. Janis is a warm yet powerful figure in the family. She has always stayed on Desmonds case about school and being a good man. Desmond answers the phone with the signature males ode to a real mother "Hey momma!"
"Hello son how are you doing today?" she says. "I'm good, just working as usual, you know me momma."

“Yes, I do know you. I birthed ya and dressed ya forever and a day. Listen Desmond momma can't talk long, but I’m calling to remind you of the family BBQ on Sunday. Me and your father expect you to be there and I don't want to hear any excuses boy!!” Mrs. Coolwater says in a loving, yet stern motherly voice. Desmond begins to give her an excuse, just like she told him not to do.

“Ma’??! But I…” Mrs. Coolwater interrupts him immediately. “Desmond I don't want to hear it!!! Now you have ducked out on us the last two family Sundays and your father and I are sick of it. You will have your narrow skinny ass here on Sunday and you’re going to church with us too!”

“Mom I can't make it to church on Sunday. I have a party Saturday night and I probably won't get in until late night.” says Desmond “You mean late morning little boy I’m not stupid. Ya heathen!! Ain't nothing out there, but some hookers that time of night. How do you expect to find a good woman at that time of night?” asks Mrs. Coolwater. “Mom I gotta go. I have a meeting in 30 minutes.” “Mmm Hmm……. don't be trying to ignore the conversation.” replies Mrs. Coolwater.

“I’m not” says Desmond. “Oh but you are, but I love you anyway and good luck at your meeting son. Go get ‘em baby!” replies Mrs. Coolwater. “I love you too mom…….. see you Sunday.” replies Desmond.

COOL NIGHTS

Chapter 10 KS107.5 OFFICES

Desmond reaches the KS107.5 offices. As he reaches the door to walk in he is approached by Lyriq who has met him at the meeting by request of the board. Desmond is irritated by first sight.

"What are you doing here?" Desmond says as he makes his way past her towards the meeting.

"Well the board thought it be in the companies best interest if I started to accompany you at all the meetings so I can stay on top of things with you as opposed to you coming back and informing everyone."

Desmond stops walking for a brief moment to look at her and say "The board huh?" He replies in a sarcastic tone as he continues towards the board room. "Yes Desmond!! They figured I might as well jump right in and start working with you. Look let's not make this hard Desmond. I respect you and the work you have done. I"m not here to compete with you. I am here to pull my weight and do my job. My concern is what's good for the Magazine, not your inflated male ego." explains Lyriq.

Desmond looks at Lyriq in the eyes and replies sarcastically once again. "Whatever! Ok we don't have time to argue over semantics. Lets go up here, work together to talk to Larry, Kendall and Kathy about doing a story in the magazine and solidify a deal with them for some remote hosting at some of our events!! Did the board tell you that Ms. Moore?" Desmond opens the door to the building and allows Lyriq to enter first as only a gentleman would do. As she walks past him she raises her nose in the air and calls him an "Asshole" under her breath just loud enough for him to hear. Desmond smiles and says "You have no idea!!" and then walks into the building behind her.

Desmond and Lyriq walk up to the receptionist desk and sign in. "Good afternoon! I'm Desmond Coolwater and my partner here

Lyriq Moore are from Fly Magazine. We are here for a 2 o'clock with Larry, Kathie and Kendall." Desmond introduces himself to the receptionist.

"Ok if you guys have a seat I will inform them that you are here." the receptionist replies. "Thank you" Desmond says. Desmond and Lyriq take a seat in the lobby waiting area across from each other as if they both have the plague. If looks could kill! Desmond grabs his phone and looks away from her as he begins to text Ms. Sincre Bouvea and chat. Lyriq rolls her eyes and looks in a different direction.

Desmond **(TEXT)**
Hey....:o)....smiley face

PAUSE

Sincre **(TEXT BACK)**
Hi!! ;o).......smiley face

PAUSE

Desmond **(REPLY)**
How are you doing today?
PAUSE

Sincre **(REPLY)**
I'm good but I would be better if we could talk instead of text?? hint-hint!!

Desmond reads the text and smiles. As Desmond was texting Lyriq noticed the way he was smiling as he was on his phone. "One of your hook-up / bootie calls no doubt??" Lyriq says to Desmond in a snide way.

Desmond looks up from his phone without moving his head, just his eye contact and says: "No, actually I'm speaking with a friend that I hung out with the other night." Lyriq smirks and says "A friend huh?"

"Yes!! Just a friend!!" Desmond responds without looking up.

"I wonder if she knows that? Lyric says with sarcastically. "Most men don't divulge that information."

"Of course she knows"... Desmond stops explaining himself and then says. "Why am I even explaining myself to you? Look lets stay professional and stay out of each others personal zone ok?

Lyriq agrees "Fine" Desmond agrees right back and says "Fine"

Lyriq says "Good" Desmond not wanting to be outdone comes back with "Great!!!" as he looks back down at his phone and begins to text Sincere again.

Desmond (**TEXT**)
Would really love to talk but I am about to go to a meeting. Will call you later k......(smiley face)

Sincere (**REPLY**)
K....(smiley face)

Just as the text conversation came to an end the receptionist came up to walk Desmond and Lyriq back to the board room "Mr. Coolwater / Ms. Moore they are ready for you. If you're ready follow me please."

Desmond looks at Lyriq and she rolls her eyes at him as she gets up from her seat. Desmond gets up and follows her and the receptionist to the room where Larry, Kathy and Kendall are sitting.

These three people are the celebrity host of the morning show in the Mile High City from 6am to 12pm. Lyriq goes in the door first followed by Desmond. Desmond goes to introduce himself and Lyriq steals the moment by introducing herself first to Kathy and then Kendal and Larry.

“Hello!! My name is Lyriq and I’m the co-director of advertising/marketing for Fly magazine and this is my co-worker and partner........” Larry interrupts Lyriq and says “Sorry doll but I was told we would be meeting with Desmond Coolwater? Is he not going to be here today?”

Desmond jumps in after his name is announced… “and that would be me........ I am He!!”

Desmond smiles a very beguiling smile as he shakes everyone’s hand and then turns his face around out of their view, towards Lyriq and his smile dissolves to a straight face as he pulls out her chair and then turns back to them and grabs his seat. “I’d like to thank you for meeting with us today. My colleague and I are here because you are the top radio team in the state” Larry U. interrupts and corrects Desmond “Uhh....... You mean in the country!!”

Desmond sits up in his chair and makes the necessary correction “Of course…” Desmond smiles… “in the country and with that being said we feel its only right that the number one radio team in the country should get the recognition that they deserve by gracing the cover of the number one magazine in the state.......i.e..... Fly Magazine!?!”

Kathy jumps right in and starts quizzing Desmond “Hmmmm......... your name is Desmond right? Desmond Coolwater?” Desmond replies with curiosity “Yeah that's me!” Kathy Lee smiles “I’ve heard a lot about you Mr. Coolwater!!” she says. Desmond looks over at Lyriq and she smiles sarcastically while rolling her eyes. Desmond responds to Kathy and says “Well I should hope that you judge me by your first impression and not by what others say?”

“Don't you worry Mr. Coolwater.” Says Kathie “Your reputation is well earned and very well respected around here. Its interesting at the same time as to why we’ve never had you on the morning show? You're quite elusive aren't you?”

"Yes, your kind of like folklore around here Desmond. You should come on the show sometime as a guest? Kendell B invites him onto the show. Desmond smiles as if he's being put on the spot, but replies with the calmest tone and smoothest posture to them. "Well thank you for the invite. I think that would be great for the magazine!!" Larry is always straight forward and as Desmond finishes his sentence Larry jumps right in and says "No, we want to interview you dude! Yeah the magazine is what you represent, but I think what my partners are trying to say is that we want to interview the cities most eligible bachelor?"

Desmond plays the bashful card as if he is actually shy and says "Oh? I see!!! So ya'll want to get me on the morning show and just blow me up?" Everyone starts laughing in the room while Lyriq just smiles.

Kendall composes himself and replies "Well not to blow you up. You're like a local celebrity Dez!! We hear about you hosting parties, doing these big model casting calls and photo shoots." Larry interrupts "I mean come on!?!?! We are 107.5!! We know these things!!" Kathy begins to hash out the deal "Soooo..... in exchange for our interview in Fly mag, you owe us a radio interview shortly after!! Deal??"

"That sounds like a deal to me. So when can we expect the interview from you guys then?" Desmond replies to Kathie. "Just let the receptionist know what date you want from us and we'll play it by ear as far as getting you on the show." replies Kendall. Desmond looks around the table at everyone and then speaks. "Cool....... well I guess that concludes the meeting here and we will get back to the office, unless my colleague has anything to add????"

Desmond turns around to Lyriq where he finds her doodling on her notepad until she notices that everyone was looking up at her and then she says. "Uh....... No!!?? I have no questions whatsoever. Desmond is the man for the job. If anyone can get it done he will and we look forward to doing business with you!!"

Desmond smiles at her with a devilish smile and turns back to the crew and stands up to shake hands and conclude the meeting. "I appreciate you guys and ladies time" He smiles seductively at Kathie Lee and then continues to speak with everyone. "We'll set up the time that works with your schedule outside and catch up with y'all soon!!"

Desmond shakes everyone's hands, Lyriq shakes everyone's hands and they exit the room. Larry just blurts out what he is thinking immediately and says "I bet he gets major tail" Kendall B looks at Larry in shock and says "That is a crass thing to say Larry" Kathy Lee chimes in while shaking her head and says "...yeah but *HE IS SMOOTH*" and I bet every bit of the gossip is true!!"

Chapter 11 ***OUTSIDE OF RADIO OFFICES***

Desmond and Lyriq are standing outside waiting on the company limo to pick them up and neither one of them even say a word to one of another. As if they are both waiting on separate rides. The limo pulls up, the driver gets out and opens the door for them. Desmond allows Lyriq to get in first like a true gentleman and then he climbs in and sits very tight to the window while she sits on the other side of the limo facing out the other window. Desmond has a cocky, confident smirk on his face. The phone rings and it is his assistant James calling to find out how the meeting with the radio station went.

"Hello this is Desmond" James speaks in his usual loud tone. "Don't be acting like you couldn't see it was me calling you ol' titty baby boy!! So how did the meeting go?" Desmond begins to speak with James as if Lyriq wasn't there in the limo with him. "So I get to the station and was met there by Ms. Moore"

James yells loudly through the phone speaker "The new chick??"

Desmond smirks as he tries to turn the volume down on the phone so Lyriq can hear their entire conversation. "Yes the new chick!! So anyway we get in the meeting and they are all there just sitting and waiting for us. Lyriq goes to introduce herself and before me.... Get this?? Larry Ulibarri interrupts her and said *I thought we were having a meeting with Desmond Coolwater?*"

James yells again "What????........" James is excited and yells "You gotta be kidding me??" Desmond responds "No! I was floored and flattered. It was so hard not to have the permafrost grin man, but you know me I played it as cool as a iceberg!" A faint voice in the background yells out the word "ICE COLD"

James laughs and says "Ice Cold!! That's cold blooded!! So did Kathie Lee just look as sexy as I imagined her to be?" Desmond answers "yeah she's a hottie bro..."

Lyriq is listening to the conversation and getting irritated. She has a look of devious proportions on her face and is trying to figure out a way to get Desmonds attention during the rest of the ride home and save face for the embarrassment back in the meeting with the radio station hosts. She turns her head starts crying in true scandalous fashion!!!!

James is going on about Kathie Lee. "Damn it!! I knew she was going to be hot in person!! Next time I'm going with you. She won't be able to stop staring at me once I give her the look!!"

Desmond laughs "Lol......... Yeah right man. She don't even seem like the type to even like dark meat!!"

James gets irritated "That's some bullshit!!! This is the second time today that…"

Lyriq begins to cry big giant crocodile tears with her back turned towards Desmond in the limo. Desmond interrupts James and tells him that he will talk to him when he gets to the office. Desmond is put off by her crying, but at the same his curiosity keeps in tune to her actions.

"Uhh..... James hold on" Desmond covers the receiver of the phone to lean over and ask her if she is crying!?!?!

"What?!?!?!?! Are you crying?!?!?!"

Lyriq hides her face and replies "No!! Just leave me alone I'm ok!!" Desmond inquires more into her situation. "Why are you crying??" Desmond reaches for the tissue dispenser in the limo and hands her some tissues "I'm fine!!" Lyriq says. Desmond uncovers the phone and tells James that he will talk with him at the office. "Hey James I'm going to let you go and catch up with you at the office."

James agrees and says "Cool!!" Desmond hangs up and addresses Lyriq's tears. "Ok?? So what is the deal?" Lyriq plays his curiosity just right in order to keep his attention on her.

"Nothing! Just forget about it! I'm fine!" Desmond continues to probe and fix the situation. "Well you got big crocodile tears coming down and your mascara is running a marathon down your face." Lyriq giggles a bit, sniffles and then she blows her nose.

"Today was just a mess!! I thought by trying to be the leader in that meeting and acting like the strong alpha female type that-that would get me to your level, but I'm noticing that I have somethings to learn."

Desmond responds with a soft cocky response."Well some things don't just happen overnight love. I worked hard to get to this level and nothing was given to me. Believe me.......... if I could've slept my way to the top I would be president by now!!"

"So what are you implying???" Lyriq is wiping her nose and looking at Desmond trying to figure what he is saying. "Uh...Uhhhh...... I'm not implying anything? What are you talking about?" he replies. Lyriq sits up in the seat and gets defensive. "Yes! You are!! You are trying to say that I slept my way to the top?!?!"

Desmond sits up. "NO!! No!!!!" Lyriq gets defensive "Well let me tell you Mr. Coolwater, I worked very hard to get myself here and it was not because I slept my way anywhere!! And for your information I…"

Desmond interrupts Lyriq so she knows he wasn't trying to offend her. "Whoa! whoa!! whoa!!! I did not say, think, imply or even try to insinuate that you slept around or even got a free ride to the top!?! I was merely stating that it wasn't easy for me to get here." Lyriq continues to collect her composure while she fixes her make up. "Well it sure sounded like it!!"

"Well I guess it would sound like that if I was crying and wasn't listening." Both Desmond and Lyriq share a laugh and then Desmond says jokingly "Although on the other hand it is hard to get to the top without a little give and take." Lyriq looks at

Desmond in surprise and appalled about his statement, but smiled and hit Desmond in the arm.

Desmond flinches and says "Just kidding!! Just kidding!!" The ride goes on while Desmond and Lyriq share a calm, tension free ride the rest of the way back to the FLY Mag offices joking and laughing.

Chapter 12 BACK AT FLY MAG OFFICES

Desmond is sitting at his desk relaxed with his blazer jacket off and around his chair. He is writing notes about the meeting with the radio station and looking down his to-do-list of clients he needs to call. He suddenly remembers to call Sincere back. He dials her number..... RING-RING Sincere's voicemail comes on.

"Hello this is Sincere and you have reached my voicemail, obviously if you get this then I am busy so please leave a message… BEEEEEEEEEEEP!"

Desmond attempts to leave a message "Hey this is Desmond and I was giving you a call to see how your day was. Kinda been thinking about you and our date the other night. Was kind of hoping to do it again sometime soon ya know?" Sincere is actually listening to Desmond leave a message because she faked the voicemail message to see what kind of message he would leave. She is on the other side laughing and cannot contain herself any longer. "So you have just....... kind of been thinking about me… huh?"

Desmond is shocked and taken back by her fooling him. "What?!?! Hello?"

"Hello!! Sexy!! I was just playing with you. How are you?" Sincere replies.

Desmond answers with a Kool-Aid smile "So you were playing me just to hear me say a bunch of sweet stuff to you?" Sincere replies "Well its not everyday I get a handsome man to tell me that they are thinking about me. I gotta take all I can get." Desmond laughs and says "Touche!! So how is your day going?"

"Not bad. Just dealing with these insurance policies and claims all day is really giving a girl a headache."

"Insurance policies? Claims? What is your profession Ms. Bouvea?" asks Desmond. "Oh nothing too big." she says. "I'm an insurance agent and I work out of an agency downtown........ selling life, health and auto. You need a policy Mr. Coolwater?" Desmond laughs "Nah, I'm fully covered with the magazine insurance already, but I would never miss the opportunity to have you cover me." There is a moment of comfortable silence between the two and then Desmond says "I mean get coverage for me if I didn't already have insurance."

Sincere giggles and replies "Uh huh..... you're a bad boy Desmond."

"No I'm not. I just have a very vivid imagination. That's all..." he replies.

Sincere feels Desmond getting more comfortable so she suggests they get together to hang out. "So anyway, when are we going to get together again? Lets do tonight?"

"I can't. I have so much work to do and I have some meetings that I need to set up with some local companies for possible side jobs that I do in conjunction with the magazine for extra money." Desmond explains. Sincere quickly becomes inquisitive. "Oh yeah?? What kind of side jobs do you do?"

"Well besides getting companies to spend their advertising dollars with the mag , they also employ me to help market them and their services by way of product release parties. I have a huge release party set up for Coors coming up soon. My next venture is this dating service. They want me to set up a high profile singles party next month." he divulges confidently.

Sincere becomes more interested as he continues to talk more. "Wow!!! You are a busy man!! No wonder you're not married or anything like that."

Desmond continues "No!?! That's not it. I just haven't met anyone worth the time to settle down with and get to know for more than a month or so. I've had some bad relationships in the past that kind of set the tone for how I view relationships and love now."

"So what you're saying is you don't believe in love?" Sincere asks.

"No, I do but maybe not in the conventional ways most view love. Know what I mean?"

Sincere laughs. "Nope! Explain?" Desmond drops his head laughs and then responds back into the phone with "Its a long story. Maybe over dinner tomorrow night?"

Sincere agrees with his dinner plans and says "Deal!! "

"Great!! I have to get back to work and make some phone calls but can I call you later?" Desmond asks.

"Sounds good" she says..."ttyl" Desmond is confused so he asks "What?!"

Sincere proceeds to break down what it means. "Talk To You later..... Mr. Coolwater...... better get hip!!"

Desmond gets cocky. "lady I am the hippest hip in the whole hip replacement factory. I made the word hip!!" Sincere laughs. "Well it sounds like you need to update your hip dialogue."

"Whatever" Desmond says as he smiles. Sincere laughs again "Byeeeeee....... Desmond. Catch ya later handsome" Desmond responds smoothly with "Adios bonita"

Desmond and Sincere hang up the phone. Desmond continues making notes as Mr. Elmhurst comes to the desk to inform Desmond that he is expected to attend a dinner with him and the board tonight to go over his upcoming plans for the magazine and its customers.

"Desmond!!" Mr. Elmhurst says "Yes sir!?" he replies as he spins around in his chair to face Mr. Elmhurst. "I'm glad I caught you before you left. The board is wanting to have a meeting with you tonight!!" Desmond repeats him "Tonight?!?"

"Yes… tonight! Is that going to be a problem?" he says. Desmond replies "No sir! Not at all..... its just that I planned on…" Mr. Elmhurst looks down at Desmond to see what Desmonds reply would be, but he decides to not give an excuse and go with the meeting without argument. "No sir.... no problem at all. Where should I meet you at and what time sir?"

Mr. Elmhurst replies with the details, time, place, etc., etc. "It's going to be a late meeting and we will be meeting in the boardroom around 8:00 p.m. so go out get some food, relax and then come back and prepare to show and prove what you're made of son! I'm pulling for you!"

Desmond responds confidently "No worries. I will be ready!"

Mr. Elmhurst takes a puff of his cigar, pats Desmond on his shoulder and begins to walk as he is speaking to Desmond…"Now that's what I wanted to hear!! I'm going to go grab something to eat, would you like to come with?"

"No thanks sir. I've got some stuff to do around here and then I'm going to run home to change because I have a fashion show to appear at tonight. The designers sent me an invite to come check out their new line and talk about possible advertising in the mag. Still working off the clock!"

Desmond waves off Mr. Elmhurst as he spins back to his work. Mr. Elmhurst continues to walk away smiling and puffing like a locomotive as he sings Desmonds praise.

"Always working off the clock. That is the kind of work that will make you partner around here Mr. Coolwater. Go get 'em kid!" Desmond yells out as he continues to type on the computer "You know it!!"

Mr. Elmhurst walks off and Desmond begins to pack up his desk and get ready to leave the office.

He needs to run home to get ready for the meeting and the fashion show afterwards. The night is young and he isn't about to let this little meeting through him off. He grabs his blazer, briefcase and takes off.

Desmond reaches the lobby of the office and walks straight out of the door and hails a taxi. As he looks out over the downtown scenery on his way home from the office to get dressed, music is playing from the radio in the background during the ride. Desmond finally reaches his house, he pays the taxi driver and exits the car.

He goes up to the door with keys in hand to put into the door and as he puts the key into the hole, the local paperboy is riding by on his bike and throws the paper with just enough stroke to hit Desmond in the back of the head and makes him drop his keys.

The music stops for just a beat for Desmond to yell out “You're late again!!! Little mother fu.........” Desmond bends down to pick up the newspaper and his keys as he continues to enter his house and mumble his cuss words while rubbing his head.

COOL NIGHTS

Chapter 13 DESMOND'S HOUSE

Inside Desmonds house its quiet as he slams the door. You only hear his shoes as he drops his bag and the newspaper. He walks over to the entertainment stand and turns on the stereo, turns the volume up to a house bumping blast as he prepares for the night ahead.

Desmond heads up stairs. He loosens up his tie, takes off his watch and walks towards the shower to get the water ready. He then takes his shirt off revealing his athletic physique and toned abs. He grabs his razor and begins to groom himself. He then brushes his teeth, takes his pants off and enters the shower.

Time is flying as he gets ready. He finishes showering, grabs his towel, dries off and wraps the towel around him. He then walks over to the closet and chooses some of his freshest designer shoes, then he matches those with his slacks. He continues getting dressed and then heads toward the living room, his phone rings and its Nicole McKnight the designer for Re'Veil fashions calling to make sure that he was going to make it tonight and that his name was on her guest list. **RING-RING**.... the phone rings!!!

Desmond answers the phone "Nicole!! How are you doing beautiful?" Nicole is a sexy bombshell with a strong sense of being and sassy attitude. Desmond would love to sex the hell out of her, but she only likes women and Desmond is cool with that, so he keeps a great friendship / business working relationship with her. Nicole yells out "I am a nervous wreck. I don't think anyone here is moving fast enough!! The caterer is late and my models seem to all be having a bad hair day."

Desmond laughs and begins to reassure her "Nicole calm down baby!! You are going to do wonderful! We have a great spread in the mag for the clothing. The models and the photos came out perfect and you have prepared for this night for over 4 months now. This show will be the bomb!!! You'll see..... take a deep breath now." She sighs and Desmond repeats his directions again…"NICOLE BREATHE"

Nicole takes a deep breath over the phone and says "Desmond you are a sweetheart as usual and you always make me feel better!! Your perfect!!! Why are you still single hun??" Desmond is looking at himself in the mirror as he straightens his clothes and then replies

"Ha ha ha ha.... aghhhh.....(SIGH).... been there and done that Ms. McKnight. I don't think any female is prepared. I'm kind of high maintenance. Plus..... I'm too busy!! Nicole is finally calm after speaking with Desmond. She confesses her attraction "Well if I wasn't in love and a lesbian, I would definitely go straight and purrr all over your body!"

If black could blush then Desmond would definitely be fuschia red. He thanks her for the flirtatious compliment and then gets back to business "I am truly honored and flattered. Ok, so back to business Nicole......... CALM DOWN!! Are you calm now?" Nicole takes another deep breath and answers him "Yes Desmond... I am as Cool as Water my sexy friend!!"

Desmond straightens sleeves and cuffs as he reassures her again that the night is going to be a success and also reminds her to breathe "Good because you are about to have the biggest night of your life and you need to BREATHE!!! Be cool and I will see you later on tonight." Nicole thanks him graciously "Thank you Desmond!! You always know what to say. I'll see you later!" Desmond tells her bye "Ciao Bella!!"

Desmond hangs up and steps in front of the mirror to fix his collar and then puts on his blazer, grabs his suitcase and heads towards the garage where his favorite toy a 2014 Chevrolet Camaro ZL1 is hidden away from the city street. He very rarely drives it, but due to time constraints between the Fly mag meeting and the fashion show he is forced to drive it.

He opens the door to the garage, walks along the side of the vehicle as if he is fantasizing about a female. He hits the button on his keychain to disarm the alarm and unlock the doors. He opens the door, puts his suitcase in the backseat, pushes the seat back and slides into the bucket seats as if he was apart of the leather it was made of.

His hand becomes an extension of the keychain as he puts the key into the ignition and shifts the gear into reverse and then backs the car out of the garage like a professional driver and burns rubber down the street.

COOL NIGHTS

Chapter 14 @ FLY MAGAZINE OFFICES

Desmond pulls up to Fly Mag offices and parks his car in the company garage right next to the company limos to avoid any door dings. He gets out the car and heads into the building entrance.

He goes to his desk to pick up his meeting notes from earlier and heads towards the meeting room.

As he gets closer to the room he notices Mr. Elmhurst and a few of the board members standing outside of the board room conversing. Desmond walks up on the group and says hello. Mr. Elmhurst introduces Desmond to them and then Desmond walks right in to take a seat before the meeting starts.

“Hello everyone!” Mr. Elmhurst points to each executive as he introduces them “Desmond I’d like to introduce you to a couple of the board members. This here is Mr. Edward Westfield one of our senior board members who has overseen our stocks and interest and international endeavors. And this gentleman here is Mr. Kenneth Kush, my partner and Chief Financial Officer.”

Desmond shakes both men’s hands and says “Its a pleasure to meet you! I am very honored to be in the presence of such great men!” Mr. Edward Westfield interrupts Desmonds flattery “Desmond you don't have to woo us young man. We are well aware of your work and the pleasure is all ours. I’ve had my eye on you for some of our international endeavors. I hear how you bring these new advertising accounts in and I’m impressed. Keep up the good work!!” Desmond responds “Thank you sir!”

Mr. Kenneth Kush adds onto Mr. Westfield's sentiments and says “Yes Desmond I share his thoughts on that.” Desmond smiles confidently and then Mr. Kush adds “....but I also feel as though we aren't getting all that we can from you young man.”

Desmond has a bewildered look on his face as if being taken by surprise by his statement. Mr. Kush continues “Which is why I decided to bring on Ms. Moore to accompany you on all of our new business acquisitions from here on out. Come on into the boardroom and we'll finish this conversation with the rest of the team."

Desmonds confident smiles and good feelings of success recognized turn to a frozen half smile and half grimace as Mr. Kush finishes his sentence. Desmond then follows the gentlemen into the room where other board members are sitting and Lyriq is seated already. Desmond takes a seat across the table from Lyriq so that he can view her as well as everyone else at the table.

Mr. Elmhurst is seated at one end of the table and Mr. Kush is seated at the other end of the table, with the other executives filling in between. Mr. Elmhurst begins the meeting with thanking everyone for showing up after such a late notice.

"Thank you everyone for clearing your schedule this evening to make it to the meeting at such a short notice. I know all of you are wondering why are we all here tonight. Well I'm going to let my partner Mr. Vincent Kush take the meeting from here and I will chime in as needed." Kenneth Kush stands up and walks to the middle of the room to demand every one's attention be on him.

"Thank you once again everyone for being here after such short notice. I want to talk to you all about the direction the magazine is going in and what our future plans are. Right now we are in a great place, but I believe we can do more. I believe we can actually take Fly Magazine to new heights with just a little bit of fine tuning, which is why I decided to shake things up a bit. Yes, we have Desmond who brings in every account he sets his eyes on and yes he brings in the big accounts every time. You might ask **What more can we ask for** or you might ask **How can we make things any better**? Well I have an answer for you? One magazine......."

Desmond sits up high in his seat listening to Mr. Kush as he explains the game plan and then Mr. Kush finishes his sentence

"....with dual factions!"

Desmond slides down into his seat like a turtle withdrawing into his shell. The whole room looks at his reaction in suspense.

Mr. Kush continues "In all our pondering and infinite thinking we are always trying to stay on the cutting edge and ahead of the smaller print competition, which is why we have decided to split the company into a feminine faction and a male faction. With this we can effectively cover all basis. I believe that in the grand scheme of things this will be a fountain of youth for us. Right now our magazine is the best, but with the present structure and Desmond bringing in the bulk of the accounts using his savvy and male machismo to sway companies...." (HE PAUSES) "......female counterparts decisions are going to get old and start seeming a bit misogynistic. We cannot and will not be viewed as the kind of print media that promotes misogyny. No offense to you Desmond."

Desmond responds with a fake look and reply "None taken sir...."

Lyriq sits in her seat not looking at Desmond, but with a snide/sarcastic smile on her face. Desmond is noticeably irritated by this, but tries to remain professional.

Mr. Kush is still speaking while Desmond is fuming with madness "So with that being said I would like to introduce Ms. Lyriq Moore. She will be heading the feminine faction of the magazine from here on out. Desmond I expect you two to be together and sharing information with each other for the benefit for the company for here on out. If there is a meeting you are having or have set up then she needs to accompany you. This includes your side ventures as well."

Desmond stands up and interjects "Wait!?!?! I get those side jobs due to my hard work and know how. Not too mention from my connections in the city's entertainment circle. The companies I have brought to this company such as coors and others only do work with me on that level because they have knowledge of my resume personally or have heard from their business relationships / referrals what kind of great job I do for businesses. No offense to Ms. Moore, but what does she have to do with that?"

Mr. Kush replies "Well from here on out Lyriq will accompany you. We need her to be in tune with you on every venture inside or outside of these doors if it is concerning the magazines business. Do you have a problem with that Desmond?"

The whole boardroom stares at Desmond and waits for his reply. Desmond looks at Mr. Elmhurst and then over at Lyriq with a fake smile and says "No! There is no problem whatsoever sir. I will make sure she stays in step."

Mr. Kush gives a watchful glance at Lyriq and then at Desmond and asks "Does anyone have any questions?"

Mr. Kush folds his hands in front of himself looking at the board members and Desmond. Desmond looks over at Mr. Elmhurst. Mr. Elmhurst looks at Desmond and winks his eye. Desmond gives another fake smile and says nothing. Mr. Kush continues "sigh......... I guess this meeting didn't take as long as I thought it would. I'd like to wish you all a good night."

The boardroom is in motion now with everyone packing up their notes and briefcases. As everyone is shuffling out of the door, Desmond sits behind and slowly packs his briefcase. Mr. Elmhurst walks over to Desmond and says "Remember what we talked about young man. I have complete and total faith in you and your ability. I know you will shine thru!!"

Desmond responds in a disappointed tone "Thank you sir." Mr. Elmhurst pats Desmond on the back and exits the boardroom. Desmond stands up, straightens out his blazer and collar, grabs his briefcase and exits the boardroom.

Chapter 15 IN THE COMPANY GARAGE

Desmond walks out of the exit door and into the garage. As he is walking up to his car he is surprised to see Lyriq leaning against his car seductively and then she asks. “So is this your fly ride Desmond?”

Desmond looks at her with curiosity as his level of irritation rises, but he remains cool as usual.

“Yes, its mine and she doesn’t like other females touching her, so if you could stop leaning on her we would both appreciate it.” Lyriq giggles at Desmond as she walks on the side of the car with a sexy strut, running her index finger down the contours of the cars hood like a sex scene from a movie as she repeats what he says........."We?”

Desmond walks up and taps her hand off of the hood of the car. He then pulls out the handkerchief scarf from his blazers outer pocket to wipe her finger prints off. “Yes, we!! Her and I…”

Lyriq smiles with her devious smile as Desmond ushers her away from his car. “You know what they say about men and these kind of cars?” Desmond is still wiping smudges off his hood as Lyriq is talking, acting like she’s not even speaking and then he replies nonchalantly with “No, I don't?? What do they say?”

Lyriq responds with “Compensation!!”

Desmond is not shocked with her response and continues around the car to the drivers side of the car in order to put some space between them as he speaks “Yep, just like I thought!”

“Well? What did you think Desmond?” Lyriq asks sarcastically.

Desmond begins to give his thoughts on the origin of this thought process “I think that was made up by some jealous person who #1..... couldn't afford it, #2...... who actually needed to compensate or my personal favorite #3...... a female who was jealous, spiteful, evil and just wanted to make a mans life hell. But that's just my opinion..."

Lyriq is standing on the other side of the car as Desmond explains his hypothesis holding her briefcase intently listening to him until he finishes and then says "I'm impressed! Very well put Mr. Coolwater. So I guess its safe to assume that you aren't compensating one bit?"

Desmond begins to fold and then tuck his handkerchief back into his blazer pocket, reaches into his pocket, retrieves his keys and then ever so eloquently replies with "Not even for a second! I don't need too!"

Lyriq laughs and then gets inquisitive "So where are you going all dressed up tonight? Huh? It wouldn't be a business venture tonight would it be? You know that you are supposed to inform me and keep me in the loop with all that!?!" Desmond smiles a devilish yet irritated beguiling smile and then answers her question calmly.

"Actually, I am invited to a fashion show by one of the magazines customers and a good friend of mine at BETA Nightclub."

Lyriq automatically assumes that she will be attending this event with Desmond. "Well I guess I better go home and get changed." Desmond gets serious for a moment when she says that sensing that she was somehow going to want to come with him and use the boards decision to hire her as the reason.

"For What? You're not coming with me?" he asks in curious tone.

"I am going with you!!" Lyriq replies.

"No your not!" Desmond says as he looks down and starts to search for the automatic unlock button to his car door on his keychain.

“Yes I am Desmond!! Did you not hear anything the big guy said?? You have to include me in on everything. Now why don't you just run me by my place real quick so I can change and then we can go?!” Desmond opens his car door and gets in. He starts his car, rolls down the window looks over at Lyriq from the drivers side and says “No thanks baby. This superhero doesn't have a sidekick!!”

Desmond then speeds off leaving Lyriq there with a dumbfounded look on her face. She then begins to walk away and Desmond backs up to her and tells her to get in. The scene fades out watching the car drive away and him tapping the brake lights as he turns on his left blinker and turns.

Chapter 16
The Fashion Show @ Club Beta

Chapter 16 FASHION SHOW / CLUB BETA

Desmond and Lyriq pull up in front of the venue to valet parking. The Valet opens the door for Lyriq as Desmond gets out. He throws the keys to the valet as he walks around the car. He and Lyriq enter the building. Both Desmond and Lyriq walk up to the door and they are greeted by security.

Desmond gives the security guard his name and lets him know that the lady is with him. The security guard allows both of them to enter.

Inside the club all you can smell is the sweet fragrances of a million different scented perfumes. As they look from left to right all they see is scantily dressed men serving drinks as well as scantily dressed women with jeweled and feathered tiara's accompanied by peacock feathers attached to the back of their costumes.

The DJ is playing a mix of, hip-hop/ trance/ rock and pop music as people are mingling, conversing and passing business cards around. Desmond whispers in Lyriqs ear that he is going to go get a drink and at the same time Nicole comes up followed by a gorgeous waitress and tray with 3 shots of tequila. Nicole hugs Desmond!

"Desmond-Desmond-DESMOND!!! You handsome man you!!! I am so happy you made it!! Say.....?" she pauses awkwardly for a moment as she scans Desmond up and down and then asks "....would you be interested in helping me out by being a model tonight? I'm missing a male model?"

Desmond is put off a bit, but not surprised by her request. He smiles and says "Uhhhh..... NO!!

Nicole smiles and then looks at the waitress and the waitress looks at Desmond from head to toe also and then she says "Bummer, I would have loved to have seen that one happen."

Desmond winks at the waitress and then she smiles. He then looks back at Nicole and says “Now YOU already knew the answer to that!”

Nicole rolls her eyes “Oh whatever Desmond. Quit being so damn modest and show us what's beneath the shirt!” Desmond starts grinning from ear to ear as Nicole continues to flirt with him and put him the spot.

“I’m a lot of things but modest and being one of your models I can't be Nicole. Besides what would that say about our professional relationship?” Nicole is very witty and responds quickly “That you're willing to go above and beyond to keep the customer happy. Who is always right may I add!!”

Desmond puts his arm around Nicole and begins to look around the club as he answers her “You were my friend before you were my customer Nicole, you can't use that against me.”

Nicole laughs and says “I bet that's what you tell all the girls!!”

Lyriq stands on the side of Desmond soaking in the whole conversation. She makes a sigh and then Desmond cuts the conversation off before it goes further in-depth while Lyriq is present.

“Uhhh........ Nicole!!?? Let me introduce you too Lyriq Moore.” He stands aside. Nicole stands there with her arms crossed while she eyes Lyriq from head-to-toe. Desmond coughs twice as too stop Nicole from eyeballing Lyriq any longer and say something.

Nicole speaks “Hello Lyriq!!” Nicole shakes Lyriq's hand. “It’s a pleasure to meet you. Are you and Desmond seeing each?” Desmond interrupts quickly with the answer before Nicole can finish the question “Uhhhh............ Lyriq is my new partner in crime at Fly Magazine, so she will be involved with all facets of operations. Inside and outside of the building.”

“Mmmm Hmmmm........ I see.” Nicole stands there for a second and then continues speaking with Desmond. “So Desmond I’m going to get back here with these models and make sure that hair, makeup and wardrobe are all going to plan. I want you and your friend to have a seat in the V.I.P. section that I have roped off. Have a good time tonight and I will be in touch.”

Nicole motions to the waitress to give them the shots and she takes a glass as well. Desmond and Nicole take the shots then Nicole says “Ciao Dessie. It was a pleasure Ms. Moore.”

Lyriq gives a fake smile and looks the other way to take the shot. Nicole walks off in true diva fashion. “She was different! What number is she in your phone...... Dessie?”

Desmond is still looking around the club and bobbing his head to the music while Lyriq is being sarcastic. “You know? You are becoming a real buzz kill. This is business not personal and you are not acting at that professional level. Now I share this position with you because I have too, but I don't have to like it!! Believe me when I tell you....... the minute you slip up or mess up a business deal because of your attitude, then we will go to speak with Mr. Elmhurst and the board!!! Kapeesh?!”

Lyriq looks at Desmond with a very devious smile and responds with “I thought you would never come around Desmond. Now we can get down to business.”

Desmond gives a look at Lyriq and nods his head and says “Good!!”

“Great!!” Lyriq comes back quickly.

Desmond looks out over the club looking for the VIP section and then walks away. He stops in mid stride across the club and looks back at Lyriq to motion her to follow. They both enter the VIP to a table with Desmond's name on the table tent. Desmond allows Lyriq to slide into the booth and then he slides in next. They both are sitting there watching the crowd ignoring each other as the night goes on.

The time is flying by when Nicole takes to the stage to introduce herself and announce that the fashion show will be beginning in a moment. As Nicole continues to introduce herself and her company the crowd begins to shuffle to the front of the runway where there are seats set up for the special guests of the city that Nicole invited to view her new line of fashion.

Desmond is sitting in his seat pointing out all the heavy hitters in the city to Lyriq that he can recognize.

"Okay, the first thing to having a key to the city is getting acquainted with all the movers and shakers. So let me start by pointing out a few shakers. Ms. Nicole McKnight our gracious host who you've met already is the owner of Re'viel clothing. The people you see sitting along the edge of the runway in the front are from our competition IMAGE MAGAZINE and that's the owner sitting to the left. His name is ISAAC LE'FLUER, his assistant Tamara Fancy and the entertainment editor Eric Graham. People consider Eric to be my white equivalent, but I don't see any resemblance of what I do in him."

Lyriq smirks at Desmond "You sound like you're a bit jealous or worried?"

"Me? Jealous? Worried? About what? Some guy who patterns his style, fashion and look around my swag?? I think not....... I'm just filling you in on the competition." Desmond takes a sip of his drink as he looks towards Lyriq. "Mmm Hmm....." Lyriq also takes a sip of her drink as she looks the other way unconvinced of Desmonds confidence. Desmond takes another sip of his drink and continues his breakdown of the people around the runway.

"Anyway, like I was saying. The people on the left side of the stage are reps from 1800 Tequila. They are one of the main sponsors for this event if you couldn't tell. I actually made the connection. 1800 Tequila and FLY mag do a lot of business together. I got that account for the mag right out of college and they've been loyal advertisers every since. Now the other group of people on the other side of the stage are different retail sellers. You got the Macy's decision making staff there and then the smaller buyers such as Marshalls and Ross chain store directors."

"Wow!! You really have this down packed!" Lyriq tries not to act shocked.

"I've been doing this for almost 5 years now. I better!!" Desmond shrugs his shoulders like its nothing.

"I'm impressed!!" Lyriq is swirling her little sword around in her drink as she compliments him.

Desmond winks his eye at her while Lyriq takes a sip of her drink and tries to lighten up a bit by sparking more conversation.

So?? Desmond?? she says. "Yes?" Desmond responds without looking back at Lyriq while he is sipping his drink again. He's attentively watching the models begin to stroll back and forth down the runway in the fall clothing line as he responds . "How is it that a strong detail oriented, successful man like yourself is still a bachelor?"

Desmond takes his eyes away from the runway for a moment to pay complete attention to Lyriq as he continues to kind of sway back and forth to the music. "That's kind of a personal non-business related question isn't it?"

Lyriq answers "Yes, but a necessary question considering all your over masculinized, misogynistic machismo you exude all the time. Desmond continues back at looking at the show, taking sips and crunching on small pieces of ice. "Nope, not going there with you lady. Strictly business!!"

Lyriq gets irritated "Whatever Desmond!!"

Just as Desmond and Lyriq start to open up, laugh and joke. A tall slender gentleman approaches the table with a suave demeanor and debonair stance. The gentleman's name is Isaac Le'Fluer the owner of Image magazine.

"Bonjor Desmond!!" He stands in front of the table with a dictator like swagger, smiling at Desmond.

"Bonjor... Mr. Le'Fluer." Desmond responds respectively. "It's always such a pleasant surprise to see you young man." Mr. Le'Fluer responds to Desmonds greeting. "The pleasure is all mine sir. To what do I owe this visit?"

Mr. Le'Fluer begins to speak..."I always wonder how you are doing over there at that piece of paper you call a magazine." He holds a martinis glass in one hand and speaks with his other hand like he is sign languaging. Desmond responds "Well Mr. Le'Fluer I can tell you that I am doing well as usual. Entering my 5th year of employment with them. I love it and I am completely intent with them as well as them with me."

Mr. Le'Fluer smiles with a sinister disposition as he replies "Mmmm Hmmm.......... I see! Well my PORTE' is always open for you young man....... (Porte' **is french for the word** "Door")

Mr. Le'Fluer then switch's his attention to Lyriq with an eye of wonder and says in French "Oh mon dieu, qu'est-ce que nous avons ici"........ (**french translation:** "Oh my!! What do we have here")

Lyriq smiles with a slight blush and then Isaac introduces himself "Bonjour Madame, et quel est votre nom?"......... (**french translation:** Hello Miss and what is your name?) Desmond goes to speak for Lyriq and tell Mr. LeFluer that she doesn't speak French when Lyriq speaks up and replies to him in French

"She doesn't understand French Mr. Le'Fluer......." Lyriq interrupts and says "Je vous demande pardon, Je comprends bien le francais. Mon nom est Lyriq Moore....." (**french translation:** "I beg your pardon, I understand French well. My name is Lyriq Moore")

Lyriq reaches her hand out to shake Isaac's hand. He takes her hand and kisses it in true international gent fashion. Desmond looks on not shocked, yet intrigued. Mr. Le'Fluer continues the conversation in English.

"Ahh.....so you know my language!!" Lyriq answers him "Oui!!" (french translation: "Yes!")

"So what are you doing hanging with Mr. Coolwater?" he asks her. "We work together at FLY magazine." she replies. Mr. Le'Fluer gives a french giggle and says "So he is your boss?"

Lyriq laughs as she glances at Desmond and then proceeds to answer Mr. Le'Fluers second "No, no, no........ we are co-workers. I have been hired by the company to oversee the feminine side of FLY MAG." Mr. Le'Fluer is in shock by her response and forgets to speak in English "Quelle est cette?"....... (**french translation:** "What is this")

Desmond intervenes "We are doing more with the company and her services will serve the mag as a great asset." Mr. Le'Fluer smiles at Desmond with a condescending facial expression "I see.... well I guess not everything is always going to be a one MAN operation. Right Desmond??"

Desmond looks at Mr. Le'Fluer and takes a sip of his drink and then replies "Well not everything is as it seems either Mr. Le'FLuer."

"Most certainly not Mr. Coolwater!! I make no assumptions at all. Just observations my talented young friend. Just observations!! I will be leaving now and heading back to finish viewing the show, but if you are interested then you are invited to come sit with me and my team by the stage."

Desmond respectively turns down the invitation "I do appreciate the invitation sir, but I believe that we will stay here and view the show from here."

“Well the offer is there and like I always say to you Desmond... My Porte’ is always open!!” Mr. Le’Fluer repeats what he said in the beginning of the conversation as he turns his attention to Lyriq.

“Thank you sir I will keep that in mind. Avoir une bonne nuit”............... (**french translation:** Have a great night!!) Desmond says.

Mr. Le’Fluer and Desmond shake hands and then he turns to Lyriq and says “It has been a pleasure Ms. Moore.” Lyriq replies “The feeling is mutual Mr. Le’Fluer. I’m sure we will run into each other again.” Mr. Le’Fluer bids Lyriq a farewell in true frenchman fashion “Revoir manquez...... En effet, nous nous reverrons”....... (**french translation:** “Goodbye miss....... Indeed, we shall meet again”)

He kisses Lyriqs hand again and walks away from the table with the same smooth demeanor that he made his introduction with. “Well!!?? He was refreshing.” Desmond is drinking his drink and looking down at the bottom of his glass as he says “Yeah..... refreshingly annoying and snake like. As usual!!”

“I tell you Desmond this jealous vibe I’m getting from you is so not like the Desmond I’ve heard these folk lore stories about.” Desmond gives a beguiling smile to Lyriq “Me? Jealous? No, I think not! Me being jealous is like Michael Jackson and Lisa Marie Presley’s marriage or like Drew Barrymore and Tom Green dating.... not real!! Very fictional........... all figments of your extremely vivid imagination. I’m merely just stating a fact. The man is a snake and he has been trying to get me to defect to Image magazine since I got out of college. He would do anything to get the upper hand over Fly magazine and I have worked hard with tooth and nail to keep him under us in every faucet. He’s like that french guy the Merovingian in the movie Matrix............ he just keeps coming back and wont go away.”

“Okay.....?” Lyriq mocks Desmond in a sarcastic tone.

"I'm being serious!! He is a conniving and will not hesitate at any chance to one up us. Keep that in mind when you are chatting with him or any other competition. Anyway....." Desmond stops his tandem and continues to sip his drink and look out over the dance floor. The music is loud and the fashion show is still in full swing.

Lyriq sits there drinking her drink and starts to bop and dance in her seat a bit. She checks out of the corner of her left eye to see if Desmond is watching, but he is focused back on the fashion show. So she decided to ask him to dance.

"So can you dance or do you just come to the club and bird watch when you go out?" Desmond looks over at her as if she just said a bad word. "I can dance, but thats not what we are here to do."

Lyriq replies "Always business huh?" Desmond confirms her thoughts "Always!!"

Lyriq ignores his response and decides to mingle "Whatever. Well I'm going to go out here dance and mingle. You can stay here and be a drag!!"

Desmond shrugs his shoulders and tells her to "Have fun!" Lyriq replies "I will......" She walks out to the dance floor and begins dancing by herself and not long after she is joined by Eric Graham the entertainment editor from Image magazine.

They are dancing and Eric stares at Desmond as if he thinks he got Desmonds date. Desmond looks at Eric with a look like "Whatever" and then looks away scratching the side of his face with his middle finger while sipping his drink with his other hand. Desmond is watching the fashion show while discreetly looking over at Lyriq and Eric talking and dancing. Desmond is bored yet pondering how he is going to deal with his present situation of having to co-exist with Lyriq as a partner at Fly mag.

The night is passing by quickly. The sounds of the club are

drowned out by Desmond's thoughts. Desmond watches the fashion show and stares out into the crowd. Everything is a haze and sort of like a scene in a slow motion movie for Desmond until he is brought back to reality. Lyriq is calling Desmond's name. As he comes too...... her voice becomes louder "desmond...? desMOND?? DESMOND??"

Desmond comes too and notices that Lyriq is talking to him. "Uhhh.....?? yeah? Yes! What's up?"

Lyriq looks at him weird and asks "Are you ok?" Desmond answers her question "Im good just a bit tired and I think I've had enough for tonight."

Just as he says that Eric walks up with two fresh drinks for himself and Lyriq. "Here's your drink beautiful." Lyriq takes the drink and says thank you. Desmond and Eric look at each other and acknowledge one another. "Well..... well........ if it isn't the cities biggest celebrity in the flesh!! Desmond Coolwater…" Desmond looks over to acknowledge Eric and replies "If it isn't Image Mags greatest **ASS**et!! Mr. Graham....." Both men shake hands firmly as they continue to look each other eye to eye.

Lyriq interrupts the tension "Cough-cough... Awkward?? Alright well I guess I better get my things."

Eric looks at Lyriq as he stops staring Desmond down and asks "Are you leaving??"

"Yes, I do believe that is my que to go." Lyriq is grabbing her purse and coat getting ready to ride out with Desmond when Eric asks "Why?" Desmond looks the other way as if subtracting himself from the conversation completely.

"Well I rode here with Desmond" Lyriq replies. "I'll give you a ride home? Don't leave yet? We were just getting started. There is an after party after this and then we will go to a restaurant that will be opening its doors just for us after that." he says. "Well that sounds like fun!! I wasn't ready to leave yet anyway." Lyriq says as she sets her stuff back down.

Eric looks over at Desmond as if he won the girl. "Great!! You don't mind do you..... Desmond??"

Desmond could care less and shows it in his body language and his response. "Nope!! Not one bit. Knock yourself out."

Lyriq gets offended that she is being pawned off "Excuse me...... I AM standing right here. I can answer for myself. Desmond I'll catch you at the office tomorrow."

Desmond gets up and says "Indeed"

"Later Desmond." Eric says in a sarcastic tone

"Adios" Desmond turns around to leave the VIP section as he replies with Adios. As Desmond is walking towards the exit Nicole is still MC-ing the show and she notice's Desmond leaving. She yells out over the microphone and introduces him to the crowd "Ladies and gentleman I'd like to take this time out to thank a friend and business affiliate....... Desmond Coolwater!!"

Nicole yells out Desmonds name and waves as he is walking out completely putting him on the spot, but he handles it in true presidential fashion and waves back as he continues to make his way to the front door. Desmond reaches the front door and before he exits, he turns to see if Lyriq was paying attention. Lyriq is clapping and shaking her head. Desmond walks out the door.

Chapter 17
Desmond's Place
#overslept

Chapter 17 DESMOND'S BEDROOM

The room is silent as the morning light creeps into the room. All the shades are still up so there is no hiding from it other than the pillow that Desmond has over his face. He is still fully dressed as if he forgot to take his close off, his phone is ringing and buzzing off the hook. Desmond sits up slowly, eyes squinting from the sunlight blinding him. He looks over at the clock and notices that he is running late to work. He has already missed the usual time at the gym with Henry.

Desmond Grabs the phone and attempts to answer it, but as he answers it, the phone stops ringing. He looks at the phone to see what other calls he has missed and he has 3 missed messages, plus two texts. Desmond retrieves his messages:

(VOICEMAIL VOICE)

Message One at 7:40am:

Hello? Hello? Desmond?? What's up this is Henry. I'm here at 24hr fitness and you aren't here bro. Are you ok!!! Give me a call. Oh and the trainer from the bicycle class was looking FANTASTIC this morning man, you missed out. I almost passed out trying to keep up with her. (LAUGH) Call me and let me know you are cool. Later!!

(VOICEMAIL MENU)

To delete this message press #7. If you want to save this message then press #9.

Desmond presses #7 to delete

Message Two at 9:10am:

Good Morning! My name is Peter Dash and I acquired your contact information from a mutual friend of ours named Vince from "The Mint". He tells me that you are quit the businessman and that i should speak to you about possible advertisement in your magazine as well as the possibilities of you consulting me on how to promote my launch party for my new energy drink. If you received this message anytime this morning please give me a call. My number is (303)XXX-XXXX. This afternoon I will be in meetings until 3:00pm, but will be free to talk or even meet anytime after that. I look forward to speaking with you and thank you for your time.

Desmond thinks out loud and says to himself "Right on Vince!! Good looking out on the business prospect."

(VOICEMAIL MENU)

To delete this message press #7. If you want to save this message then press #9.

Desmond presses #7 to delete

Message Three at 9:45am:

Desmond this is James. You know? Your assistant from that place you work at. I'm curious as to why you don't have yo ass here right now. Mr. Elmhurst has been asking for you. The reps from Coors has called like 3 times today. You didn't forget we had the model shoot this afternoon did you?? Oh yeah I caught your girl Lyriq at your desk snooping thru your notes and messages. You might want to watch out for that chick. She is poison!!!! Call me when you get this. I was able to intercept some of your calls by forwarding your desk phone to my cell. I got some messages that you want to hear ASAP!! Remember that bitch is POISON!!!! James hangs up the phone.

Desmond hangs up from his voicemail immediately to call James back. Desmond is dialing the number with some urgency. The phone rings and James picks it up on the second ring "Man what in the hell are you doing? Shit is out of control here. Mr. Elmhurst is looking for you, but don't worry I covered for you. I had your calls forwarded to my phone so I could keep things moving for you. Last night must have been crazy." Desmond sighs "Not really. I got home and laid down thinking. Accidently fell asleep and didn't set my alarm."James yells out playfully "We don't have time for that Coolwater come on now. We got a call from Chauncey Billup's sports agent and he is down with our proposal."

Desmond gets excited "Shut the hell up?!?"

James is excited as well "No seriously!!! He said that Chauncey is 100% in for the interview and photoshoot with the championship rings and everything!!! We are the greatest team man!!! We like Batman and Robin, Butch Cassidy and the Sundance kid, Shaq and Kobe, Jordan and Pippen, Captain America and Bucky?!" Desmond laughs "Man shut up!! You're a trip!! Maybe you are in the wrong business. I think you should become a comedian some day."

"Don't sleep on it. I just may and then you can be my manager." James jokingly suggests and Desmond agrees to the offer. Deal! Let me get off this phone and get dressed and make it to the office.......What time is the photo shoot?" Desmond asks. "About 2:00pm...... Hurry up!!! This chick is really shark swimming past your desk every 15 minutes or so like can't nobody see her. She acting real Bell, Biv, Devoe........ Poison!!!" James sings the last line of the 90's hit "POISON" by Bell, Biv, Devoe.

"Okay cool!! I will be there in a bit and James??"

James peps up and says "Yeah what's up?"

"Thanks" Desmond says. "Thanks yo ass..... get in here before I have to trip the bitch in her high heels or something." James hangs up the phone and in the background of the room you can hear Bell Biv Devoe's song Poison playing!! The last part of the song plays as the scene fades to black.

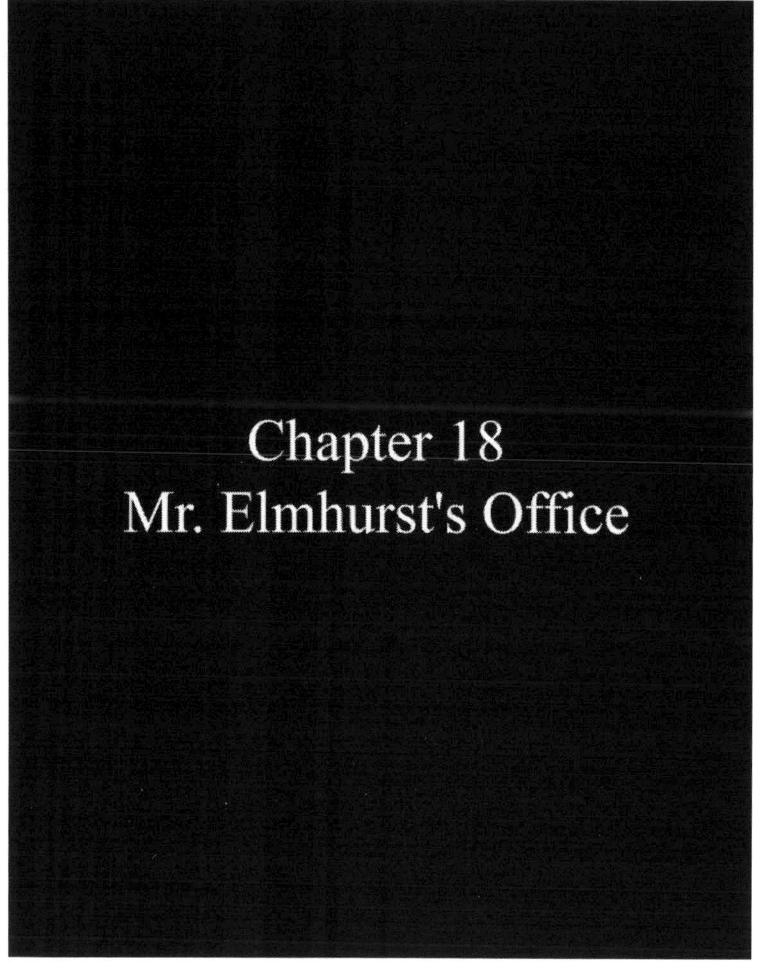
Chapter 18
Mr. Elmhurst's Office

Chapter 18 MR. ELMHURST'S OFFICE

Desmond makes it to the office about an hour an half later and heads straight to Mr. Elmhurst office. He walks past James desk and drops his bag off and gives him dap. As he grabs the doorknob to the office the scene slows down and he looks to his right side and notices that Lyriq is eyeballing him attentively as he walks into the office. He kind of frowns at her as he turns the doorknob and enters the office. The scene goes back to normal speed.

"Mr. Elmhurst I apologize for being late into the office. I don't have any excuses other than I overslept. I went to the Re'Veil fashion show last night with Lyriq. We stayed for a while just so I could make sure that everything went without a hitch and then I ended up leaving a bit early." Mr. Elmhurst is sitting in chair listening to Desmond explain himself as he pulls his cigar out of the box and cuts the end of it. Then once Desmond has finished he tells Desmond to sit down. "Its ok son… Sit down, sit down for a minute. Lets talk."

Desmond takes a seat and listens attentively. "Desmond I have known you for almost 5 years now. I hired you right out of college because when you walked in that door and sat down you were on a mission. You had a drive and ambition about you that I couldn't compare to anyone or anything I have seen in awhile. You have since grown into quite the interesting young man. You made yourself a name here in the city and some other parts of the country and outside for that matter. I'm loving it. However, you have allowed yourself to become flawed?"

Desmond sits back in his seat with a curious, yet worried look on his face. His emotions are starting to race as he asks Mr. Elmhurst "Why do you say that sir? What do you mean by all this?" Mr. Elmhurst explains "I say all that to say this? You have been so good at being great that you haven't ever had your metal tested Desmond." Desmond is dumbfounded by Mr. Elmhurst's statements "What ?!?"

Mr. Elmhurst can see that Desmond is getting perturbed so elaborates on his statement. “Desmond you’ve never had your balls weighed son!!! Its easy to be at the top when you start out at the top. I’m not saying you haven’t worked your ass off all these years. I’m just saying that you are too comfy and we need edgy and testy. We want more for the magazine. We need to go from a regional publication to a national/international publication. We need to know that you are ready for that.”

Desmond goes from legs being crossed and comfortable to sitting up in his seat… “I can do that Mr. Elmhurst. I am edgy!!! I am ready. I have competition out there and everywhere I go. I was just at the fashion show last night and the competition was there. Image magazine was there sniffing under the skirt of the hard work I did for that event. I fight tooth and nail to get these accounts by any means necessary!!”

Mr. Elmhurst senses Desmonds uneasiness and begins to try to settle Desmond down. “Desmond calm down. We are not downplaying anything you have done already. We appreciate the work and look forward to getting more from you. You have yet to reach your full potential and that is amazing considering everything that you have accomplished at such a young age. There are some that would argue that you slept your way to the top, but I can firmly stand up for you considering everybody above you are male.” Mr. Elmhurst laughs a big hearty laugh as he breaks the tension a bit. Desmond laughs and loosens up a bit and then replies “Don't tempt me!!”
Mr. Elmhurst is still giggling a bit, but looked at Desmond with a curious look after that statement.

“Listen son I just want you to know that we still back you up here at the magazine and to not lose your grip on the goals ahead here.” Desmond nods his head and says “Indeed sir!!”

Mr. Elmhurst takes another pull from his cigar as he continues to speak “Now, with that being said I heard last night went great, but had a hiccup?” Desmond sits back up straight in his seat taken back by his statement and repeats what he says “A hiccup?? What kind of a hiccup?"

"Well from Lyriq's point of view you left the event early. Did not stay until the end and there were some potential clients to round up. From her assessment of the night, you missed some key role players and she had to pick up the slack due to your lack of enthusiasm for the job at hand? She also stated that Image magazine was there and had a chance to capitalize on this? Is that true?"

Desmond gets frustrated by this false claim by Lyriq, but continues to explain himself. "I did leave early sir, but I assure you that Image had no chance of taking anything from us or gaining on us." Mr. Elmhurst sits back is chair relaxed. "Well I just thought I'd check with you. This isn't the time to let your slip show. She's gunning to take over the whole department. She has this cunning yet conniving disposition about her that gives me a cold chill every time she is around. Almost like she can taste blood."

"Yeah....... she rubs me the same way." Desmond agrees.

"You don't let her rub anything and keep an eye on her. This one is off limits!! You hear me??? Off limits!! Kapesh?" Mr. Elmhurst sits back up in his seat with his elbows on the desk to make sure his point is understand and made very clear.

"Understood sir." Desmond shakes his head and replies.

"Alright. I'm glad we had this talk. I am about to get out of here and go to my dentist appointment and then go golfing. Get out of here and get to work." Mr. Elmhurst barks.

"Will do. Have a great day!!" Desmond gets up from the seat feeling irritated and fired up by Lyriq overstepping her boundaries by trying to give a report to Mr. Elmhurst about him, but he decides to let it slide for now, continue working with her and not say anything. As he exits the office he looks over at Lyriq's desk with a glare and then he smiles at her. She is on the phone, but she gives a fake sassy grin back.

The scene fades to the ending part of **"BELL, BIV, DEVOE's song "POISON"** as Desmond walks thru the office and they stare each other down.

Chapter 19 COORS PHOTO SHOOT

Desmond and James are on location for the Coors photo shoot. They are sitting and enjoying the scenery as tons of models walk around in all white attire. Some are dressed in winter apparel, while others are dressed in spring and summer apparel. Both men are dressed in white sitting in the photographers seat with dark shades and tanning boards like they need to tan. As they sit there lounging and catching some sun they talk about the fashion show, the interview with Chauncey Billup's and the models at the photo shoot.

"I need to do something!! Desmond says. James sits motionless as he asks his question. "What are you talking about??"

"I'm talking about Lyriq man. She is trying to ruin me. The Coolwater brand is under fire here. She is **deliberately** trying to ruin me." Desmond says as he sits motionless in his chair as well.

James is zoned out with his sun glasses on shaking his head as he repeats everything that Desmond says "Deliberately…"

Desmond carries on talking, thinking that James is listening "I mean this chick is systematically attempting to erase all the hard work I've done by undermining me and going behind my back."

"Systematically, undermining, going behind ya back" he continues to repeat everything that Desmond says.

"The thing I don't get is how can the mag do this to me? Its like they are trying to get her on the job training from me. Get all of my contacts and connections and then let me go."

"Yep and let you go!!....." James agrees with Desmond still repeating Desmonds every word. Desmond turns his head over towards James who is leaning back in his chair still holding the tanning board with his dark shades on, eyes closed, repeating everything he says. "Are you listening to me?" Desmond asks.

“What?? Yes, I hear everything you are saying, but what do you want to do? James says. “Nothing! Sit there and let her take over. You do know that once I’m fired and gone then you are next!! Right??”

James sits up abruptly in his seat, then dramatically falling out of his position after hearing Desmond make his last comment. He starts going off on an adrenaline filled tantrum. “What?!?! Awe HELLLL NOOO!!! We gotta wack her ass Dez!!! We could trip her down the stairs. The janitor owes me a favor for hooking him up with some Nuggets tickets. We could get her whacked and rolled in a carpet.”

Desmond looks at James out the corner of his eyes as he is talking “Really?? James?!?! Really???”

Desmond is looking at James with a look of disgust and frustration. “Yeah!! WHAT??....” James looks at Desmond with a look of lost bewilderment.

Then Desmond asks “....and how many times do I have to tell you to stop scalping our company tickets!!! Those are for the employees, not for you too hustle with.”

“You weren’t complaining when we went on that double date with the **FEATHER FREAKS**” James laughs as he reminds Desmond of that night.

Desmond and James both look up and gaze off into the sky for a moment having flashbacks of that night and all the sex charades they had that night. Then he agrees softly as he remembers and snaps back to reality. “Man!!!.......... stay focused!!! We have got to keep her from taking over and keep US winning!!”

“Your right!! James agrees.” Both Desmond and James sit back down and slouch in their seats with their glasses on while models continue to walk back and forth in front of them. Desmond then brings up the Chauncey Billup's interview. “SO what did

Chauncey's agent say about the interview?"

"Well he was a little lax-a-daisy about it, but he definitely said that Chauncey was with it. It's going to be hard catching him due to his schedule though." James informs Desmond. "Call his agent back and ask him to give us a time when he plans on traveling back home for a bit. We may have to schedule a phone interview and ask for rights to use pictures in the mag. If so then I want pictures of him in his Knick's uniform as well as his other vintage uniforms such as when he was with the Timberwolves or Toronto.... oh and definitely Detroit. It's a must that we have pictures of when he was first with the Nuggets and then recent pictures of when he got traded back home and the new Nuggets uniform.......... cool??

"Done deal. I'll call him first thing in the morning!" James confirms. "No, lets get this done today. I don't care what time it is in New York. Let's make sure he understands we are serious about this and that we want this interview done as soon as possible."

James shakes his head and says "Sounds good." Desmond and James are sitting there quietly soaking in the sun again. Just as they both get comfortable again Lyriq shows up dressed in all black amongst everyone else that is dressed in all white and breaks the mood. "So this is what you do on company time?

Both Desmond and James sit up. James takes his glasses off and says "Oh look the storm clouds just rolled in and blocked the sun!! I guess I better get out of here before the tornado comes in and blows us all to OZ. I sure would hate to meet the wicked "Bee-WITCH"....ya know?!?

James gets up from his chair and gives Desmond the heads up nod as he packs up his tanning board under his arm and walks towards Lyriq, stops, pulls his glasses down to the rim of his nose, looks Lyriq up and down and then slides his glasses back up and walks away. Lyriq makes a sassy face back at him as he walks away. She then takes his seat next to Desmond who is still leaning back in his seat and relaxing.

Desmond replies to her question "Here Slumming it today huh???

Lyriq sits back into the seat that James was sitting in and pulls her purse up. She then pulls out her make up and begins to freshen up her make up in her mirror. "Nope, just working and making sure everything is handled professionally."

Desmond sits up in his chair and folds up the tanning board. "Yeah I've noticed. Good work with the fashion show last night. I hear you handled everything professionally!?!" Desmond says with complete sarcasm making Lyriq get on the defensive. "Look....... you left early and a few things was going on that I thought you should have been there to see and/or handle. I noticed what needed to be done and I fixed it. I didn't mean to make you look bad partner. I was just trying to cover OUR behinds and make the company look good."

Desmond sits in his seat and does not move a muscle as he stares at Lyriq and replies "Partners huh?? Lyriq answers quickly "Yes!! Partners!!" Lyriq extends her hand out for Desmond to shake it. Desmond looks at her hand for a moment and then shakes her hand. "Great!!! Thats-that. So since you were gone this morning I took the liberty of looking at your calendar of events and I noticed that you helped promote the Christopher KID Reid comedy show at the La Rhumba room tonight?!?!?! Why don't we go together??"

Desmond sits up in his chair straight and takes his glasses off so he could look at Lyriq seriously "Hey you can't just be going to my desk and going thru my things like that."

"Well you haven't forwarded me anything yet and I am supposed to be kept in the loop with everything you do." she says. "I feel violated. What is this coming too?" Desmond asks. "It's just a partnership Desmond. We have to work together remember??"

Desmond looks at Lyriq and slides his glasses back on, but he continues to sit up straight as he watches the photo shoot and converse with Lyriq. “Yeah I remember.”

“So how about it? You and me go to the comedy show together?” Lyriq goes back to the initial question.

Desmond never looks over at Lyriq as they are talking. He then says “Sorry, I already have a date for that event.” Lyriq smiles and slides off of her seat seductively. “Well..... it sounds like I’ll be going stag then. I’ll see you there Mr. Coolwater.”

Lyriq struts away like a sleek cat. Desmond watch’s her exit with a turned on yet irritated stare.

Cool Nights

Chapter 20 @ FLY MAGAZINE OFFICES

Desmond is headed back the office after the Photoshoot to check messages, make some callbacks and catch up. He gets to his desk and notices that his planner with all of his contacts have been moved and put back in the wrong place. Desmond grabs his planner and sits down at his desk. As he is flipping thru his pages of the planner he is getting more and more upset. Just then Cindy walks up to the desk to speak with Desmond.

"Hi Desmond" Desmond looks up for a moment to acknowledge Cindy and then looks back down at his planner. "Hey Cindy. How can I help you."

Cindy looks around before she answers his question as if to make sure no one can hear what she about to say. "Well technically its not me needing the help per say." Desmond looks back up at Cindy to see what she is talking about.

"Okay? You have my attention. What's going on??" he asks. "I probably shouldn't be telling you this because I could get fired and I don't want to get fired because I love my job, but I really felt like you should know." Cindy begins to speaking at the speed of light telling Desmond everything that she has witnessed go down in the office during his absence.

Desmond's head is swirling back and forth before he grabs her and says "Cindy!! CINDY!!! CINDY!!! Just calm down, SLOW DOWN and tell me what's going on alright?"

"Okay so I was making copies at the printer and sending faxes like I always do, when I noticed that Ms. Moore was at your desk. She was sitting there and it looked like she was making phone calls and going thru some stuff on your desk." Cindy informs him.

"She was on my phone making calls?" Desmond asks calmly. "Yeah that's what it looked like."

“I see...... Hmmmmmm well that explains why my planner was out of place.”

Cindy is nervous and she frantically asks Desmond “You're not going to tell anyone I told you are you? Please don't!!” Desmond assures her that she is ok. “Don't worry Cindy you're safe. What are you doing here anyway? Its like almost 5:00pm?”

“Mr. Elmhurst has me doing some document shredding this evening and I promised I would have the storage room organized as well.” she says. “Ok I Gotcha. Well I really appreciate the heads up Cindy. I owe you one!!” Desmond reaches out and touches her shoulder.

“Nah, this one's a freebie for you Dessie” Desmond packs up his bag, grabs his coat and kisses Cindy on the cheek as he leaves the office.

Chapter 21 DEEP THOUGHT /LIGHTRAIL

Desmond is riding the Lightrail home. He is sitting by the window and staring at the mountains as the light rail train speeds by everything at light speed. You can tell that he is deep in thought. Just then he decides to call Sincere and invite her out to the comedy show. He dials her number and waits for her to answer:

RING-RING and then it goes straight to voicemail: "Hello!! This is Lyriq I appreciate your call. I apologize if I missed you, but if you will leave your name, number and the reason you called. I will call you right back. Thanks!!!"

BEEEEEEEEEP

Desmond starts to leave a message. "Shit!! Hey Sincere this is Desmond. Of course you know that already. Uhhh....... I just wanted to invite you to a comedy show tonight. I got some free tickets to see…"

Suddenly Desmonds phone is beeping and it is Sincere calling on the other end. He then leaves the message and answers his other line. "...well this is you calling on the other line so I will hang up with you and then talk to you." He laughs as he clicks over and answers the phone.

"Hello beautiful!!" Sincere smiles on the other end of the phone as she responds. "Well hello Mr. Coolwater. How have you been stranger?"

"Wheeling and dealing as usual." Desmond replies. "I figured you forgot about me and moved on."

Desmond laughs at her and then says "....moved on??" Sincere answers "Yeah. I haven't heard from you in a couple of days and all."

Desmond explains what's been going on lately. "Yeah it's been a little hectic with my job and new business acquisitions and all. Had a fashion show I had to attend slash work at the other night and today we had a photo shoot all day so I was on the set."

"I bet there were all kind of sexy, voluptuous models walking around huh?" Sincere asks in a semi jealous tone. Desmond responds with a smooth reassuring answer. "None more beautiful and may I add voluptuous than you." Sincere sighs. "Whatever Desmond. So what's new?"

"Well I was calling because I have tickets to a comedy show that we have been promoting in the magazine. Do you remember the hip-hop group KID-N-PLAY?" Desmond asks. "Yes!! I loved them!! Me and my girls used to do their dance moves and watch their movies all the time. My favorite was Kid. He was so sexy with his big ol flat top!! I just loved his high yellow sexy ass!!"

Desmond laughs at her and continues to speak about the show as well as invite her. "Funny you should say that. He is now a comedian and will be here tonight. The mag co-sponsored the event with the club so we get free tickets to the event. I was wondering if you would accompany me to the show tonight?"

"I think I may be available tonight. Let me check my schedule????...... Hmmmmmm alright." she replies. Desmond smiles and asks her in a flirtatious tone. "You got room for me in your busy schedule lady?"

"That's what we are trying to find out Coolwater. So what time do I need to be ready?" Sincere says.

"Let's do this? The show starts at 8:00 pm so I'll come get you around 6:30 pm so we can grab a bite to eat and maybe have a drink. Then we can go to the show?" Desmond says. "Well I'm not hungry cause I had a late lunch and I'm going to be here at the office finishing up a few things. Plus my office is significantly closer to La Rumba than where I live so how about you come get me from here around that time? Deal?" she says.

Desmond responds jokingly “Ugghhhh stinky??” Sincere laughs and replies in a sassy, but cute tone. “I know you didn't. I never stink!! I have a shower here at my office that I utilize often. Thank you very much!!”

Desmond chuckles a bit. “Oh well my bad Ms. Sincere. I should have never doubted you.”

“Never!! Doubt me!!” Sincere says in a haughty sassy tone. Desmond sits back in his chair and smiles at her and then says “Ok so I will be there in a bit then.”

“Uhhhhh? Don't you need my address?” Sincere asks. “Yeah I guess that would help me from circling the entire downtown area right?!”

“Yes! I’ll Google map it and send you the directions via email. You can get emails on your phone right?” Sincere asks in a sarcastic, yet sexy voice.

Desmond answers with a smooth response. “Come on now lady I am the king of hi-tech gadgets!! Nothings better than my Android spank you very much!!!”

Sincere laughs and says “You wish!!.” Desmond laughs again and says “Alright I’ll be there in a bit!!”

“Ok… bye” she says.

They both hang up the phone. Sincere looks around the office at her female co-workers and they are all smiling big smiles while they work. She looks up from over her computer and says “What??..” She smiles to herself.

Chapter 22
Sincere's Office

Chapter 22 SINCERE'S OFFICE

Desmond pulls up in front of Sincere's office. He looks down at his phone in order to make sure that he has the correct address. As he is confirming that he has made it to the correct destination he looks into the mirror to make sure everything is in place. He does the Dougie and then exits the car with flowers in hand, headed towards the front door. As Desmond reaches the front door he is taken back by a group of cute ladies all rushing out the door talking and laughing. One of them bump into him and then says sorry. All of them look at him as they walk past him gossiping in a whispering voice to each other and smiling at him.

Desmond smiles and heads into the office where Sincere is sitting at her desk still working, but looking refreshed. Makeup and hair is flawless. She stands up and she is beautiful all the way down to her toe nails. Desmond scans her from top to bottom and does a big Kool-Aid kid smile showing all of his teeth.

Sincere smiles and blushes at Desmond's smile of approval. "SOOoooooo?.... This is awkward?? Aren't you going to say something?"

Desmond snaps back to reality "Uhhhhhh....... yeah!! Yes, hello beautiful!! I'm sorry. I was wordless there for a moment. You look great!!"

Sincere smiles at him and asks "You like?" Sincere poses and then turns around in a circle. Desmond claps as if he was at a fashion show and uses RUPAUL voice to say "Fantastic, Fabulous and FIERCE!!" Sincere blushes and then says "Thank you Desmond!! The flowers are beautiful!! Are those for me?"

"Of Course....... I figured I would deliver them myself instead of having them delivered by a stranger." Desmond replies as he hands Sincere the flowers. They hug each other and then Sincere says "I like that." Desmond steps back from her as he says "I figured you would appreciate that. So are you ready to go?"

"Yeah, let me shut down my computer and grab my purse. I'm going to put these in some water really quick and then we can go." she replies. Sincere heads to the back room. As she turns and walks toward the back room the scene slows down. Desmond watches her walk. Sincere reaches the sink in the back and Desmond see's her from the side as she bends over grabbing a vase from beneath the sink. She is talking, but Desmond cannot hear her because he is daydreaming while he watches her move around. In the background you can hear music from **OUTKAST**......"I Like the Way you Move". Desmond snaps back into reality as Sincere is walking back towards him calling his name

"desmond? desMOND?? DESMOND!!" Sincere repeats until he answers her.

"Uhhhh?? Yea-Yeah-Yeah!? Desmond finally snaps out of his trance. "Were you listening to anything I was saying?" she asks.

"Yes!? Yes I was!!!" he replies in a dazed tone. Sincere looks at him with a weird confused look.

"Uh huh......... So when the show is over I'm going to need you to bring me back here to get my car ok?"

"Not a problem at all. You're in great hands with Coolwater insurance. I'll get you back to your car!" Desmond answers. Sincere smirks and repeats him "Coolwater insurance huh?"

"That's right!! I insure you." Desmonds replies back. "We'll see about that mister." Sincere then heads towards her computer and bends over to press some keys and give the command to log off computer. Desmond's mind slows down again as Sincere is bent over the desk at the computer. Desmond is daydreaming again and Sincere is still talking away totally oblivious to what Desmond is thinking or daydreaming about. The song by OUTKAST comes on again and his eyes are scaling Sincere's body from head, down to arch in her back, past her thigh, over her curvy calf muscles, right down to her heel and arch in her foot sitting in her high heels.

Desmond is in awe of one of the most beautiful woman he has ever laid his eyes on. Sincere stands back up with her coat in hand and is ready to go. As she is walking towards him he looks her right in the face.

Everything is perfect perfection from her hair, to her eyeliner, eyeshadow and lipstick. Desmond is thinking "She is perfect" and he has never had this feeling before. Desmond is now fantasizing about her and him being married in the front yard of a big house, with kids running around the yard safely kept in by a white picket fence. At that moment is when Desmond comes too and Sincere is standing right in his face smiling and blinking her eyes at him.

"Hello!?!?! Desmond are you ok?" Desmond shakes his head to clear his thoughts. "Yes!! I am great!! Are you ok? You ready Freddy?" he asks her. "Yes I'm ready…" she replies and then Desmond motions towards the door and says "Lets Go then!"

They both head towards the door. Sincere walks out the door first, looks at Desmonds car and she says: "Nice car" Desmond responds in a cocky tone "I know huh...... You like it?" Sincere answers nonchalantly "It's aiiiight!!"

Desmond walks up to the passenger door and opens it so Sincere can sit down. Desmond closes the door and strides around to the drivers side. Sincere opens the door from the inside. Desmond grabs the car door and looks up to the sky with a shocked face and says "THANK YOU GOD" in a whispering tone. He sits down in the car and places the key into the ignition. He is about to start the car when Sincere begins to say what everyone has said to Desmond about his car.

"You know what they say about men with these kind of vehicles?" Desmond smirks and says "Yeah I keep hearing that........ But that doesn't apply to me though." Sincere looks at him with a puzzled look and replies “Oh yeah?? Why is that?”

Desmond looks at Sincere with a devilish smile and replies “Because I have all the essential tools to not make it true!! Desmond then starts the car as Sincere gets ready to reply. Desmond then floors the gas pedal and peels out to make her head whip back into the padding of the seat. “Now that was a pretty overly confident and cocky thing to saaaaaayyyyyy......” she says as the
car speeds off from curb.

Chapter 23 CLUB LA RUMBA

Outside of the club there is a line of people scaled along the side of the building waiting to get in and get some seating before its all gone. Desmond and Sincere park in the back. Desmond turns off the car and walks around to Sincere's side to open the door for her. As she steps out of the vehicle a song by BRUNO MARS...**"OUR FIRST TIME"** is playing in the background. They walk towards the back door to gain entrance and avoid the line in the front of the building. Desmond and the security guard nod at each other as they give each other dap before the guard stands aside and allows Desmond, plus Sincere to enter thru the VIP entrance. Inside the club is lively as they walk thru sheer white curtains into a dimly candlelight room where people dressed in blazers and form fitting skirts and dresses are mingling.

Desmond leads Sincere to the table where they will be seating for the show. As he pulls out the chair she sits down in true lady like fashion and he pushes her in. He then sits down in the chair beside her. The scene is energetic with people dancing around them, talking and smiling. Desmond is waving to some friends and acquaintances while he scoots into his seat. He then waives at a waitress to come to there table. She makes her way over.

"Hello! Would you like to order some drinks?" the waitress asks.

Desmond looks at Sincere who is noticeably having a great time so far, grooving back and forth to the live music to ask her what kind of drink she would like.

"Ms. Bouvea"

"Yes??" She says as she is moving to the rhythm.

"What would you like to drink?" Desmond asks. Sincere looks at the waitress with a smile and
replies "I would like a Chocolate Martini please." The waitress writes down Sincere's request and then turns to Desmond to ask

"And what would you like sir?"

"I'm simple. If I could just have a Heineken and a shot of Crown Royal for now please" he orders his drink. Sincere looks at him jokingly and says "Wow!! Big dog." she says. Desmond lets out a big dog bark "WOOF!!" Sincere, Desmond and the waitress all share a smile and a giggle.

"Ok so I'll get your orders together and be right back." the waitress says and then Desmond says thank you. "This is nice!!! I love the setup and everything. How did you get into doing all of this?"

Sincere asks inquisitively as she continues to dance in her seat. "Well when I was in college I studied marketing and advertising with a minor in business. I didn't really have much money and the student work program wasn't really my style if you know what I mean. Too much style for that." Sincere perks up after his answer and says "Ummm......? Excuse me?? I did the student work program and it worked out well for me."

Desmond corrects his high and mighty comment by apologizing. "Sorry..... I didn't mean any disrespect by that. It just wasn't for me."

"Okay.... carry on with your story." Sincere accepts his apology "So what I would do is promote events on and off campus. By the time my junior year of college came around, I was already making enough money to afford an apartment off of campus and I didn't really need the financial aid, but I would accept just enough to pay for the rent. I was on an academic scholarship already."

"Hmmmmm........ Well aren't you just an over achiever." she says sarcastically.

"No just a hard worker. I didn't have time to get caught up in the hype. I wanted to get my degree and get out as soon as possible. So once I graduated I already had some job offers and Fly

Magazine was one of them. I had an opportunity to go to New York and do the whole big city, big newspaper thing, but I opted to come back home where my family was and where I could do some good for my city." Desmond responds to her sarcasm. Sincere is very impressed with Desmonds reply. "Well from what I can see you are doing well for the city. Maybe you should run for Mayor next?!"

Sincere smiles and speaks with a sarcastic tone. Desmond picks up on it and replies "Ahhhh sarcasm.......... I love it!"

Sincere gets semi serious for a moment. "No really that is impressive. You are a very intriguing individual Desmond. I have never met anyone so driven before. I bet your parents are very proud." she says.

"Well that's a different story. My mom is the compassionate one who always took care of me and my siblings needs, while my father was the hard-nosed blue collar worker who was never home and when he was home it was like he wasn't. Tough family dynamic...." Desmond's vague explanation makes Sincere a little more inquisitive. "So how is you and your fathers relationship now?"

"The same. We don't talk much." Desmond answers.

"....why??" Sincere asks

"He's a hard one to read. I love him, but I'm done trying to make him proud. I feel like he barely acknowledges that I even exist. Tough love..." Desmond starts to get a little uneasy as he sits back in his seat and crosses his arms. Sincere stops bobbing from side to side and touch's Desmonds hand and says "I'm sorry Desmond. I didn't mean to pry."

"Don't worry about it beautiful. I'm good!! Let's have a good time and not talk about that depressing stuff." he says. "Deal!!" she agrees. Desmond smiles at Sincere. The waitress comes back to the table to bring them the drinks they ordered.

"Ok here we go. One Chocolate Martini for the lady, a Heineken and shot of Crown Royal for you." The waitress sets napkins down and then the drinks on top of them. Desmond says thank you and then goes to ask how much he owed, but the waitress informs him that the tab has already been taken care of.

Desmond and Sincere look at the waitress with curiosity and asks… "Oh really? And who do I need to say thank you too?" he asks.

The waitress points over across the room and replies "The lady over there with the two gentlemen in the suits waving her hand is the one." Desmond takes a look around the waitress and the waving lady is Lyriq sitting with the promoters of the show. Desmond waves back with an irritated presidents wave and smiles as he sits back in his chair. The waitress walks away.

"Desmond you are a popular guy. Got ladies buying us drinks." Sincere asks

"Not really." Desmond replies

Sincere takes a sip of her martini as she says "What do you mean?" Desmond begins to briefly explain who Lyriq is. "Long story, but the short version is she is my co-worker/partner that the magazine just hired to oversee the feminine side of things in my department." Sincere is stirring her martini as she sips it and continues to sway to the music. "Oh that's cool! Right??" she asks.

"Maybe for her, but not for me." Desmond replies. "Why?" Sincere asks again looking totally lost.

Desmond looks back over at Lyriq while he is explaining to Sincere who she is and watching her mingle with the promoters of the show. Desmond knows the two gentleman as acquaintances, but not personally.

Lyriq keeps looking over at Desmond while she is conversing with the gentlemen almost in a taunting way to Desmond.

Desmond continues to explain to Sincere who Lyriq is “Because she is trying to make me look bad and move me out of the department, so she can take over the whole thing. She doesn't think I’m hip to her game. But I see what she’s trying to do loud and clear.” Lyriq smiles an evil sexy smile at Desmond while he’s talking about her to Sincere.

“Well that sounds crazy Desmond!! I don't like that girl already and I haven’t even met her.” Sincere says. Desmond smiles at Sincere and scoots closer to her. “Ahhhh...... it’s nothing. Sometimes a little healthy competition brings out the best in people.”

“Depends on what kind of competition we are talking about.” Sincere says.

“The kind of competition where both parties win a prize maybe??” Desmond replies. Sincere gives a seductive smile at Desmond and replies with “Everyone loves a win-win situation right?”

Desmond nods his head and matches her seductive smile with an equally smooth half smile and wink as he agrees. Both Desmond and Sincere are having a great time grooving to the music and talking. The crowd is filled with energy, laughing and dancing as the band plays the music before the comedian takes the stage. The D.J. announces that the show will start in 5 minutes and Sincere gets up to go to the ladies room. As Sincere is headed to the ladies room Lyriq passes her by walking towards Desmond. The scene slows down as Sincere and Lyriq pass by one another and give a **“If Looks could kill”** kind of look at each other.

Lyriq smiles as she cuts her eyes and continues on her path towards the table where Desmond is seated.

Sincere is still walking and watching Lyriq as she heads towards the table. She was so occupied that she did not see the waiter and collides with him, making a crashing sound as all the drinks fall to the floor.

Sincere is embarrassed. She helps the waiter to his feet, she is emotionally apologetic as she covers her face and enters the ladies bathroom crying. Desmond hears the commotion, but did not notice that it was Sincere that was involved. As he sits there sipping on his beer Lyriq walks up and sits down.

"Hello Desmond" she says. "Hello Ms. Moore. You look rather stunning tonight." Desmond compliments her as she sits down.

"Yes, well it was nothing. It only took me 30 minutes. Its not much you have to do to natural beauty." Lyriq replies with the confidence of a bonafide diva. Desmond looks at her and smiles. Then he replies after sipping his beer "30 minutes huh? I can tell…"

Lyriq looks at him with a weird look after his rude statement and asks "What is that supposed to mean?"

"With all that natural beauty and brains you forgot to pull the tag off. But I bet neither one of those gentlemen that you are with over there bothered to mention that." Desmond says as he takes a sip of his Heineken "You just think you are so smooth don't you?" she asks.

"I definitely have my less than smooth moments love, but not many." he replies as he is sitting back in his chair.

Lyriq sits up straight in her seat and arches her back with all the sexual prowess of a temptress on the prowl and then replies "Touche'........... so I've been sitting with the promoters over there and they wanted me to invite you and your less than graceful date over to the table. Would you like to join us?"

"Nah, my date and I prefer to be alone tonight, but thank you." he declines their invite. Just then as Desmond is telling Lyriq no, the waitress comes back to the table with two shots and says "THese shots are from the gentlemen over at VIP table #3."

The waitress sets the drinks down and walks away. Desmond looks over at the table and waves at the gentlemen as they put their shot glasses up. Lyriq puts hers up and nudges Desmond to raise his.

Everyone takes their shot in unison. Desmond gives kind of a grimace after the shot and says "Patron!!! WHooooaaaa!! Didn't expect that."

Lyriq takes her shot without a flinch or grimace on her face, smiles at Desmond and says "Little bit too much for you to handle there young man? Take it easy. This will put hair on your chest."

"I'm afraid to ask how many of these you have taken then." Desmond replies with razor sharp wit.

Lyriq is taken back by his quick come back, but laughs anyway. "Ha ha........ very funny Desmond. Listen I think it would be in good taste to come over to the table and at least speak with the promoters don't you think?"

"Of course!!! I always greet the customers, but I don't just run right up to them. I let them marinate for a bit." he replies. Lyriq toots her sexy lips and then slides her chair out slowly enough to catch Desmonds noticeable attention and then says "Marinate huh? Whatever!! I'm headed back to the table."

"Happy trails Ms. Moore" he says. She replies with "Always, oh and by the way your date is very cute."

"Thank you. I know this…" Desmond smiles and nods his head confidently.

Lyriq then informs Desmond about Sincere's incident "...but you might want to go check on her. She ran into the waiter on her way to the restroom and didn't look too happy." Desmond sits up and looks around Lyriq to see if Sincere was ok or if she was still out there with the waiter.

Desmond says "Thanks"

"Anytime Dessie......... bye-bye!!" Lyriq gets up and the dress she has on is as smooth as her skin is and very form fitting. Desmond is still looking for Sincere and as Lyriq walks away she walks in front of Desmonds view and he begins to stare at the arch in her back that is supported by the very slim, but sexy muscles that surround it. As she is walking away everything slows down again and Desmond is mesmerized by her walk. He notices every line and strap on her dress that cross cut over her open backed dress. As she walks away Desmond begins thinking to himself:

(inside thought)
"I don't see a panty line at all. I wonder if she even is wearing any???"

Lyriq is just about back to the table and as if she heard what Desmond was thinking, she turns her head to look back at him. She smiles seductively, winks and waves her finger at him like....."No, No, No" / "Naughty-Naughty" and then turns around and continues sitting back down at the table.

Just then Desmond snaps out of his trance and remembers Sincere.

Sincere is the only one in the restroom. She is standing in front of the mirror crying and trying to wipe her face. Once she gathers her composure she begins to reach in her purse for her make-up.

She is talking to herself and giving herself a pep talk. "Oooh come on Sin get it together girl. You're not even with him and you're getting all shook up over him already." she says to herself.

Sincere turns around to grab some toilet paper and dab the corner of her eyes so she can stop the tears from ruining the rest of her make up. She turns back to the mirror and looks at herself. She reaches into her purse, pulls out the mascara and begins to fix her eye-liner.

She then begins to powder her face and fix her lipstick. She then steps back and look at herself, takes a few poses to see how she is looking, she puffs up her lips like she is blowing kisses at herself and fixes her breast in her dress.

Desmond is still at the table and decides to finally go and check on Sincere who has been in the bathroom for some time now. Desmond gets up from the table and begins his journey to the women's restroom to check on Sincere. Desmond has to pass by Lyriq and the other promoters as he heads to check on Sincere. As Desmond is headed to the bathroom he feels a hand grab his and lead him in another direction. It's Lyriq leading him to the table to speak to the gentleman.

Desmond looks at Lyriq and follows her lead to the table reluctantly. They arrive at the table and Desmond says hello to the gentleman as they both sit there speaking to one another. The gentlemen's names are Travis Vasquez and Mitchell Helsberg. Two well known comedy show promoters. Desmond addresses both of the guys.

"Good evening fella's hows it going?"

Travis is the first to respond to Desmond. "What's up Mr. Coolwater. Pleasure to have you in the building. You don't ever show up to the events anymore." Mitchell is Travis's partner and he chimes in next.

"Yeah...... what brings you down tonight?"

"I decided to come down and check you guys out. Make no mistakes I always know what's going on with your shows, which is why we are all still in business together. You guys are doing a great job as usual." Desmond says.

Mitchell nods his head and says "Well thank you sir. We appreciate that."

"Why don't you and your date come over and sit with us?" Travis asks. "I appreciate the offer, but we are kind of doing the date/alone time kind of thing." Desmond declines Travis's invitation.

"Always the Lone Ranger" Mitchell replies. "......Or on a mission." says Travis

"Ha ha........ nah just relaxing gentleman. That's all. I do appreciate the offer, but we'll stay at our table."

Lyriq sits down and says "Alrighty then. Suit yourself Mr. Desmond ***Too Cool for School*** Coolwater."

Desmond smiles and replies "You people have a great night and congrats on the show tonight. I know it will be a smash and we will be doing more business soon." Travis sits back in his seat, takes a sip of his drink and then gestures at Lyriq as he says "Well with what Ms. Moore is telling us, I think we will be doing a lot more business with the mag in the near future."

Desmond looks over at Lyriq with a puzzled look and says "Is that right? Well I'm sure she'll fill me in soon about it."

Lyriq is sipping her drink as she looks over the rim of her drink at Desmond as he stares down at her. She then says "You know I will."

Desmond nods his head at her as he wishes everyone a good night. Desmond walks away with a troubled look on his face as he makes his way to the restrooms to check on Sincere. As Desmond reaches the door to knock on it Sincere opens the door looking even better than she did when he picked her up from the office.

She looks Desmond in the eyes and smile. Desmond smiles back and says "WoW!!"

Sincere plays coy and says "What?" Desmond is still in a daze from how beautiful she is. He then says "Nothing. I mean?? You look marvelous!!"

She starts to blush as she tells him "Stop it Desmond."

"No! I'm being serious!!! You look even better than you did 10 minutes ago. I love this date already. I mean I've never been on a date where she kept getting more beautiful as the night went on." he continues to compliment her as they walk back towards their table.

"...without alcohol that is." Sincere replies sarcastically. Desmond cracks a smile at Sincere and says "I reject that last statement. I don't go out with just anyone or as they call them on "Jersey Shore" GRENADES!!"

Sincere laughs and says "I can't believe you would even make a reference to that show."

Desmond laughs. "Hey what's wrong with JERSEY SHORE? I like that show."

Sincere replies "Whatever!! Lets go sit down you nerd."

Desmond puts his arm out for Sincere to take and walk with him back to the table. As they are walking back to the table the DJ announces the comic that's about to take stage. Desmond and Sincere reach the table as the music volume is turned down and the lights are dimmed. The comedian takes the stage.

Desmond and Sincere are sitting at their table laughing and having a good time as the comedian is working the crowd and doing his act. In the background people at the show are laughing and having a great time. Sincere and Desmond are laughing and sipping their drinks. As the show progresses on, there is a couple of times that Desmond and Lyriq make eye contact as if checking on one another. Both Desmond and Sincere are sitting close to one another while watching the show, intimately talking into each others ears.

The show is sexually charged with energy. As it goes on drinks are served, laughs are happening and the show is an overall success.

Chapter 24 INSIDE DESMOND'S CAR

Desmond and Sincere are driving back to her office. The scene is being narrated by slow music in the background and both of them grooving. Desmond breaks the silence by saying "Soooo? What did you think about the show?"

Sincere is smiling as she sits on the passenger side. She then replies "I loved it!! I had a great time with you tonight once again. Its amazing how you have all these connections and how you pull so many different facets of entertainment in the city together all under one roof. I'm quite impressed. Is there anything you can't do?"

Desmond is pulling up to the front of the office. He turns the music down and replies "Yeah there is a few things I can't seem to get right." Desmond looks at Sincere as he is saying that. Sincere looks at him in a sweet seductive manner and asks "Oh yeah and what's that Mr. Coolwater?"

Desmond responds with "I can't seem to get close enough to you!?" Sincere looks at Desmond and leans over the armrest enough to make him meet her halfway and then motions with her index finger coaxing him to her. Desmond sits up and meets her half way over the arm rest. They both are face to face as Sincere reaches up for Desmond's face to pull him closer to her face and then she says "I think you are one of the most amazing men I have met. You are smart, intelligent, funny and cute."

Sincere kisses his cheek after she makes that statement and then Desmond responds "Just cute huh?"

"Incredibly!!" Sincere pulls his face straight with hers and kisses him on the lips for the first time.

They begin to kiss slowly and passionately. The music starts to play in the background as if narrating the movements of their lips locking. As the music plays and they continue to kiss there is an abrupt knock on the driver side window and the music stops playing. It’s a police officer looking down on them and shining the light in the car.

“Excuse me sir and Ma’am” Both Desmond and Sincere look at each other and start to laugh. Then Desmond reiterates what he said initially about never being able to get close enough to her by saying “See?? See what I mean?”

“What?” Sincere is clueless at first and then Desmond repeats his earlier statement before they kissed “I can never seem to get close enough to you.” The officer looks at both of them and then says “It’s pretty late you two and it’s probably not too smart to be parked here at this time. Nice car could get you robbed sir. Ya know??”

“Most Definitely officer. I was just dropping the lady off at her car.” Desmond agrees. “Okay, well I’m going to let you two finish up here while I make my rounds, but please wrap this up.” The officer says before he takes off.

“Yes sir we will right now.” Sincere replies. The officer walks away and Desmond slides back down in his seat with a disappointed look on his face. Sincere looks at him with a smile and says “Awwe come on? Why the sad face? I had a great time / WE had a GREAT time tonight. I think this is a perfect end to the most perfect night. You don't?”

Desmond looks up at Sincere smiles and agrees. “Good!!! So you can walk me to my car now?” Sincere says after he does. “But of course!! What kind of gentleman would I be if I didn't do that?” Desmond responds.

“You would be a horrible date. I would have to tell my girls about you.” she says. Desmond looks at her in shock and asks “What!?! You're not going to tell your girls about me?” Sincere looks at Desmond and says: “No!!”

Desmond gets out the car, walks around the car, opens the door and says “No?!?!? Thats kind of cold-blooded don't you think?”

Sincere steps out of the car and replies “No! If I tell them everything about you, them hoochies will be all in my business. Trying to take you.” She then walks up to Desmond and looks up into his eyes, smiles and walks off towards her car. Desmond smiles and shuts the door as he walks behind her to catch up, while she walks to her car. She walks up to her car and unlocks the door with her automatic door key. Desmond opens the door and says “Allow me to get that for you.”

He opens the door as she walks around him to get into the car. She then throws her purse in the car and pulls Desmond closer to her to kiss him again. As they lock lips she raises to her tippy toes. He wraps his arms around her and she moans a sexy moan as if surprised she is being swept onto her tippy toes. They are kissing and locked into a passionate moment when the patrol car rolls past and the officer lets the siren rip one time to startle them. He then says “Lets get it moving people.”

The officer smiles as Desmond and Sincere turn to look at him. He then drives off.........

“Well I guess this is it for now.” Sincere says. “Just for a little while. I look forward to seeing you again..... soon!!”

Sincere looks over at Desmond and asks “Well how about this weekend?”

“I would love too, but I’ve got work and a family function on Sunday.” Sincere looks down at the ground and then Desmond touches her chin and replies “....but I think maybe we can catch up Sunday evening for dinner and/or movie?”

“How about both at my place??” she says. Desmond looks shocked and responds

“Oh really??”

“Yes really!!” she replies. “I’ll cook and you can choose the movie. Deal?" she continues.

Desmond agrees as they reach Sincere's car. Sincere then says "Well you be safe driving home
Mr. Coolwater. I really enjoyed my night tonight." She sits down in her car and Desmond shuts the door.

Desmond looks at her says "I enjoyed your company the most. Maybe you should just stay and keep it going."

Sincere laughs "Nope, I'll leave something to think about for now." Desmond backs away from her car door and says "Somehow I knew you were going to say that."

"I'll see you Sunday Dessie!!"

Sincere starts the car and shifts into gear. She blows a kiss to Desmond as she pulls away. Desmond watches her drive away as he stands in the middle of the street, waving and saying to himself

"Goodbye...... Ms. Bouvea"

The night fades out as she drives down the street passed a couple of green lights and turns down another street.

Chapter 25 AT THE GYM WITH HENRY

Desmond and Henry are in the locker room with their lockers open. The shower room is filled with men walking around shirtless, shirts on no pants, with towels and fully dressed and heading out to work.

Desmond is sitting in his towel and still dripping wet from the shower. Henry is almost dressed and they are speaking candidly about Desmond's change in mood and his work drama. Henry is putting on deodorant and buttoning up his shirt, while Desmond just sits there resting.

"Man I gotta tell you. Lately you have not been yourself." Henry says. Desmond looks up at him with a confused look. "What are you talking about man?"

Henry speaks up again not missing a beat. "I'm saying that you are here, but you aren't here. You seem so distant and gone in the wind. This is not the Desmond I know. This drama at the workplace got you real blurry. Where's ya focus at??" Desmond sits up from his slumped position and says "Bro I got a lot going on. Too much going on."

Henry is tucking in his shirt and straightening his belt. "Too much going on for the Great Desmond Coolwater??"

"Don't start man." Desmond says in a low tone.

"No, I'm being serious!! This just doesn't sound like you. Can you hear yourself?" Henry sits down next to Desmond and continues to speak "Listen man...." Henry pauses before he goes on... "for as long as I've known you which has been a pretty large portion of our lives, you have always took on any and all challenges. You have never complained or walked around with your tail between your legs unless you and your dad were having problems. I don't know what you are thinking right now or where you're at with all this change that's going on in your life at the moment, but you need to find that peaceful medium. Get rebalanced and push forward. Reformat your game plan bro and stop with all this long ugly face shit. You real ugly right now!!"

Desmond begins to laugh as well as Henry. Henry stands up, puts his blazer on and gives Desmond a couple of taps on his shoulder as he grabs his bag from his locker, shuts the locker door and walks away.

Desmond stands up and heads to the steam room. He grabs a another towel from the clean towel rack, throws it around his neck and enters the steam room.

Chapter 26 BACK @ FLY MAG OFFICES

The office is alive as usual on a early mid-Monday morning. Desmond is walking thru the hallways towards his desk and gets intercepted by Stacey. Stacey passes a message to Desmond to go to Mr. Elmhurst's office after he gets to his desk.

"Good morning Desmond."

Desmond looks at Stacey with a seductive smile and replies "Morning Stacey. How are you this morning?" Stacey smiles back with her usual cougar like style and says "I'm great this morning. Thank you for asking and Mr. Elmhurst wants to see you in his office after you get settled in."

"Ok, sounds good. Thank you." Desmond nods his head

Stacey goes to turn away and walk as Desmond says "Hey Stacey?"

"Yes Desmond?" She looks at him intently waiting on his question. "Do you ever feel like Angela Bassett in How Stella Got her Groove back?"

Stacey stands there and sizes up Desmond, smiles and says "No, never. I don't like younger men and I'm nobodies cougar." Desmond laughs, makes a cougar sound and puts his fingers up like claws as he continues walking by. Stacey smiles and continues passed Desmond towards her destination. Desmond walks to his desk and sits down his briefcase and blazer. As he is about to walk towards Mr. Elmhurst's office, he meets eyes with Lyriq as she sits at her desk. Once again as he makes his way to Mr. Elmhurst's office they give each other looks. Lyriq gives a very devious smile yet still in a professional manner. Desmond gives a half smile and turns his head forward towards Mr. Elmhurst's office. Desmond knocks on the door and Mr. Elmhurst motions for him to come in.

"Desmond how's it going young man?" he says. Desmond sits

down as he answers him. “It’s great Mr. Elmhurst. Just been working as usual and locking down more accounts for the company.”

“That's good-That's good. Listen I wanted to bring it to your attention that Ms. Moore has been making big strides with her marketing and connecting with the customer at extremely fast rates.” Mr. Elmhurst tells him. Desmond sits up in his chair with a confused look and says “What does that have to do with me sir?”

“Well for instance she has locked down a key promotion company and also in talks with Ford to advertise in the magazine.” he replies.

“What promotion company?” Desmond asks.

Mr. Elmhurst shuffles thru his paperwork on his desk, pulls up a piece of paper and hands it to Desmond. Desmond takes it while still looking at Mr. Elmhurst and then gazes at the paper. “What the ……..?!? Mr. Elmhurst these promoters are people that we have already worked with. I have secured plenty of events and promotions with them thru the magazine. What has she done so special??”

Mr. Elmhurst is sitting in his chair puffing his signature cigar as he listens to Desmond. “Well Desmond it seems she has managed to secure a year's commitment with the gentlemen at the company to only promote with Fly mag. That's a pretty good deal.” he says. “Mr. Elmhurst that is a bad deal. I have worked with these guys for a couple of years now and purposely chose not to lock us into any contractual obligations with these people. They are snakes and are always looking for a way to get over. If you don't mind me saying sir....... this is a foolish move.” Desmond says.

Mr. Elmhurst can see the concern on Desmond’s face “Calm down. I understand. The board however is looking at this in a different light.”

“What do you mean sir? For one there is no communication going on between us and she is not keeping me in the loop with any deals that she’s working out. What kind of co-partnership at this position is going on?” he asks.

“I understand your frustration Desmond and I am watching her closely.” Mr. Elmhurst reassures Desmond.

“She is deliberately going thru my desk when I am gone. She is fingering thru my contacts and systematically picking out all the big dogs first. Its not a mystery Mr. Elmhurst.” Desmond continues to explain. “Well moving forward I can't just go point the finger at her, but I will be watching. Meanwhile you need to stay on the upper path and keep doing what you do best and thats FLY MAGAZINE. Understand??” Mr. Elmhurst asks.

“Yessir I do.” Desmond agrees and then gets up to walk out of the office when Mr. Elmhurst calls his name. “.....And Desmond?” Desmond turns around and says “Yes sir?”

“Make no mistakes the board is watching. I’m pulling for you, but you have to be diligent and stay on the path.” Mr. Elmhurst warns him. “Yessir I will indeed.” Desmond walks out of the office and immediately focuses his stare towards Lyriq's desk. Lyriq is focused on her screen and does not look up to acknowledge Desmond passing by. As Desmond starts to look away Lyriq smiles while still staring at her computer screen as if she knows that Desmond is looking over at her. Desmond looks away and continues to walk towards his desk. As he reaches his desk he is met by his assistant James who is sitting on his desk waiting.

“Alright now this chick is starting to get on my nerves.” he says. Desmond walks up to James and motions with his thumb for James to get off his desk.

“Yeah tell me about it.” Desmond replies. “I heard she got City One promotions (**Travis Vasquez** and **Mitchell Helsberg**)?”

James says. “Man? How many times do I have to tell you about listening in on the office meetings?” Desmond asks. “I didn't listen in man! I was reading lips!!” he says.

Desmond looks at James in shock and asks “You can do that??” James shakes his head with a cocky overly confident nod. “Hell yeah!!”

Desmond is still looking at him with an expression of disbelief and then speaks. “Whatever!!! ANYWAY...... yeah she got them to sign a years promo contract with the mag.”

“But I thought you said that would be a bad position for the mag?” James asks. “I did and I still believe that. Somehow she got the in ad with them and they were able to convince her to do the contract after years of trying to convince me.”

James gets irritated. “So this bitch is going behind your back and trying to connect with all the contacts that you have made for the mag and rework deals?”

Desmond shakes head and says “Yes”

James takes a look over at Lyriq. “That scandalous, scamming ass hoochie train”

“Yeah and what's worse is I don't know what other contacts of mine she has gotten a hold of? She must have really gotten a good look at my black book.” Desmond says.

“Don't I always say: Des you should lock that thing up.” James reminds him. “I know..... I know...... I just never expected to have to defend my job against this though. I always felt like I had this under control.” Desmond replies.

James continues “I told you she was sneaking on your desk the other day so this really shouldn’t come as a surprise.”

“You and Cindy caught her on two different occasions…”

Desmond recalls "I've got to come up with a plan to stop her before she steals all my connections and my our jobs away."

"Yeah cause right now it looks like she is sleeping her way right to the top and about to steal YOUR job away from you." James says to him while excluding himself from the problem.

Desmond looks over at James after he makes that statement. James is staring out across the office in a daze ignoring that Desmond just looked over at him for his statement.

"Maybe I'm going about this the wrong way Mr.Wright!?!?" he says. James looks over at Desmond with a curious look and asks like Gary Coleman in Different Strokes.

"WHAT YOU TALKING ABOUT WILLIS?"

Desmond smiles with a sneaky demeanor and then replies "Well you know the old saying? If you can't beat 'em then join 'em right?!?"

"Uuuuuh?? Right??" James replies with a puzzled look on his face as they both stand next to the desk and Desmond begins to secretly unhatch his plan.

Cool Nights

Chapter 27 PHASE ONE @ FLY MAGAZINE

Desmond begins to un-hatch the first phase of his plan after him and James finished conversating.

Lyriq is working at her desk, Desmond walks up to her appearing to be preoccupied with a phone call on his cell.

He walks up to the desk and Lyriq looks up over the rim of her glasses as she is typing to see what Desmond wants. Desmond asks the person on the other side to hold while he hands her a piece of paper and explains what its about. "Hey Sarah hold on for a minute while I hand a coworker of mine a document please." Desmond puts the phone on his shoulder as if covering the receiver and then hands Lyriq the piece of paper and then says "Here is a schedule of what we will be doing with the next promo. I'd like to meet for food this evening and discuss this. Will that be a problem??"

Lyriq takes the paper and looks at it awhile and replies "Uhhhh..... no, no, not at all."

"Ok sounds good. Lets meet in the company carpool after work and have a driver take us somewhere." he says and then goes back to his call. Lyriq is trying to listen in on his conversation while he turns his back to her, Desmond looks over his shoulder and notices her eavesdropping and begins to walks away.

Lyriq seems lost, but answers as if he would actually hear her "Ok…"

Desmond goes back to his desk after wrapping up his conversation on the phone to start making follow up calls to everyone that he had meetings with during the week......i.e. Ike, the K.S.107.5 morning team and also some callbacks to potential clients. Desmond's first call is to Ike in order to set up a time for his interview and where? Desmond dials Ike's number and the phone rings. After 5 rings Ike finally picks up the phone.

“This is Ike…” he says. Desmond introduces himself. “Hey Ike this is Desmond Coolwater from.....”

“Fly Mag..... yeah what's happening? When are we going to do this interview or are you calling to bullshit me?” Desmond sits up in his seat and says “No, no, no, no...... actually I’m calling you to confirm when, where, and what time next week we could get together?”

“Next week is a busy week. Let's say Tuesday evening around 7pm if that’s not a problem??” Ike replies. Desmond begins to pencil in the date and time on his calendar as he answers him “No, that sounds great. Where are you thinking we can do the interview at?”

“The studio!! That's where I’m going to be at. That's my office, that's where I conduct business bro come on now.” Desmond sits back in his seat smiling. “I like the idea and I will be there at 6:50 p.m.”

“Oh and Coolwater?” Ike says. Desmond puts the phone back to his head. “Yeah??“Don't bring your friend this time. My boys are a little edgy and moody. They don't like all that loud noise and acting around them alright?”

“Will do sir. I’ll just show up by myself.” Desmond laughs to himself as he replies. “Yeah...... that would probably be safer. I’ll text you the address” he says.

“Cool as water. I’ll be there” Desmond says. Ike hangs up the phone and Desmond writes some notes down on his notepad as he gets ready to make his next call to the radio station. Desmond picks the phone back up and dials the radio stations office to set up radio interview with the team. The phone rings twice and the receptionist picks up the phone.

“Thank you for calling KS107.5 how may I help you?” Desmond answers her promptly “Hi! This is Desmond Coolwater and I’m calling to confirm an interview that’s supposed to be set between the morning team and myself." The receptionist replies "Yes, Mr. Coolwater they have been waiting on you to call and set that up. I was instructed to let you know they are available all next week. They would also like you to make an appearance on the Tuesday morning show. Is that possible?"

"They were serious about that huh??" Desmond asks. "Yes sir they were. Is that going to be a problem? she asks. "No, not at all. Of course I'm available......... actually lets do this? How about you schedule me in for the morning show and then we can do the interview for the magazine right after the show?" he requests. "Sounds good. I will schedule you and the team for that. We look forward to having you on the show Mr. Coolwater."

"Me too. Thank you for your time and have a great day." Desmond hangs up the phone and pencils the date in the scheduler. He then begins to make another phone call when he receives an alert from his cell phone. Its a text from Sincere.

Text convo between Desmond and Sincere

"Hey there handsome!! I hope your day is going well. How are you doing?" Desmond begins to smile while typing and replying to her text.

"Hellooooo Beautiful!! I am great. Just working and trying to save the world one advertisement at a time. you know me. How are you doing today?" **(SEND)**

(REPLY) "I'm GREAT!! I'm extremely tired, but I am in a good mood. I just wanted to tell you that I had a great time with you last night. I look forward to seeing you again." Desmond sits up in his seat like an excited sports fan at a game while texting.

"I had a great time with you last night as well. I'm looking forward to seeing you again soon…"**(SEND)**

(REPLY)"....As soon as Sunday night for dinner and a movie right??"

"Of Course!! If I could hang with you any sooner I would...."**(SEND)**

(REPLY)".....I would love too, but you're kinda too busy for me Mr. President. *wink*"

"lol...... ok so you got jokes! It's not what it seems sexy lady. We just met at a very busy time for me, but we will have our time soon. I'm feeling you!!...."**(SEND)**

(REPLY) "....I'm feeling you too. =o)"

"Good!!! That means we are on the same wavelength then. I would love to see you tonight but I have to be at a dinner meeting this evening to discuss the week's business ventures and stories we are going to post in next months issue as well as discuss details about our annual fashion show…"**(SEND)**

(REPLY) ".....Exciting!!! Well I know you are a busy and I don't want to bother you, but if you aren't too busy then shoot me a text or something. Hope you have a great rest of your day and look forward to seeing you soon sexy man........ xoxoxox muah!!"

"Exciting?? Not as exciting as being with you, but its my job to make it exciting for others so I have to do it… lol I look forward to seeing you. Hope you have a great night and I will talk to you soon beautiful....." **(SEND)**

(REPLY) ".... Later ;O)"

Desmond smiles as he reads her final text with the smiley face added and then slides his phone closed. He looks at his watch and realizes that he better get back to work and make some more calls before the end of the day. The scene fades out with him picking the desk phone back up and making more calls.

COOL NIGHTS

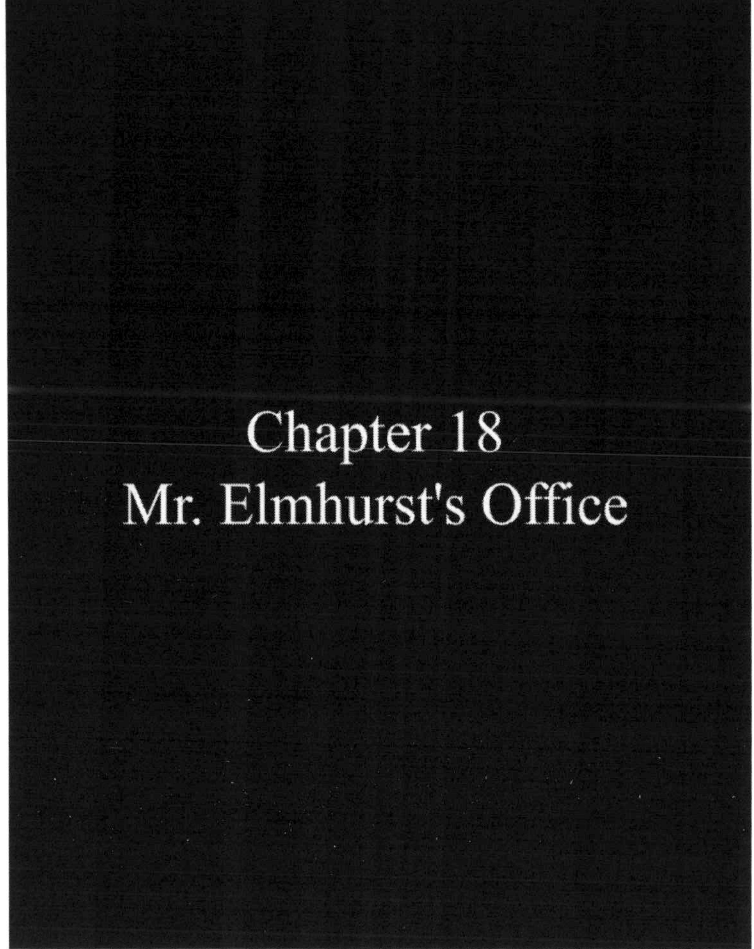
Chapter 18
Mr. Elmhurst's Office

Chapter 28 DESMOND AND LYRIQ GO TO DINNER

Desmond and Lyriq are having dinner at Casa Bonita's Mexican restaurant. They are discussing the previous business week and going over what needs to be done in the upcoming week. "So its been quite the week for you Ms. Moore...... new job, added responsibility, some business leads that led to a few new accounts with Fly Magazine........ etc., etc., Congratulations and welcome to the team!!" Desmond lifts up his drink to toast with Lyriq and she raises her glass as well. Lyriq smiles with a coy, beguiling smile almost as if she wasn't trying to be the two-faced, devious, underhanded bitch she really is.

"Thank you Mr. Coolwater.... thank you."

Desmond nods his head. "You are very welcome it is well earned." They both cheers and take a drink.

"So?? The reason I wanted to get with you this evening is because this week was sort of a rocky one, plus I feel that we may have gotten off on the wrong foot."

Lyriq smirks as she looks the other way and rolls her eyes. "Yeah!! You have been kind of an asshole!!" she says sarcastically. Desmond smiles and continues talking... "So I figured we could get together and kind of unwind a bit, have some great food, a few drinks and discuss some things."

"Ok, shoot....." Lyriq sits attentively listening. Desmond looks perplexed, but carries on with his convo.

"Well first off how's your food?" he asks.

Lyriq wipes her mouth with her napkin after taking a bite and says "It's good. I like it......... why? Did you have the cook poison me?" Desmond smiles devilishly. "Yeah... can you taste the Decon??" He then proceeds to take a bite of his food. Lyriq stops chewing her food, very calmly swallows and then takes a long drink of her wine. Desmond finishes chewing and wipes his mouth. “I’m just kidding..... just kidding. I wouldn't do that too you.”

“Yeah..... ha ha ha........ sure you wouldn't.” Lyriq cuts her eyes as she looks at him.

“I wouldn't!! You believe me don’t you?” Desmond asks.

Lyriq sits up in her chair a bit as she takes another sip of her drink. “Thats hard to believe considering how your assistant James has been eyeballing me all week.” Desmond cracks a smile. “Yeah well he’s a bit on the crazy side anyway. Ignore him.”

“Mmmm Hmmmm…” Lyriq rolls her eyes unconvinced. “Anyway, the reason I wanted to come here is because Casa Bonita’s is our Restaurant / Cuisine spot in the next issue of Fly mag.”

“Really?? This place??” Lyriq looks kind of puzzled.

“Of course!! Look at is architectural structure, look at how the decor opens up the further you venture into the establishment. I think this is a great place to do a review on. There is a fire juggling act and a diver will dive into that pool down there in the next 10 minutes. They have a mini show that happens every 20-30 minutes.”

Lyriq looks around the restaurant. As she is surveying the entire place she is drinking her martini and mentally critiquing it entirely.

“Hmmm.... soooo why are you wanting to help promote this place?

“Because they paid me!” Desmond says in a sarcastic tone, but laughing while he begins to make his point. “....let me explain? I decided to help them promote the business so they can increase business. I know the owner, because I used to work for him. He actually gave me my first job. This place was my first customer when I was fresh out of college and just getting started with Fly Magazine. The owner told me that he would invest in me until he had no more money because he believed in me that much! So you see? This place is an important place. Kind of like that very first dollar that you earn. Know what I'm saying?"

Lyriq listens to Desmond intently for a bit before she decides to speak. "Desmond I had no idea that you were so sentimental and soft......." her serious expression melts down to a playful smile. Desmond smiles, holds his drink up and motions to cheers with Lyriq.

As the time continues to fly by they continue talking, laughing, taking shots of Patron and eating their dinner. The whole evening is narrated by the sounds of Robin Thickes song **"BLURRED LINES"**. While Desmond and Lyriq are talking business, watching the show, and consuming shots of different Patrons the time begins to blur and phase into a collage of the nights events. The night ends with Desmond and Lyriq walking into the parking lot. Both Desmond and Lyriq go to the Company vehicle to head home. The driver has the door open and they both enter the vehicle.

Lyriq is giggling as they both settle into the limousine. "So I had a great evening Desmond. I feel like we really got a chance to see eye to eye. What do you think?"

Desmond is sitting on the other side of the car really feeling good after all the shots. He is swaying back and forth smiling and putting up make believe glasses on his face with his hands. Just then he falls back into the seat and keeps bobbing his head to the music. Lyriq then leans over the seat about half way and motions for him to come here with her finger.

Desmond moves up and Lyriq slides her legs across his legs and they both unleash all their sexual tension they've had towards each other since they met.

As they are making out the lights flicker in and out like a camera with a short in it. First you see them sexing each other up, then it goes black, then you see them again making out with her on top, goes to black, him on top, goes to black and then with Lyriq leaning against him kissing him seductively. The night closes out with Ludacris's song **"MY CHICK BAD"** playing in the background.

Chapter 29 BAD NEWS AT THE PARK

It's a brisk morning and Desmond is finishing his jog, heading towards the parking lot, he walks toward his car thinking about last night with Lyriq feeling guilty. He shouldn't have done any of it for numerous reasons, but the two most important one's he is thinking so deeply about is that he works with Lyriq and he is falling for Sincere hard. Lyriq still can't be trusted and Desmond knows that its going to become even more of an issue now that they have slept together. Just then his phone rings. Desmond answers the phone while sitting in his car. Its James to inform him about a party that Lyriq is hosting with Eric Graham from Image Mag tonight.

"This is Desmond."

"So what time are we going?" James asks.

Desmond is untying his shoes as he answers James question. "Going where?"

James pauses on the other side of the phone before answering. "Are you serious or are you just joking? I really hope you are joking!?" Desmond sighs and then says "Just tell me what's going on man?" James begins to explain to Desmond what's going on. "You know you are one sad case my brother. Lyriq is co-hosting a party with Eric Graham from Image Mag tonight!"

Desmond goes from being calm and tired from his workout, to being shocked and agitated instantly as he asks "What? You kidding me right? You had to hear that wrong?!"

"Des..... Have I ever lied to you or misinformed you about anything in the 3 years we have worked together?" James asks him.

"No" Desmond replies. "Have I ever bullshitted with you when it was time to be serious?"

"No" he replies again. "Well then you know that I am always on my business swagg..... all the time my friend. Please believe it!" James says. "Right.... of course. So what's the story then. Fill me in....." Desmond aks.

James clears his throat as he begins to inform Desmond about the planned events. "Well word has it that she has been cross-promoting this event for about a week now at The Church over off Lincoln St. in downtown. Needed to find somebody with the connects for the club which is why she went with Eric Graham cause she knows that no one worth their weight in the city would just up and cut throat you like that."

"Except.....?" Desmond says. James interrupts Desmond and finishes his sentence for him. "Thats right you guessed it......... except Eric Graham!! This broad has been sneaking around your desk and turning your connects over to Eric this whole time."

"Scandalous bitch!! I mean last night we...." Desmond stops and at the same time James interrupts him again. "Desmond?!?!? You didn't? Did you??? You did.... didn't you?" Desmond sits on the end of the phone just staring out thru the park in a zone and then he responds "Yep...."

"Damn bro!! You just couldn't keep it in your pants this time around huh? Just had to poke a hole in the enemy too man!! Damn." James laughs sarcastically as he makes fun of Desmond. Desmond answers reluctantly. "Yeah man I know. Slept with the enemy last night and it was good too! Woke up this morning with that weak leg twitch still bro."

James laughs again and says "So what!!....... You're going to wake up Monday morning with that I need a JOB twitch!!! Wake up!!! She is pulling your job right from under your nose and you're too busy and full of yourself to see it. Get ya shit right Desmond. I'm going tonight to check this bullshit out and I advise you to get your mind right. Meet me there or we both may be looking for new jobs!" James gets mad and hangs up the phone on Desmond.

Desmond looks at the phone and throws it to the floor of his car, slams his car door, starts the car and peels out. The day passes by fast as Desmond continues to fume and his anger builds. He gets ready to go to the Church nightclub to see what Lyriq and Eric Graham has put together, as he gets dressed he continues to have flashbacks of speaking with Lyriq the night before as well as replaying what Mr. Elmhurst warned him about.

Desmond finishes getting ready and by that time its time to go. He grabs his coat and his keys and heads out the door.

Chapter 30
The Church NightClub

Chapter 30 THE CHURCH NIGHTCLUB

Desmond pulls up to the Church nightclub and sees a line around the corner of people who are waiting to get in. Desmond parks across the street and gets out of the car. As he is walking up to the line he goes to get in line, James sticks his head out the door and spots Desmond. He motions for Desmond to come to the front of the line. James slides the bouncer a $20 to let Desmond in and they both head inside of the club. Desmond is following James through the crowd.

The venue is packed wall to wall and Chris Browns song "WALL TO WALL" just so happens to be playing as well. They finally make way to a table where James sits down with a female companion. Desmond sits down and cases the entire club looking for Lyriq. James bends over to speak to Desmond.....

"So what you going to do huh?" he asks. "I'm going to lean back and watch the festivities. I'm going to watch how she reacts when she see's us here. I mean she had to know that we would find out."

"Which means she literally does not give a FUuuuuuuuuuu........." Just as James is finishing his sentence Lyriq comes strolling up smiling, welcoming Desmond and James as if nothing is wrong.

"Hows it going boys?" she smiles. James looks at her with a look of disgust as he turns his back to her as if she wasn't there. Lyriq smiles and looks toward Desmond. "Well hello there Ms. Moore. Quit the party you having going on here? Was this part of **OUR PLANNING** or did I miss the memo?" he says. Lyriq smiles promiscuously as she gets ready to answer Desmonds questions.

"Look Desmond... You have been playing hardball with me so I had to turn it up and start making my own connections here in the town." Desmond looks at her without blinking. "So you conspire with the competition? How do you think Mr. Elmhurst is going to take this? Or the board for that matter?"

Lyriq looks back at Desmond nonchalantly and replies “Frankly Desmond..... I don't care how Mr. Elmhurst takes it. My job is to bring in more business to the magazine and take it to the level that you couldn't take it too, because of your limited vision.... See what you fail to realize is that I was brought on by the board not Mr. Elmhurst.” Desmond is standing there fuming and wordless for once in his life, he doesn't know what to say and that in itself is adding to his frustration. James is floored and begins to start talking to Lyriq, but Desmond puts his arm in front of James to stop him from saying the wrong thing and getting himself fired. Just then Eric Graham from Image Magazine walks up to them.

“L Boogie!! What's up beautiful!” Eric walks up and hugs Lyriq immediately. He then turns around and looks at Desmond like he has dog shit on his shoe. Desmond looks at him without a blink or a move. James gets mad and begins to push towards Eric. Desmond puts his arm out again to hold him back. Eric then says “Well, well..... look who we have in the house! If it isn't Desmond Coolwater.....” He says sarcastically. “What do you think about our little swarray we put together here? I mean you have to admit...... this is pretty live and its happening in YOUR CITY.” Eric begins smirking. “.......and you're not hosting it?? I mean damn!! That has to burn! Just a little bit right?”

Eric smiles with a thug like swagger while waiting on Desmond to respond. Desmond smirks back and then says “I must say....... you’ve got it going on here.” Speaking sarcastically the whole time.

“It must feel good to be able to slither around the elite huh? It must be one of your biggest accomplishments to be able to say **“I threw a party worth going to for once”**. Desmond turns and smiles at James while talking ”.....**in my sorry ass career!”**

He then straightens the smirk like smile off of his face as if his face never had an expression on it and continues. “So if you want to be happy about that accomplishment then please… be my guest.... be happy." Eric is standing there with a stupid-jealous look on his face and Lyriq realizes that the conversation is becoming volatile so she steps in and begins to change the subject quickly "So gentlemen lets all part ways. Eric we have some business to tend too. Desmond you and your crew have a nice night, matter of fact why don't you guys go enjoy V.I.P. on us as a friendly gesture."

Lyriq begins to pull Eric away from the situation. Desmond and Eric are locked in a death stare at one another as Eric walks away. Just as they are out of view, James yells out "No thanks!!"

As Lyriq and Eric walk away Desmond begins to zone out. The rest of the night as he sits there at the table with James and his date, they all party hard, taking shots and mixing drinks. The whole time Desmond is still upset about the altercation as well as the expected betrayal from Lyriq. The night continues to carry on and Desmond is drinking heavily, but not stumbling. Desmond finally decides to go to the restroom and he gets up from the table. James is too busy with his date to notice Desmonds absence.

Desmonds strolls thru the crowd in a daze headed towards the bathroom, he bumps into people a few times, but finally makes his way into the men's room. He goes to the urinal, unzips and begins to go. As he stands there his mind is racing, his anger has been bubbling all night and he is now ready to just go home.

He finishes and walks over to the sink where he washes his hands and splashes water on his face to snap out of it. He dries his hands off and walks out of the restroom back into the club. He walks over to the bar to get another drink. As he is there waiting for a waitress to help him, a beautiful dark-skinned lady is on his right smiling, Desmond smiles back. The young lady walks away seductively and Desmond watches her walk away, as he draws his attention back to the bar he is met face-to-face with Eric Graham smiling at him a few feet away.

Eric stares at Desmond for a moment before he speaks "What

does it feel like to lose?" Eric asks.

Desmond turns his attention away from Eric and back to the bartenders then says "I don't know.... you tell me?"

Eric laugh turns into a chuckle. "You just can't get over how I won this time huh? I mean the very thought of being 2nd best right now has you so jealous and mad that your ego is just swollen like a pussy." He chuckles again. Desmond laughs with him, yet never acknowledges Eric enough to look at him.

"Don't you have somewhere else to be other than sitting here and bugging the shit out of me? Why don't you go somewhere-where I can't see you....... as usual. Loser!" Eric turns towards the bar and the bartender automatically tends to him.

"Let me get you a shot." Eric offers, but Desmond says "No thanks I can get it myself."

"I insist..... let me get this last one before the bar closes." Desmond rolls his eyes the other way and says "Whatever" Eric orders two shots of Fireball Whiskey. The bartender pours them up and serves them to both of them. Eric holds his up and makes a toast. "Cheers! To friendly competition......"

Desmond hesitates to join in and against his best judgment, he puts up his shot glass to cheers. Just as he raises his arm to take his shot, Eric throws the shot in his face and punches him square in the mouth.

Desmond stumbles back, but at the same time he has the balance to set his shot glass down without spilling his drink.

Eric rushes him and they are entangled in a brawl that clears a space in front of the bar. Desmond blocks the next swing from Eric, counters it with a throat chop, a 2 punch combo and then smiles.

Eric stumbles back, shakes it off and puts his hands back up.

Desmond goes in to swig but, Eric blocks Desmonds advance, then comes in with a flying knee and a right cross. Security rushes in to break everything up, but the two men are so adrenaline driven that they break free simultaneously and go over each other one last time.

The scene in the club slows down to a Matrix type speed as both men extend to collide and punch each other at the same time. The blow from both punches landing knock both men to a knee and they are then tackled by multiple guards.

James runs over to try to pull some security guards off of Desmond, but he is grabbed and escorted towards the door with his date following close behind. The security guards begin to ease up off of both men and Desmond gets up from the floor. He is still surrounded by a few guards waiting to escort him out of the club. He snatches his arm away from a guard as he attempts to gather himself after the fight.

He just happens to be right by the bar where is shot was still waiting. He wipes his face, straightens his blazer jacket and then reaches for the shot of fireball whiskey and downs it. The security goes to grab his arm and he snatches his arm away again as he walks past Eric and the security guards.

Desmond is walking thru the crowd and spots Lyriq as he is walking out. He winks at her as he is pushed out the front door.

Desmond is looking for his keys and as he finds them he looks up to see the Denver police is sitting there watching him with the lights flashing. Desmond makes a sigh, shakes his head and drops his keys to the ground. The police arrest him and take him in.....

Chapter 31
Desmond's In Jail
#longnight

Chapter 31 DESMOND IN JAIL

Desmond is sitting in the holding tank with 7 or 8 other people being detained for the night. He has this pissed off look on his face trying to think about who he should call to come bail him out.

As he sits there thinking, another inmate waiting to be bailed out sits next to him and Desmond looks over at him. He just so happens to be staring back at Desmond waiting to get a confrontation started, but Desmond looks over at him and then diverts his attention elsewhere in the cell.

Desmond walks over to a corner, puts his back against the wall and stares at the ceiling deep in thought.

Night turns to day very quick and a limo pulls up in front of the station. The driver gets out and goes to the other side of the vehicle to let the passenger out of the car. Mr. Elmhurst steps out the vehicle smoking his signature cigar. He is dressed in golf gear and has a scowl on his face like everyone else who steps in front of the building. Mr. Elmhurst makes his way into the building to bail Desmond out.

Not long after Mr. Elmhurst walks into the jailhouse, both he and Desmond are walking back out.

Riding in the limo, the tension is very tense. Desmond attempts to speak first, but Mr. Elmhurst interrupts him

"You've got more class than this Desmond...... I am very disappointed." Desmond sinks down into his seat a bit further and says "I know...... this was definitely immature. I must admit but......"

Mr. Elmhurst cuts Desmond off again as he is trying to explain. "But nothing Desmond. When you are out at functions such as this one then you have to be presentable and represent the magazine in a professional light at all times! This is beyond immature young man. You have allowed someone or something to get under your skin and you showed your ass in public."

"I know sir" Desmond puts his head down. "The board is considering suspending you. What do you think about that?" says Mr. Elmhurst. "Considering this all started because of them....." Mr. Elmhurst interrupts Desmond again.

"How is this their fault? Because they brought in a little friendly competition?"

Desmond answers his questions in a frustrated tone. "Friendly?!?! There is nothing remotely friendly about Lyriq. She is a sneaky, side-winding, two-faced snake. Did you know that she helped promote this event with Eric Graham from Image Mag?"

"Yes, I did....... didn't you?" Mr. Elmhurst replies.

Desmond looks perplexed by his reply and asks "No, but..... why would you ok this? Isn't it a conflict of business??" Mr. Elmhurst pulls out another cigar and cuts the tip off of it as he answers Desmonds question. "Not when she isn't using any of the magazines resources to do so."

Desmonds disgust is growing as the conversation continues, but he keeps his respect for Mr. Elmhurst at a professional level. "She has been sneaking on my desk and stealing my contacts. How do you think she has been able to get it all together so fast and efficiently?"

"DO you have proof of this?" Mr. Elmhurst stops from lighting his cigar, looks at Desmond very intrigued by his accusations.

"I have witnesses" Desmond replies. "So you don't have proof then? Just a couple of people who said, she said and he said right?" he ask Desmond. "Mr. Elmhurst its more than that." says Desmond.

Mr. Elmhurst continues with sparking his cigar and speaking. “Yes, it is more than that Desmond.

Your spoiled! You don't know what it feels like to not win. Right now your ego is shot and you can't handle it, but I tell you one thing...... you better get your shit together. Get your ego and feelings in check!! This is business and you have made this personal young man.”

Desmond is looking at Mr. Elmhurst trying to hold back his emotions as he delivers some of the toughest advice he has given him so far and then he says “I understand Mr. Elmhurst.” Mr. Elmhurst can see the frustration on Desmond’s face and eases up on him a bit. “Listen Desmond........ take today to relax. Think about what you need to do in order to get back on track. When you get in the office come talk to me and we’ll talk about the week.”

“I will sir. Thank you for bailing me out.” Desmond says. “Not a problem son.” Mr. Elmhurst replies. The driver pulls up in front of Desmonds place. Desmond opens the door and gets ready to shut the door when his curiosity sets in and he bends back into the door and asks “Just out of curiosity Mr. Elmhurst..... How did you know I got arrested last night anyway?”

Mr. Elmhurst simply replies “I received a call from Lyriq this morning.”

Desmond has a look of bewilderment on his face as he steps back from the car and shuts door. The limo pulls away from the curb leaving Desmond to his thoughts. He walks into his house and begins to get dressed to meet his mother at church.

Chapter 32
@ Church

Chapter 32 CHURCH

Reverend Parker is having an exceptional day, the whole congregation is standing at the moment singing and giving praise. Desmond is sitting down next to his mother listening, but not really there in church mentally. Desmond is too busy going over last nights occurrences in his mind. Desmonds mom notices Desmonds disconnect, grabs his hand as she smiles, rocks back and forth while listening to the choir. Reverend Parker stands up as the choir is finishing and begins to speak to everyone.

"Today is a special day. Like everyday we are so blessed to have another chance to praise the lord. Today however is special because we are up early singing for the lord, we are stomping and yelling for the lord almighty and I know he can hear us. Do you know why? Well even if you do know I'm going to say it anyway..... See you got up out of bed and the sun was shining bright right?? Right??"
(The crowds responds with a RIGHT)

He continues...."You got up this morning and the air was fresher than you remembered the air the day before and You didn't feel any aches or pains this morning did you?"

(The crowd answered him with a no and some just shook their heads no)

"You looked over at the one you love and smiled at them. Had another chance to say good morning! Can I get an AMEN?!"

(The crows says "AMEN" and then some yells out "KEEP GOING REVEREND")

"Can I get an Amen because you are here in Gods house and definitely in his favor! See I prayed this morning for you....... I pray every morning, but this morning especially because I wanted something specific today. I said **"God can we please have a FULL HOUSE today"?** Can we get everybody in here from the windows to the wall. We are the best club, the most exciting place you can be in right now! Right here with me, the congregation and the choir. Right here in the house of the lord listening to the word..... Amen!!"

(The Entire crowd says "AMEN")

The reverend continues on preaching and around the entire church all you see is people enjoying themselves. The church is rejoicing the lord.

Chapter 33 MOMMA'S ADVICE

Desmond and his mother are walking in the parking lot towards the car. Desmond's father is right in front of them as they stroll. Desmond extremely quiet and hasn't said a word while walking. Mrs. Coolwater notices her sons uncharacteristic silence and begins to try to console him.

"Son.......... what is wrong? Why are you so quiet and solemn today?" Mrs. Coolwater asks.

Desmond keeps his head down and replies "It's nothing momma. It's been a rough week and things at work aren't going....." Mrs. Coolwater stops walking, turns towards Desmond and finishes his sentence "Your way?" Desmond looks up "What? No!"

"Yes, things aren't going your way and the great Desmond Coolwater is having an issue with that. Listen son. I'm your mother, I have been around a long time and your whole life the issue has always been that you didn't do well with competition or loss." she says.

"Mom...." Desmond goes to explain and gets cut short by Mrs. Coolwater. "Dont mom me Desmond I know that's what it is whether you admit it with me out loud or come to that realization when you are all alone. You're just like your father and look at him now." Desmond looks over at his dad. "What do you mean by that.......?" he asks.

Mrs. Coolwater looks over at Desmond, places her hand on his face for a moment and then looks over at Mr. Coolwater as she explains why. "Desmond your father is a bad loser, but thats because when I first him he had no reason to act otherwise. He was always winning at whatever he chose to do. Whether it was sports or business he couldn't lose. His particular sport just so happened to be football. HE ran that ball with all out abandon. He was the best in the state. Desmond your father made it to college on a scholarship and he played one whole season before he was hurt in a preseason scrimmage. He was never able to comeback from that. Do you know why?"

"Why?" Desmond asks while he stands there with a curious look on his face waiting on his mother to explain. "He never knew what it felt like to lose in order to know how it felt to rebuild and come back from a loss!! Desmond you have to learn how to lose in order to fully understand and appreciate what winning is about!! Baby I don't wish any bad on you. I only hope the best for you, but I want you to learn this lesson with open arms. Embrace it and then overcome it. I fear you haven't learned anything yet, but I do believe in you and what you are capable of. You will get past this. See you at the house later for dinner."

Desmond stands there speechless as his mother delivers the final word. She kisses Desmond and walks away letting go of his hand. As she walks away towards the car, Desmond's father stands there holding the door for her. She gets into the car and Mr. Coolwater shuts the door. He looks at Desmond and says "See you at the house son." Mr. Coolwater walks around the car as smooth as Desmond would, but smoother and gets in. He starts the car and pulls out. Mrs. Coolwater waves as they pull forward out of the parking lot.

Chapter 34 DESMOND'S HOUSE

Desmond is sitting on his couch trying to relax and still thinking about the night before. On the tv is Eddie Murphy's movie "BOOMERANG". While Desmond is sitting and watching tv, his phone is blowing up from people like James, Sincere, Mrs. Coolwater, etc., etc. Desmond waits for a while to call back Sincere. He sits there staring at her phone number as he sits there and pondering what to tell her. He finally decides to call her.... The phone is ringing and Sincere picks up on the 4th ring. "Hello there handsome how are you doing?" Desmond pauses for a moment as he sinks back into his couch. "I'm cool. Just was a busy weekend. Had some meetings and a couple of disagreements."

While Desmond is speaking Sincere is cooking on her end of the phone in anticipation for Desmond to tell her what time he was going to come over for dinner like they planned. "Well I am sure it's not anything that can rattle you right? I mean not Desmond Coolwater" Desmond smiles but it fades away from his face as he gets ready to deliver some bad news to Sincere.

"Hey look Sincere I know this is short notice and I do apologize, but I just can't make it tonight." Sincere's happy excited tone leaves her voice as she continues cutting vegetables, trying to hold her composure and not sound upset. "Oh??" she replies. Desmond can hear her disappointment and tries to explain. "I'm sorry it's just been a long weekend and I am tired." Sincere makes a pouty face while still cooking. "Ok, well I understand. I mean........ I guess I'll just take all this food to the office tomorrow for the ladies to eat."

"I am truly sorry." Desmond sits up and puts his hand on his head as he continues to apologize to her. "It's just not a good night." Sincere stops cooking and sits down as she speaks to

Desmond. “Ok well I will let you go then. I hope you have a better night and get some rest.”

“I will. Hey I’ll give you a call this week and make it up to you alright?” he says in an awkward tone.

“Sounds good Desmond....... Bye.” Sincere sounds increasingly disappointed as she says bye. Desmond is feeling even more down after letting Sincere down. “Goodbye Sincere” he says. By the time Desmond gets out goodbye to Sincere she has hung up already. Desmond sits there for a bit and continues to watch “BOOMERANG”. As he is watching the movie once again his phone rings and its his mother. “Desmond Kenneth get off of your couch and get over here for dinner now!!”

“Mom........ how do you know that I am even at home?” he asks her. Mrs. Coolwater pauses and then answers him “Uh? Because I am your mother and I know exactly how my son acts when he his down. It’s been awhile since I have seen you like this so its not too far fetched that you still act the same way you used too, which is just withdraw from everything and everybody.”

“I’m on my way momma” Desmond smiles to himself and gets off the couch to head to his parents house.

Chapter 35 FAMILY ISSUES

Desmond pulls up to his parents house in Aurora where on the porch there is a crowd of people drinking beer and having a great time. Desmond parks his car and then sits there trying to get himself together before he has to deal with all his family. He turns off the car, takes a deep breath and then gets out of his car. As he gets to the porch he is met by his uncle Mario who is his mother's youngest brother who is always under the influence of alcohol, but by far Desmonds best uncle out of the other three brothers his mother has.

“Desmond!!! Hey nephewwwwwwwww!!! How's its going boy!?!” Uncle Mario yells from across the street. Desmond smiles a genuine smile for Uncle Mario and replies as he walks up “What's up uncle Mario. I’m good. How are you doing?” Uncle Mario walks up and puts his arm around Desmond as they walk up towards the house.

“I’m as cool as the other side of the pillow nephew. Gotta keep it ice cold like my tall can here.” Uncle Mario gets a kick out of his own smooth vernacular always. Desmond and uncle Mario make it to the porch where Desmonds brothers Gerald and Marvin are sitting talking to each other. Gerald stands up and gives Desmond a handshake and a hug. Marvin keeps sitting and just looks over at Desmond with a “What's up” nod.

“Little bro! Whats up man! How are you doing?” asks Gerald.

“I’m good G, just been chillen big bruh” Uncle Mario walks past the two while they talk. “Hows the job treating you man? I mean it must be good because you rarely come around anymore.” Gerald sits back down in his chair next to Marvin on the porch.

"Yeah its been hectic with all these new accounts I've been getting for the magazine." Desmond replies.

Marvin chimes in on Gerald and Desmonds conversation. "Yeah baby bro.......long time no see. Down thee throwing parties downtown with the yuppies. It's a little too hood for you this far east huh?"

Desmond chuckles at Marvin as he walked over to shake his hand and hug him. "Come on now. You know it isn't that. Its just that the people I deal with don't do business out this direction man. They don't see the attraction in the real estate out here."

Marvin laughs and then says "That's why you are in the position you are in now right? Its your job to sell them on bringing the business out this way."

Desmond kind of chuckles. "Where would they possibly want to bring the business out here Marvin? Huh?" Gerald looks over at Marvin with a shocked expression and then looks back at Desmond. "Damn, baby bro are you that detached from where you are from?"

"No, but...." Desmond replies. Marvin interrupts Desmond before he can reply. "Yeah!! Look at him Gerald? He's too wrapped up in that booshie bullshit. That's alright little bro keep that yuppie booshie bullshit where it belongs......downtown in the city." Just then as the conversation is getting heated, Desmonds sister Desiree comes out, hugs on him and then leads him by the hand into the house.

"Hi Dessie!!! Look at you!! My baby brother the big time businessman. Come in the house mommy is looking for you."

Desmond walks into the house with Desiree as Marvin and Gerald keep the conversation going with Uncle Mario. Desiree leads Desmond thru the house to where Mrs. Coolwater is sitting in the kitchen setting the table for dinner.

“Momma Desmond is here!” she announces.

Mrs. Coolwater walks over and hugs Desmond. “Just in time for dinner honey. Good you made it for family time son. Desiree go get your father and tell him dinner is done.........no matter of fact Desmond go get your dad from under that car in the backyard please.”

“Ok…” Desmond says as he walks past his mom and she hits him on his butt. He walks down the stairs and towards the garage where his father is working on his car. As he gets closer you can hear sounds of Bobby Womack. Desmond walks into the garage and his father looks up at him and says “Pass me the wrench please.” Desmond walks over to the counter, grabs the wrench, hands it to his father and then says “Hey pop.....mom sent me out here to get you for dinner.”

“Yeah well you can go back in now and tell her that you spoke to me. Thanks.” he replies and then sticks his head back under the roof of the car. Desmond goes to walk off back to the house and his emotions stop him in his tracks. He decides to go back and give his father a pierce of his mind.

“You know something?” Desmond says. Mr. Coolwater steps back from the car and grabs the rag to wipe his hands while he listens to Desmond.

“No, what's on your mind Desmond?” Mr. Coolwater asks.

Desmond just starts to emotionally unload everything. “You never have more than 2 or 3 words for me. I mean what have I done so bad that you can never speak to me. I see you speak to Gerald and Marvin all the time. What is it about our relationship can't you get along with huh?”

Mr. Coolwater stands there looking at Desmond and says “I don't know what you are talking about.” Desmond looks at him, starts to walk off and then comes back one more time.

“No, of course you don't. Why would you? I mean you never ask me anything about how I’m doing or how's my job or how's life? Let one of your favorite boys come out here and you're just all conversation, but for me nothing. I’m sorry that I am not like your other sons. I’m sorry that I haven't met your expectations, but this is my life and you can either accept it or not, but I am still your son......”

By this time Desmond has raised his voice enough to get his sisters attention and she is looking thru the screen door. “Son, you are mistaken I do care about you...... ” Mr. Coolwater says trying to reach out, but Desmond has suddenly blown up and decided to go into the house. He walks towards the door, swings the screen open and rushes past Desiree as he makes his way to the front door. Just then Mrs. Coolwater yells from across the house and says “Desmond Kenneth! Don't you walk out that door. Come here!”

Desmond walks back towards the kitchen where Mrs. Coolwater is and listens to what she has to say “Go back out there!” she says.

“I am not going back out there momma. Why would I ?” Desmond asks. “....because I said so, that's why. He loves you and just wants the chance to explain to you. He is not like you in that way son. Some things are just hard to say and he is one person who would love the chance to do a better job of that with you...... even if you don't believe it! So go back out there and give him a chance." Desmond nods his head and goes back outside where is father is bent over back in the car.

Desmond walks back into the garage and straight up to his father. Mr. Coolwater stands straight up and looks Desmond in the eye, grabs the rag, wipes his hands and begins to speak. "Son I love you. You are my baby boy and all I ever wanted for you is to be successful!! Well you're doing that and I didn't do any of it for you. Son you are a man and I respect that to the highest degree. I am so damn proud of you. I never wanted this kind of relationship with you, where we can't talk, can't come to each other and talk."

Desmond looks down and away from Mr. Coolwater as if he is only there listening because his mother told him too and then he interrupts his father "You and me...... we are nothing alike. It's like I'm not your son. It's like with Marvin, Gerald and Desiree you show them all the love a father can show them because they could play basketball, run track or throw that football, but with me...... nothing?!?"

Mr. Coolwater reaches to put his hand on Desmonds shoulder, but Desmond backs away by stepping back. Mr. Coolwater pulls his hand back and starts to wipe his hands with the towel again.

Desmond gets irritated, but continues to speak.....

"You got nothing huh? Nothing to say to that do you? Nothing I have ever done has been good enough for you! It's not enough that I was top of my graduating class in highschool right?

Nah...nah….not good enough that I was voted most likely to succeed or that I went to school on a full ACADEMIC scholarship…… a full fucking scholarship and didn't cost you SHIT…"

Desmond yells and at the same time Mrs. Coolwater yells from the house at Desmond. "Watch your mouth Desmond Kenneth!!" Desmond looks over his shoulder towards the house, then cuts his eyes back towards his father who never stopped staring at him and continues to speak, but with a more lower yet sharper tone.

"No, it wasn't good enough that I graduated in 4 years and got a job right away without having to move back here under your roof. I don't ask you for nothing! Do you want to know why? It's because I don't need anything from you...nothing. The exact same thing you have given me my whole life.... nothing!! What do you have to say to that……. huh?"

Mr. Coolwater looks at Desmond with a smile plus a small chuckle, yet as a hurt father. He looks down at the car, back up at Desmond and then leans against the car.

"You know son. I remember the day you were born. The day you took your first breath and I knew just by looking at you, that you were going to be the one out of all my children to go the furthest in life. Since you were a baby in these hands."

He holds up his hands like he is holding an infant. "I have been proud of you. I watched you push any ball I ever gave you away and pick up a book instead. I guess as a man whose only special skills was sports and cars, that's all I really had to offer you other than the shirt off my back. Maybe me working 12 to 15 hour days to keep a roof over you and your sister and brothers heads was too much. Or just maybe the hot meal that you got every night or the clothes on your back was just me showing you how much that I didn't love you...... right? Every single night that I got home and you were in bed I would kneel by your bed and pray while holding your little tiny hand in mine. I hoped that one day you would understand the hopes and dreams that I had and still have for you."

Mr. Coolwater walks around his car as he speaks to Desmond. You can hear his footsteps. Desmond is still standing there with a smart / sarcastic look on his face and then says "Yeaaaaah whatever…"

Mr. Coolwater looks over at him, cracks a half cocked smile and then says "Why don't you just leave huh? I have tried to speak to you with every loving bone I have for you and all you have for me is a bunch of nothing….."

Desmond interrupts him and says "How does it feel huh??" then chuckles as he turns his back and starts to walk back towards the house. Mr. Coolwater begins to speak again except this time his voice is different. "The difference is that you can't be man enough to deal with the truth and I know how too now. I'm willing to change and try. You're too stubborn to try to change and that trait right there son you get from MEEeeeeeeee…" His voice has become weak, raspy and winded. Mr. Coolwater suddenly grabs his chest and collapses to his knees on the floor. The rag he's holding falls to the floor slowly as well as some tools hitting the ground making a loud ting and twang sound.

Desmond runs over to his fathers aid. He is yelling to the house for help as he pulls his father up on his lap and hugs him close to him. Mr. Coolwater is laying there limp on Desmonds lap as

Desmond rocks back and forth with him.

Time seems to slow down as everyone runs from the house into the garage to see what has happened. Everybody is screaming and yelling for Mr. Coolwater to respond. In the background the song *"**CHANGE IS GONNA COME**" **by Sam Cooke*** is playing on the radio.

"Daddy….. daddy…. daddy" Desmond is yelling.

The chaos is interrupted by the paramedics rushing in to Mr. Coolwater's aid. They are trying to pull him from Desmond, but he is in shock and his brothers has to pull him away from Mr. Coolwater so the paramedics can start to work on him. As they pull Desmond to his feet, Mrs. Coolwater grabs Desmond in her arms and hugs him.

The night ends with Desmond watching on while the paramedics are putting his father into the ambulance and his mother climbs into the back with Mr. Coolwater. The door shuts on both his parents and the ambulance pulls away from Desmond as his brothers and his sister walk away with Uncle Mario towards the house. Desmond watches the ambulance go down the street.

Chapter 36 VISIT DAD IN HOSPITAL

Desmond walks into the hospital room where his father his hooked up to all kinds of wires and his mother sitting there with her head on the bed while holding Mr. Coolwater's hand. Desmond walks over to his mother and lays his hand on her shoulder. She brings her head up with a smile towards Desmond, touches his hand and lays her head on it as well. She stands up and fixes her shawl and then bends down and kisses Mr. Coolwater on his head. Her and Desmond walk out of the room and begin to talk.

“How's he doing?” asks Desmond.

Mrs. Coolwater looks back into the room before she answers. “He is doing alright baby. The doctor said that he was lucky to survive this heart attack. If you weren't out there, he could have been laying out there for God only knows how long.” she says.

Desmond looks down and says “I’m no angel momma. The only reason I was still out there and the only reason he probably even had a heart attack was because of me.” Mrs. Coolwater softly grabs Desmond's face. “Oh no honey don't say that. Your fathers health hasn't been the greatest and I had been trying to get him into the doctors office for a while now about his chest pains.” Desmond gazes up at his mother with a confused look on his face. “How come you have never told me about this before mom?”

“....Because your father Desmond. He is a proud man and doesn't want everyone making a fuss about his health and what he needs to do. He has taken care of us all for so long that having to let people take care of or worry about him would just make him feel.” she replies.

"Feel what?" Desmond asks. Mrs. Coolwater starts walking down the hallway a bit and replies. "Well honey........ like less of the wonderful man he has been. Like less of the strong father that you kids have always seen from him at all times. Even when he was tired from working all day and everything else."

"Typical...." Desmond mumbles to himself. Mrs. Coolwater stops walking once again and looks Desmond in the eyes. "Typical?? He is your father Desmond. He is the person, the loving father and man that has kept this whole family together all these years. He loves you with all his heart Desmond. If you could just get over all those memories of him not being the stereotypical father that you see on tv and notice him for what he has been too you. You will then realize that he has been trying to reach out to you in his own little ways for along time now. You have to open your heart up to him and let go of all that so-called pinned up hate for your father. He loves you Desmond......He loves you and is so proud of you! GO sit with him Desmond, go to him and speak to him. He can't speak right now, but he can hear you honey......... Go!"

Desmond hugs his mother and then agrees to do what she has asked him to do. "Ok momma I will. I don't know what to say to him, but I will sit with him."

"Once you can let go of your anger then your heart will give you all the words you need. Now go in there and sit with him. I have to go home for a bit and get dinner started. I will send your brothers or your sister up here in a bit." Mrs. Coolwater assures Desmond he will find the words.

Desmond and his mother hug each other again and Mrs.

Coolwater walks down the hallway towards the elevator. Desmond watches her and then walks towards the door and goes in. As Desmond walks in and takes a long stare at his father, he tries to figure out what to say to his father. He walks over to the same chair that his mother was sitting in and sits down. He looks over to his fathers hand that's just laying there open as if he has been waiting for Desmond to come in and take it.

Desmond stares at his father's hand a while before he reluctantly takes his hand. Desmond stares at all the wires going in and out of his father, he then grips his father's hand and lays his head down on the bed.

Time flies by as Desmond lays there thinking of when he was a child and his father played with him and wrestled with him as a little boy. He remembers how his father would take him driving and let him sit on his lap like he was driving. Desmond comes back to after being in deep thought and starts to speak to his father while he sleeps.

"How did we get here pop? How did we fall apart huh? I mean where did I go left and you go right. I always felt like you didn't like me much cause I didn't want to play a sport. Have you ever noticed how slew footed I am dad?" Desmond chuckles to himself. "I always felt like I was just awkward and had no athletic ability whatsoever, but you always made me get out there. Over and over and over again."

Desmond looks at Mr. Coolwater as he lays there resting and continues to speak to him even though he doesn't reply back. "I guess that was your way of teaching me lessons. It's funny but I swear I sit and shine my shoes for like an hour before I can get myself to put them on and I know I get that from you." He chuckles again.

"I can remember sitting there watching you shine your shoes for hours. I can remember watching you ironing your dress slacks before you and mom would go out on date night. I can remember the smell of that cologne....Aww man was the name of that cologne?? What was that cologne?? **GREY FLANNEL**...........yep that was it right there........**GREY FLANNEL!!!!**"

Desmond smiles and just laughs as he holds his fathers hand and reminisces. The whole time he never realizes that his father is responding slightly every time he laughs and speaks about a memory. "Ok ok ok.........I know you would remember this? Remember when we were all in Texas on that road trip to Aunt Diane's house and we had to stop like 100 times because we all got food poisoned somewhere along the way. I mean between you yelling at us about not stopping until we got to auntie's house, mom yelling at you to pull over for us and you farting and passing some of the worst gas I can recall in life..." He chuckles again and says ".... that was the funnest trip I ever had right there."

Desmond stares up at Mr. Coolwater and notices his eyes watering. Desmond reaches to grab a Kleenex and wipes his father's tears away. He then sits down and continues talking to him. "I'm sorry dad. I'm so sorry for not being man enough to come talk to you. I love you. I love you with all my heart dad, please don't go away from me, from us......please be ok. I have so much to tell you. I am just going thru the toughest time dealing with work lately. I'm losing my edge to a person who is stealing everything from me.

Everything I have worked for his slowly, but surely being taken from me. I have never known what it feels like to lose. What it feels like to have to fight for something because I have always been the best at whatever I wanted to do, so there was never an issue."

Desmond puts his head back down and lays there for a minute. As Desmond is about to get up and walk out after his long conversation with his father, Mr. Coolwater squeezes his hand. Desmond looks up and Mr. Coolwater's eyes are watering and running again, but he is still squeezing Desmonds hand as if he didn't want him to get up and go.

Desmond smiles and sits back down. He wipes his father's tears away and begins to talk to him some more.

COOL NIGHTS

Chapter 37 DRAMA AT THE OFFICE

The atmosphere is busy. As usual employees are moving around with urgency trying to meet and make deadlines. Desmond is sitting at his desk working. Lyriq is not at her desk yet and James is nowhere to be seen. Desmond has yet to get suspicious because James never misses a day and normally pops up when you least expect. Desmond is typing away when Cindy the office intern rushes up to his desk in a frenzy about something.

"Dessie, Dessie, Dessie" Cindy rushes Desk. Desmond replies "What Cindy? What? I am not in the mood today ok? What is it? Cindy senses Desmonds irritation and is kind of put off by it which cause her to slow down and speak calmly. "Well I heard about the little...ummm….scuffle that you and James got into at The Church nightclub and…" Desmond interrupts her. "Wait a minute? Uhh the scuffle that James and I got into?"

"Yes, it's all around the office." Cindy answers Desmond as if he is supposed to already know it. "There was no James and me getting into a scuffle. I got into the scuffle…" Desmond says in a sarcastic tone.

"Well you might want to go into the boardroom cause I think they are getting ready to fire James for it…." Desmond jumps up and rushes to the boardroom where James is sitting across from Mr. Elmhurst, Lyriq and Mr. Kenneth Kush, the Partner and Chief Financial Officer at Fly magazine. Desmond walks right into the meeting without caring about the intrusion.

"What is going on here?" Desmond asks as he walks into the boardroom. Mr. Kush sits up in his chair and looks right at Desmond. "Why don't you tell us Mr. Coolwater? From what I'm told here your assistant is the cause of a lot of harassment and bad moral around here in the office, according to Ms. Moore? What do you have to say about this?"

Lyriq looks at Desmond and he stares back at her. "Mr. Kush I don't know if that is true sir. Yes, James is my assistant, but he works under my direction and…" Mr. Kush cuts Desmond off "So then you are responsible for his behavior and how he had treated Ms. Moore?"

"Mr. you are completely wrong about this see…" James tries to speak up and then Mr. Kush cuts James off as well. "Your explanation is not needed young man. You are in enough trouble as it is."

Mr. Elmhurst finally speaks up. "If I may add in their defense Kenneth this whole dual gender faction split of the magazine was a big surprise to these guys and maybe it was a bit unexpected."

"Yes, that may be but that doesn't excuse their unprofessional behavior." says Mr. Kush. Desmond tries to get in a word. "Mr. Kush James has been a great asset to me as well as a model employee to this company, so why is he under fire right now?"

Mr. Kush walks toward Desmond as he replies "I was told that you gentleman were engaged in a scuffle in a local nightclub a few nights ago and I will not put up with employees ruining the name and not representing us in a professional light. I don't know who started it, but what I do know is that one of you if not both of you should have had the respect to not engage in it at all. I am thoroughly disappointed with both of your behavior and frankly Desmond I expected more of you."

Mr. Kush looks at Lyriq on his way back to his seat. Lyriq stands up and walks into the middle of the boardroom past Desmond straight up to James. “James I have been watching your conduct here in the office and out on assignments these past few weeks and I must say I am not happy.”

“Wait a minute? This isn't her place? Mr. Elmhurst what's going on here?” Desmond interrupts.

Mr. Elmhurst replies to Desmonds plea for an answer. “Desmond we have to let James go based off of Ms. Moore's claim of harassment. We do not tolerate that here at Fly magazine. James you are aware of this strict code of conduct right?” Mr. Elmhurst says as he looks directly at James.

“Yes sir I am, but in my defense I love my job here at Fly and I would never put that in jeopardy for anything worth it or worthless…” James responds to Mr. Elmhurst as he looks directly at Lyriq.

“Nonetheless James a claim has been made to this office and we have to remove the issue moving forward. You are hereby fired and your employment terminated. Your things have already been placed in a box and at the security desk. Please follow these guards to exit.” Mr. Kush says. James looks at Desmond and walks past him. As he walks past Lyriq he jumps to scare her. Lyriq jumps back as if James was really going to do something. James laughs as the guards grab his arms and escorts him towards the exit. As James is pulled out in true James fashion he yells out…

“I told you she was a scandolous hoochie traaaaaaiiiiiiiiin Desmmmoooooooonnnnnndddd!!!”

The exit doors slam as James yells out! Desmond looks at Lyriq with a scowl and then looks at Mr. Kush and Mr. Elmhurst and asks? “Is there anything else I can do or help you gentlemen with or can I go back to work now?”

Mr. Kush looks at Desmond. “Desmond you are skating on thin ice young man. The only reason that I didn't fire you is because of Mr. Elmhurst's fondness of you and your track record here the past 4 to 5 years, but I will be watching you.”

Lyriq speaks after Mr. Kush. “Desmond I really want this relationship to work. I really believe that we can take Fly Magazine to the next level.....internationally if we both put our heads together and work hard.” Lyriq walks over to Desmond and extends her hand to him. Her back is to the others in the room and she gives Desmond a devilish no good grin then she says very lightly “You should probably shake my hand and play nice. Wouldn't want them to think anything would you?” Desmond shakes her hand reluctantly and then looks over at Mr. Elmhurst. Mr. Elmhurst gives him the nod and he leaves the boardroom.
Desmond is sitting at his desk as others are staring at him and walking past spreading rumors. Just as he gets ready to try and work, Stacey the office secretary walks up.

“I heard about what happened to James, Desmond. I’m sorry. I know you guys were really good friends.”

Desmond keeps looking at the keys as he is typing and then looks up at the screen. “Thanks Stacey. He was a damn good assistant and they don't make them like that anymore.” Stacey shakes her head, laughs and then says “No they don't. Keep your head up Desmond you will come up with something.” Stacey pats Desmond on the back and then walks away. Desmond sits up in his seat and just then his cell phone rings and its James calling him…….

"Hello" James speaks after Desmond. "Man I ought to blow the whole entire building up!!"

Desmond sits back and jokingly says "Damn man even the disability rehab joint upstairs?"

"YES!! Fuck them too!!!!" James replies. "Ummm......Damn, can you at least wait for me to get out of this place before you go psycho ape shit??? " he says. Desmond laughs a bit, but gets back to serious really quick. He decides to walk away from his desk so people cant hear his conversation.

"You better hurry up!!! Shit aint funny right now." James says.

"James I am really sorry for this happening to you man. This shit has gotten way out of hand. I mean she has only been here a week and a half. She has single handedly managed to move in on my contacts, shake hands with the enemy and do a joint party venture as well as getting you fired." Desmond sympathizes.

"Yeah she's the devil bro…… I mean this chick has got us both beat on this one. Did you see the look on her face as Mr. Kush was talking to us? It was like she planned this whole thing out before she even knew who she was up against?"

Desmond shakes his head as he replies. "Yeah she had that look like nothing could touch her in that boardroom. I just can't get over how Mr. Elmhurst was almost helpless in there?"

"That's what the hell I'm saying. It was almost like he couldn't do anything for us." James raises his voice.

Desmond is leaning against the wall deep in thought as him and James talk. “I know!?!?! Listen James I have to get back to work, but I will call you back later.”

James responds “Cool. I’m going to go drink and try not to blow anything up!”

Desmond sits up in his seat and says “Hey bro don't do anything stupid! I’m going to work this out and get us both out of this mess. I promise.”

Desmond hangs up the phone and heads back to his desk. As he sits down at his desk he looks over at Lyriq's desk and she is sitting there working with a smirk on her face like she knows he is looking over at her. Desmond turns his chair so his back his towards her. He then calls his mom to check on his father.

“Hello” Mrs. Coolwater answers.

“Hi mom.” says Desmond. “Hey baby how are you doing?” Desmond leans back in his chair. “I’m alright. It’s been one hell of a day already. How's dad doing?”

“Well he is up and ok. He’s talking a bit and smiling a little bit as well. Are you going to come see him today?” she replies. “Yeah….it will probably be this evening before I go home. It’s been a crazy day for me. They fired James today.”

“No!?! They fired your assistant James? Why?” Mrs. Coolwater asks in a shocked tone.

Desmond looks over his shoulder to see if Lyriq is looking over at him. He then turns back in his seat and continues talking. “It's hard to explain it all right now momma. I mean for nothing really, but I'm going to clean this mess up that I allowed to happen due to my inability to cope with change though. I tell you that."

"Hmmm? Sounds like you have a lot on your plate son." Mrs. Coolwater says. Desmond nods head and says "I do mom…..I do."

"Well I know that you will figure it out baby. I remember when you were a baby and you would fail at something or you couldn't do it at first, your father would be right there making you do it over until you could master it. You will fix this and master this problem like normal. I have faith." Mrs. Coolwater says with confidence. "Thanks momma. I love you. Tell dad I will see him later."

"I love you too and I will tell him to expect you this evening. Goodbye baby boy." she says "Bye mom" Desmond says back as they both hang up the phone. Desmond sets his cell phone down and then turns to his computer to continue working. Desmond decides to pick up his laptop and go back to the boardroom where he can make calls to his clients without Lyriq and everyone else over his shoulder. As he is walking down the hallway he notices that Mr. Elmhurst is not in his office.

He gets to the boardroom and enters the room, closes the door behind him and locks it. He sits his bag and laptop down then goes to draw the shades open to show another picturesque day in Denver, Colorado.

Desmond sits down and begins to make his calls. His first call is to Peter Dash……….the phone rings and Peter picks it up on the

3rd ring.

"Hello this is Peter Dash how may I help you?" he says. Desmond introduces himself. "Mr. Dash this is Desmond Coolwater, Vincent's friend. How are you doing?"

"I'm doing great Desmond. Thank you for calling me. I know you are a busy man." he replies. "No problem at all Mr. Dash. I apologize for taking so long to call you back." Peter laughs and then says "Hey first of all........if we are going to do business together then you can't call me Mr. Dash alright?" Desmond laughs as well and continues with the conversation. "Cool. So tell me about your business then Peter?"

"I am in need of your assistance Desmond. I am launching my very own energy drink and I need help with a complete marketing / advertising package." Peter replies. "What kind of marketing, advertising and/or promotions are you doing so far?" Desmond asks.

"Well as of right now I am just lining all my ducks up. I have national and international distribution for my product, but no staff or employees to help me out. I am a grassroots kind of guy with just enough money and connections to pull this off. Vincent was telling me that you are the man when it comes to marketing / promotional know how and can really help get my name out there?"

Desmond smiles with a confident grin and replies "I'm humbled by the referral from Vincent. Vincent and I are really good friends so a friend of his is a friend of mine. I would love to help you get started."

"This is great news Desmond!! Where do begin?" Peter asks.

Desmond takes a seat at the boardroom table, grabs his pad and pencil from his bag, then begins to detail the first steps of the marketing plan. “First things first........ Get me your logo’s, website address, company colors and any other ideas you may have via email so I can have my marketing team get started on some mock internet campaigns.”

Peter is taking notes as well, while Desmond runs down the plan step by step. “Consider it done immediately!” Desmond switches the phone to other side of his head as he continues. “Secondly, lets also plan a day for you to come into the office for a meeting with my time and I so we can meet face to face and rub our heads together. I will contact you with some meeting dates and launch dates. Sound good?”

“This is good Desmond. You are as great as Vincent said you were. I am impressed already.” he replies.

Desmond drops the pen and stands back up to look out the window at the mountains again. “Well let me put some work in first and then I’ll take that compliment then. I will email you later today with some calendar dates to see what works best for you?”

“Deal! Sounds good and I look forward to working with you. Have a great rest of the day sir.” Peter says and Desmond replies “Ditto”. Both Gentlemen hang up the phone and Desmond writes down some more notes in his planner. He sits back in his seat reflecting over the conversation before he dials the next call. Desmond then dials up Chauncey Billup's agent. The phone rings and Fredrick McGaul’s voicemail comes on . “**This is Fred and I am not available right now. If you are interested in booking or scheduling any artist or athletes on our roster please leave a detailed message for your specific artist and/or athlete as**

well as the occasion. I will call you back as soon as possible. Thank you and God Bless!!"

Desmond leaves a message. "Hello Fredrick my name is Desmond Coolwater and I am the entertainment director with Fly Magazine here in Denver, Colorado. My assistant James Wright has contacted you a few times and I have received word that Chauncey has agreed to an interview with us for our hometown celebrity issue. Please contact me so you and I can get the ball rolling on the dates. I know that the season is in full swing and your window for scheduling is slim so please contact me at your earliest convenience so we can get this going ASAP. My number is (720) 641-7501. Thanks in advance."

Desmond hangs up the phone and starts writing some notes in his planner. As he is finishing up his notes he looks up to the glass wall and see's people walking past the door. Just as he gets ready to get back to calling his assignments he notices that Lyriq is walking past the door so he hangs up the phone. She looks through the window as she is walking past and waves at Desmond. Desmond waves back sarcastically, turns in the seat, picks up his cell phone and walks towards the window to look outside. He then decides to give Sincere a call. The phone rings a few times and Sincere picks up.

"Hello" a sexy voice says from the other side. Desmond smiles as Sincere's voice turns into a sensual vibration to his eardrum. "Well hello beautiful"

"Hi stranger!! I thought I scared you off or something." she says. Desmond grabs the chair, pulls it over to the window where he was standing and sits down right in front of it . "No, not at all. It's just been a crazy past couple of days. Drama and business just does not mix."

"Yeah.....it never ends well. So other than that how is your day going?" she replies.

Desmond leans back in his chair. "Uhhhhh.......a little more of the same at the moment, but it would get better if I could see you later for dinner? What do ya say?"

Sincere sits there for a moment in silence before replying. Desmond gets impatient and says "Hello?" and then Sincere answers him. "I'd say that-that would be an awesome idea, but you stood me up the other night so I don't know how excited I should be or get?"

"Be excited! Be very excited!" Desmond smiles as he replies. "Ok! Well I'm excited then. What are you wanting to do?" she asks. "Well I'm thinking that we will go to the Rodizio Grill for dinner and a glass of wine, then head over to this other spot where they are having a live band along with artist painting during the performances. It's an art benefit. You down?" he asks as he twiddles the pen between his fingers waiting on her to answer.

"Oh fun! Ok so then lets plan on getting together around 7:45 p.m. at the restaurant then." she says.

"Great see you there then." Desmond says. "It's a date!" she replies. Desmond checks his watch. "Yes it is."

"Alrighty then. See ya there handsome." Sincere hangs up the phone. Desmond hangs up his phone, sits it down, looks back at the inside office window and everyone is done walking past. Desmond is very excited to see Sincere this evening. Desmond continues working, sending emails and making phone calls when

Lyriq suddenly enters the boardroom to ask how he is doing.

“Hello Desmond how's it going?” she says. Desmond sits up in his seat as he is working. He then looks up at Lyriq with an irritated look but entertains her presence. “Hello Ms. Moore…….what can I do for you? Lyriq sits down on the edge of the table seductively and crosses one leg over the other. “Well, well, well, Mr. Coolwater I see despite today's festivities you still find time to get to business.”

Desmond is sitting there typing up his notes and setting dates for events. He never looks up at Lyriq to acknowledge her and then he says “What do you mean Ms. Moore? Surely you didn't think I would be bumming it and all down did you?”

Lyriq’s body language changes as she speaks. “Don't play coy with me Desmond. I know there is some bad blood flowing right now.” Desmond continues to keep typing while she is talking. He never looks up at her once while he is working.

Lyriq tries to continue to hold conversation, but Desmond stops typing, looks up at her, sits back in his seat and says “Lyriq you just got one of my good friends axed today. Not to mention you have been stepping on my toes and trying to make me look bad since you got here, so don't sit here like we are all good and you have been a victim of a mysterious circumstance. Remember who you are dealing with…..” Lyriq stands up and walks around the table. As she is slowly walking around the table she begins to speak to Desmond.

“Desmond you are in no position to badger me. You have been running this place like it was your personal playground for some time now. You’ve had this entire magazine under your thumb and now I’m here. Things are going to change. Things are going to start being ran my way or...."

Desmond straightens his posture in his chair fully engaged in what she is saying as he asks ".....or what?"

Lyriq leans over the table towards Desmond's face and says "Or you too can be let go just like James."

Desmond looks right into Lyriq's eyes and then sits back into his seat completely beside himself that Lyriq would have the gall to even say what she just said. "Oh you're the boss now huh? Handing out pink slips and all that?"

Lyriq walks around the table while running her freshly done fingernails across the glossy dark wood table and replies "I'm not the boss yet, but its only a matter of time Desmond. See the truth is that you haven't been as effective as you think you have been for a while now and you are this close to being let go yourself. Yeah I bet you think Mr. Elmhurst can save you, but he is like minded and he thinks the same way according to him and Mr. Kush's meeting earlier."

Desmond is sitting in his seat fuming, but he is doing his best to be as cool as possible. Desmond manages to chuckle and says "You know.......its been awhile since I have had some healthy competition so keep them coming. I have no worries about my job."

Lyriq stands straight up and then says "Make no mistakes Desmond. This is not a joke. This is not a competition.........this is a takeover and you are on the wrong side of the playing field. You are dispensable, you are replaceable and if you don't watch your ass then you'll see how far I am willing to go to get you terminated as well."

Lyriq smiles at him. Desmond crosses his arms and leans back in his chair some more. Lyriq turns around, walks towards the door and just as she is about to exit she says

"......And Desmond?" Desmond is still looking at her. "Yeah? What?"

Lyriq smiles as she stands there in a sexy stance. "The other night was great. I loved it and I must say your reputation is definitely well deserved, but don't get it twisted. Great sex never out trumps money and power." Lyriq turns around and leaves the room with a cold chilling breeze behind her. Desmond is still sitting there for a minute in shock. He then picks up the phone and calls James back to hatch his plan. The phone rings 4 or 5 times before he picks up.

"Hello" James answers. "James! I need your help and I need it right now" Desmond says as he looks over his shoulder to make sure no one is listening to him.

"Lay it on me then!!" James gets ready for the plan.

Desmond begins to lay the plan out with James about calling in a bomb threat in order to clear out the building, so he can check out Lyriq's desk and get some clues to what kind of angles Lyriq really has.

Chapter 38 PHONE BOOTH/BOMB THREAT

James is at a phone booth across the street and down a couple of blocks from Fly Mag offices. He is chewing gum and waiting on Desmond to give him a call. As he stands there a group of extraordinarily fly latin ladies walk past and he decides to walk away from the phone booth to follow them. As he is speaking with the ladies, getting acquainted, his phone rings and it's Desmond.

He ignores the phone call at first to keep speaking with the ladies. He then snaps to his senses, runs back to the phone to find an old lady has occupied it and is rummaging thru her purse in order to get the right change. James is standing there trying to be patient and the lady just keeps talking to herself while trying to count change.

"Hey lady can I help you?" James asks her. "No!!! I am fine but thank you" she replies as she turns back to looking for quarters for the phone.

"Yep" James stands there impatiently as the lady continues to search for change and then James loses it and says "Ok lady that's it!!! I tried to wait but you not having the correct change could get me into trouble. " James booty bumps the lady out of the way and starts to put the change in the machine. Just as James is putting the remaining change into the machine the old lady comes back and booty bumps him back. James falls to the ground and the lady starts to hit him with her purse.

James is kicking and yelling as he struggles to get back on his feet. The lady stops hitting him and begins to walk back towards the phone. James phone rings and he checks it to see that its Desmond.

The lady is at the phone trying to use James change and quickly dial her number. James jumps back up, puts the old lady in a headlock and begins to dog walk her around the phonebooth, screaming and yelling like he is pumped up for putting an old lady in the headlock.

The old lady is struggling to get out of the headlock that James has her. “You little disrespectful heathen!! I am a lady. Weren't you raised better than that?” James is at the phone by now breathing hard and dialing the number to Fly Offices to call in the bomb threat. As the phone is ringing he looks back at the old lady and says “Old lady do I look like I am the respectful type. Get your old geritol smelling ass out of here before I do the headlock dance on you again!!”

“You ugly little mother fucker! I hope you get old one day and your dick stop working!!” she yells out.

“I bet you do ya old arthritic orangutan looking……” Just as James is finishing his sentence and trying to catch his breath, Stacey the Head Office Secretary answers the phone. “Thank you for calling FLy magazine. How can I help you?” James gets into character and then says “Yeah! You can help me bitch!”Stacey’s face goes from calm to a concerned frown as she says “Excuse me?”

“Yeah you heard right ya old wrinkly cougar!!! You can help me… I want you too…” Just then the old lady comes back at James attacking him ferociously with her purse and then some other old women all join in to start beating him with their purses as well. He manages to get out the bomb threat before he is overtaken by the geriatric mob of mad women.

James is tussling with the phone and fighting off the angry gang of women. He yells out
"Bitch I will…" James is still trying to hold his composure, but the sounds of tussling can still be heard as Stacey listens on. "Who is this?" she asks.

"This is a bomb threat!! You old bitch……get out of that building before I blow all you idiots up!!" he yells through the phone. Stacey hangs up the phone and instantly calls security to alert them of the threat. Everyone is being ushered out of the office while Desmond is sitting in the boardroom continuing to type away and smile to himself .

Desmond then gets up and walks towards the door. He opens it up and a few more people are still running to get out of the building. One employee says to Desmond… "Desmond there was a bomb threat man. Get out of here asap!"

Desmond looks at him and replies with a fake sense of urgency. "Hell yeah!! I'm just checking to make sure everyone else is out of here! See you out there!"

"Okay good!! See you out there." the employee says frantically as he runs down the hallway.

Desmond continues down the hallway to the main office. He is looking around to make sure no one is in the office so he can carry out his plan. He then goes over to Lyriq's desk and begins to inspect the area for clues to what she is up too. He runs across some business cards from people he knows. He then opens up her desk drawer to find a mess of snacks, snack wrappers and women hygiene. He is looking thru her desk and comes across a notepad with some passwords written down that help her remember how to get into her desk.

“Bingo!! Who writes down their passwords anymore?” Desmond says out loud to himself. Desmond continues to start logging into Lyriq's computer. He sits there while the computer boots up. He is looking around to make sure no one is around. The computer is finished booting up and Desmond goes straight for Lyriq's email inbox.

The first email that pops up is an email from Mr. Kush telling Lyriq to have a great night and to inform him of the outcome first thing in the morning. Desmond then goes on to the next email which is from Travis Vasquez with City One promotions and he instantly gets a salty look on his face. He begins to speak to himself out loud.

“I told James and everyone else that these guys are no good for business and what does this chick come here and do? She ties us into a contract with these shady mutha’s……”

Desmond starts going thru other emails and comes across the email talking about the event that she is hosting tonight and he didn't know anything about it. Desmond sits back and is instantly frustrated. Just as he gets a little too comfy, he hears people coming back and begins to frantically put things back where he got them from. He closes her drawer as well as locks the computer, but he forgot to close her email out and he tries to stop the lock, but its too late. He pushes her chair in and runs towards the restroom.

Lyriq is walking back towards her desk and notices Desmond walking towards the restroom….. She goes back to her desk, looks around to see if anything is out of place. She starts to boot up her computer, as it comes up the first thing she notices is that her outlook inbox is up and its on the email from Travis Vasquez of City One Promotions. Lyriq looks around to see if Desmond is in sight, but he is long gone already.

Chapter 39
The Bank Bar And Grill On Colfax Ave

Chapter 39 BANK BAR AND GRILL

Desmond is sitting at the bar having a Heineken and waiting on James to arrive. He is playing with a book of matches. Sparking each match one after another one until the bartender comes over and takes the box of matches from Desmond looks at him strange and says

"Damn Pyro…" Desmond smiles and takes a drink. Just as he is putting his drink down he receives a text from Cindy from the office with a video attached and the message says "I figured you would get a kick out of this one. Let me know if there is anything I can do to help too…..Lol"

Desmond pushes the video button and it starts with James booty bumping the old lady from the pay phone and then it shows him walking around with the lady in a headlock. It then flashes to James on the ground with 4 old ladies beating him down with their purses while he is kicking and swinging his arms.

Just as Desmond is laughing and about to watch it again James shows up with a bandaid on his face in a couple of places. Desmond jumps back in shock. "DAMMMMMmmmmmnNNN!?!?! What the hell happened to you?"

James sits down and throws his cell phone on the bar. "You know what the hell happen Desmond don't play stupid." Desmond smiles and says "What are you talking about?"

James looks over at Desmond both eyes fixated on him and his cell phone as he slides into the seat at the bar. He straightens his blazer as he tries to get comfortable and then waves to the bartender and gestures for 2 shots. He then looks at Desmond and says “Whatever asshole…”

“Yeah well Cindy just sent me a video and I must say..... you never cease to amaze me dude.” Desmond chuckles. James looks over at Desmond before he takes his first shot and says “Fuck You Desmond!! Fuck you….thats all I have to say” Then he takes his shot, makes a funky face and then coughs.

Desmond puts his hand on James shoulder. “I appreciate you bro…” James shrugs his shoulder slightly to get Desmonds hand off of him and says “Yeah-yeah”

“No I mean it truly! You are always backing me up and doing whatever it takes to make sure I win and I won’t forget about you.” Desmond says as he is taking his shot. James takes his other shot, makes another funky face as he swallows it. “You better not. Who else is goes out and fights a gang of tripple OG geriatric grandmothers? And win?”

Desmond laughs. “Only you could pull that shit off I tell you that.”

James continues to straighten his blazer as he tries to get comfortable in his seat, but just kind find the right position on the hard bar stool. “Fucking “A” right……...ME!! SO what did you find out?”

Desmond finds another book of matches and begin to light a match and just as he sparks the match, the bartender comes by again and grabs it with the wet rag he was using to wipe the bar down. he then looks at Desmond with his lips turned up as he continues to walk by. Desmond continues to explain to James what he found. “Well she definitely has connected herself in with Mr. Kush for sure.”

James finds another book of matches and goes to spark it, but this time the bartender walks past and snatches it from him on his way back to the other side of the bar. James mean mugs him as he walks past.

"I knew it!! What else?" James replies.

"She has somehow managed to keep everything she has done a secret from me since she started. She has a party this evening at Beta." Desmond explains. James gets hyper as he bangs his fist down on the bar and begins to raise his voice a bit. "Yeah I told you we couldn't trust her man. I told you.... So what's the plan from here?"

"I'm going to the event she is having tonight to see what's going on." Desmond replies. "Man you have to confront her! You have too!" James says gritting his teeth as he attempts to keep his voice down.

Desmond shakes head. "Nah, I can't just go at her like that. It will just get me fired next and that won't help either one of us now would it?" he replies.

James agrees and nods his head. "Truth! Well I'm going to go home and get dressed and then meet you there." Desmond looks over at James and says "No, that wouldn't be a great idea. You just got fired my man I don't think she would even let you in or at least let you stay for long.........know what I mean?"

James jumps as he says "Man fuck her!" Desmond shakes his head as he is finishing off his Heineken and then says "I did and it wasn't all that.......trust me." James laughs and then makes a serious face while looking at Desmond. "Your dick is going to get you caught up Dirk Diggler! Need to keep it to yourself sometimes."

Desmond looks over at James, nods his head and says "That may be true, but not today." Desmond stands up, pulls out some money to pay for his and James drinks. James takes Desmonds shot and orders up 2 more shots. "Give me a call when you need me. I will be updating my resume."

"Don't get it done too fast. Fly magazine is where you will be working at. Consider this time away as a vacation. Don't get too comfy."

Desmond says as he shakes James hand and walks toward the door.

Chapter 40 Dinner WITH SINCERE

Desmond is sitting on the bench in front of the restaurant waiting on Sincere to show up and he decides to play Angry Birds on his cell phone as he waits. A couple of minutes pass by and then Desmonds attention is interrupted when a cab pulls up and out emerges the most beautiful woman Desmond has ever seen. Desmond turns the game off and then stands up. As he puts his phone away he is walking up to Sincere with a very handsome smile on his face. Sincere comes right up to Desmond, hugs him with both arms around his shoulders and then speaks in his ear…

"Hi handsome. How are you doing?" she says

Desmond is taken back by her beauty and just stands there for a moment. Sincere looks up at him as he smiles down at her and she smiles back. "I'm doing well beautiful. It's been a long week / weekend you name it. Too long to go without seeing you too!" Desmond replies.

Sincere nods her head and says "Agreed! I must admit……the other night was a little disappointed that you didn't make it over. I was in the middle of cooking dinner and everything. But I'm over it now though…"

Desmond looks Sincere right in the eye, apologizes with a deep apology, then goes in and kisses her on the lips. As they embrace Sincere raises up on her tippy toes and Desmond pulls her in closer. She makes a cute little noise and then pushes away from Desmond slightly enough to break his embrace, but still stay in his arms.

"Hmmmm…I guess I'll accept your apology Desmond. I mean anyone who kisses like that needs to be forgiven from time to time." Desmond gives her a very sexy, smooth half smile and says "Just from time to time huh?"

Sincere wipes her lipstick off of his lips a bit and smiles. "Yeah…… just sometimes. Sometimes you have to just work for it. Nothing is going to be easily given to you all the time Mr. Coolwater." Desmond touches his lips after she touched them and replies "I can respect that Ms. Bouvea…"

"Can you really?" Sincere says sarcastically.

"No doubt" Desmond answers confidently. Desmond motions towards the front door. Sincere takes the cue and begins to walk towards the entrance. Desmond rushes to the door to open it and Sincere walks right in. They are both met by a waiter who walks them to a seat right away. Desmond waits for Sincere to sit down and then he grabs his seat as well. The night is going well and they are having a great time conversing with each other. They both are having dinner, laughing and enjoying each others company.

Seductive smiles and gestures are exchanged as they sit in the booth and finish dinner and drinks. They finish dinner and both head to the cocktail / cigar room. They are both having a great time playing different card games on the table and laughing at each other. The entire evening is playing out while the song "**TURN OFF THE LIGHTS**" by **Charlie Wilson** is playing on the background speakers.

They're finishing up playing games and begin walking out of the game room. Desmond has his arm around her shoulders and Sincere has her arm around his waist. The song goes off as they leave the games behind. Desmond and Sincere are standing outside of the Rodizio Grill talking. Desmond decides to invite

Sincere to the event at Club Beta so he can check out what Lyriq is doing and still be able to spend time with Sincere since they are having a great time.

“I have had an awesome time tonight with you.” Desmond says.

Sincere hugs up to him closer and smiles with a blush. “Tonight was very fun and your phone didn't ring not once??” Desmond pats on his blazer jacket pocket and says “I had my phone on vibrate.”

“Oh I see!!” Sincere makes a face at Desmond and punches him in the arm. Desmond flinches
and says “No, seriously… I just didn't get a call. It’s been kind of weird for me lately.”

“Yeah you keep saying that. Tell me about it……” she says.

Desmond tilts his head as he looks at Sincere, almost shocked that someone would be interested in his day besides his mother. “Well how about this? Instead of leaving so early this time. Why don't you accompany me to this event at Club Beta for a while and then I will escort you home?”

“Well I caught a cab here. Did you drive?” she asks. “Nope I rode the light rail here. Desmond replies.

Sincere steps back with attitude and replies “Do I look like a Light Rail kind of girl?” Desmond smiles at her and then says “That is where I met you right??” Sincere smiles and says “Touche”

“Lets go catch the light rail and talk more.” he invites her to walk with him by putting his arm out like a true gentleman.

Sincere accepts his invitation and takes his arm. Both of them have made it to the light rail station found a seat and waiting for the light rail downtown as the discuss what's been transpiring in Desmonds world. "So Desmond what has been going on with you honey? Why have you been so stressed out huh?" Sincere asks.

Desmond is rubbing on her hand as they sit close to each other, waiting on the train. "Well its a long story…" Sincere looks around and says "Looks like we have nothing but time here?" Desmond smiles and starts to talk to her about things that have been happening.
"Well first my father had a mild stroke" he says. Sincere's facial expression goes from smiling to concerned. She grabs Desmonds hand and says "O my God Desmond!! Is he ok?" She asks.

Desmond's face has a concerned yet cool demeanor too it. "Yeah he's getting better day by day. I was there and we were arguing when he collapsed so it was double the shock and triple the heartache on my end of things." Sincere grabs Desmonds hand in hers and begins to rub on them as she listens intently to him.

"How long ago did this happen?" she asks.

Desmond looks over at her from the corner of his eye while he continues to look down a bit, head still hanging low. "It happened the day before yesterday."

"Sunday?" she replies. Still in shock from the news, but even more concerned now about how fresh the incident is for Desmond.

"Yeah" he responds to question in a solemn tone.

She sits up and to the side a bit while talking to Desmond now. "How come you didn't tell me then? I mean I was so hurt by not being able to see you and I would have preferred to be there for you that night!"

Desmond looks over at her with an expression of curiosity as he kind of smiles at her. "Sincere let me explain something to you?" Sincere sits up as Desmond begins to explain. "Shoot!?" she says in a attentive and bubbly voice.

"I have never been in love before. I have never even felt a feeling close to love before. Well before now anyway…" he says. Sincere sits there and gazes into Desmonds eyes as he is speaking, with a stare that could melt the tundra off of the coldest heart in a Siberia. She then asks "So what you're saying is that you're feeling some kind of way about me then."

Desmond shakes his head and replies "Yeah….well I……..sort of ……..I guess I'm trying to say that I am kind of catching some kind of feelings towards you.........yeah I can say that." Just as Desmond finishes his sentence Sincere grabs his face very fast and begins to kiss him passionately.

Desmond is overtaken by the kiss, but wraps his arms around Sincere as they kiss. As they are kissing the light rail comes rushing by with enough force and wind to blow papers and other things around them. The door opens up and the contender sits there watching. Desmond and Sincere stop kissing and smile at each other. They both get on the light rail, find a seat and continue the conversation.

COOL NIGHTS

Chapter 41 @ CLUB BETA WITH SINCERE

Desmond and Sincere reach Club Beta after riding the light rail and walking from the Union Station stop. Sincere goes to stop and get in line, but Desmond pulls her to come with him to the front of the line. He tries to speak with the security guard overseeing the line.

“Hey I’m Desmond Coolwater from Fly Magazine. I usually don't have to wait in line when I come here.”

The security guard looks at Desmond like a nobody and then checks his list. “Well I don't have you on any list and we're not giving anybody special treatment tonight, so you’ll have to wait in line like everyone else.”

Desmond is taken back by the security guards attitude. “Look man I come here all the time. I know you know me? What's the reason for this treatment?”

He looks at Desmond again after scanning the crowd. “Look Mr. Coolwater is it........? Like I said there is no special treatment tonight. You are not on any list of mine and nothing has been said to me about you getting in past the line or for free for that matter so just go wait in line or you can leave.”

Desmond is in complete and total shock. “Let me speak with the manager.”

“He’s not seeing anyone right now sir so please... Just as the guard is telling Desmond that he can't see the owner, the owner walks up.

“What's the issue here?” he asks as he approaches them.

He nods his head towards Desmond and says "This guy here expected to get in past the line and for free. He was just asking to speak with you."

Desmond chimes in right after the guard finishes. "Hey my man we do business together all the time. Why am I being treated like this?"

The club owner and the guard chuckle at Desmond and the owner says "Tonight we are not accepting any special guests or requests Mr. Coolwater. Please just get in line and wait like everyone else. You will get in ok?" he says as he smiles back at the guard.

Sincere grabs Desmond and pulls his hand with her towards the line. Desmond is still riffing and arguing with the two gentlemen. Sincere pulls him closer to her and they walk to the end of the line to wait like everyone else.

"Baby calm down" she says.

Desmond is furious and says "No, this is crazy! I mean I do business with this club all the time. I just orchestrated the best show they ever had a few weeks ago. I just got their restaurant the best review in the city from Fly Magazine!!"

"Hey look!?!?! Well you're with me and lets just have a great time together right now ok?" she says still trying to calm him down.

"You're right.....You're right........ I'm cool........I'm calm..." Desmond takes a deep breath. Just as he is saying that Travis

Vasquez and Mitchell Helsberg are walking past and notice that Desmond is in line waiting to get in like a regular patron.

"Oh shit!! Trav peep this out........ If it isn't the ever elusive Desmond "*Keys to the City*" Coolwater. What are you doing waiting in line bro?" Mithcell says with a hint smart ass in his voice. Travis Vasquez chimes in as well. "I mean this is a picture perfect moment right here. Desmond Coolwater is waiting in line to a City One Promotions party."

Desmond is getting irritated while the gentlemen are talking. "What the hell is going on here? Since when do you make me have to wait in line and pay?"

"Well Desmond lets just say that we got a chance to lock in with the magazine for a years worth of promo at a very cheap price and we didn't need you to do it." Mitchell replies. "Yeah and you been keeping us out for a long time now. Don't act like we couldn't see what you were doing."

Desmond stands back and crosses his arms as he realizes what the gentlemen were trying to do. He smiles and says "Ohhhhhh...........I see!?!? So you get a little side bush from my so called co worker and you think you're in the "In Crowd" now huh? I guess you are those guys now huh?"

"Well you are outside our party trying to get in aren't you? Who's really the lame here?" Mitchell responds. Travis Vasquez begins to speak to Sincere. "Hey pretty girl.......why don't you come on in with us and leave this bum outside."

Desmond steps up to Travis ready for confrontation, but Travis never flinches or moves. Sincere steps in between them and looks at Desmond. Then she replies "No, I think I am just fine out here with my man. Besides once you eat Filet Mignon……….you never go back to Pork Chops." Desmond looks at Sincere and smiles. Sincere smiles back at him and wraps her arms around his arm.

Mitchell is taken back by her response and says "OOOOoooooooooooohhhhhhhh now that was cute! Well I guess we better get to business then. I mean there is no reason to be out here arguing with the customers and common people in line. Right Travis?" he asks Travis as he begins to walk away. Travis looks Desmond up and down and gives a thug like smile at him. "Yeah we have business to tend too. Lets roll."

Both Gentlemen walk past Desmond and Sincere towards the front door and are let right in past the line. "Pretty slick comparing Filet Mignon to Pork Chops! I liked it!" Desmond looks at Sincere and repeats what she said.

Sincere blows on her fingernails and wipes them off on her shirt in a cocky way and then says "What can I say huh? I'm good."

"Yes you are. Thanks for sticking up for me. " he says to her.

Sincere smiles and kind of blushes a bit. "No problem. I couldn't have those little guys putting my future "KIND of LOVE" down."

"You are too much! Never cease to amaze me lady." he says. Sincere is standing there just as fly as the first day Desmond met her as she says "Yeah I have heard that before." Desmond pulls her closer to him while they wait in line and have a great time with each other.

Desmond and Sincere finally make it into the club where it is packed from wall to wall with people partying and having a good time. There is a band playing and Sincere is holding Desmonds hand as they walk thru the club. Desmond finds a booth and points to it for Sincere to see. Desmond lets Sincere sit down in the booth first. They are both enjoying the band and whispering in each others ears smiling back and forth at each other. Suddenly, Desmonds friend Nicole walks up……

"Hey Dessie!! I have not seen you forever! How are you?" Desmond stands up and hugs Nicole and then introduces her to Sincere. "Hey Nicole this beautiful lady here is Sincere Bouvea…... my future uh uh uh……..?" Desmond looks at Sincere with a puzzled look on his face and Sincere reaches her hand out to shake Nicole's hand and replies "Uh lets just say future to be determined"

Desmond looks at Sincere and says "Future to be determined? You are just full of some good ones this evening." Sincere smiles and says "Yes I am…"

Nicole interrupts… "Well I must say I am pleasantly shocked and excited to meet you. I have known Desmond forever and I have never heard him talk about a future anything of his besides a business deal he was involved in so you are a first. Sincere smiles at Nicole and replies "So I have been told."

Nicole crosses her arms and smiles. She looks at Desmond. "Desmond she is quite witty so far. Can I sit down with you guys for a bit?" Desmond gestures for Nicole to sit down. "I'm going to go get some drinks. Nicole you still drinking the same thing?"
"I'll never change Desmond….You know what I like" she says. Desmond nods at Nicole and then looks at Sincere "Sincere what would you like?" he asks.
"I would like a…" Desmond interrupts and finishes what Sincere

was saying “A Chocolate Martini right?” Sincere smiles at Desmond.

“You remembered!” she says. Desmond winks at her. “I did. I remember things that are important to me.” Nicole is just in shock while watching Desmond interact with Sincere. She scoots in closer to Sincere and says “Desmond I am just speechless right now. Now Shoo-Shoo go get our drinks so Ms. Bouvea and I can speak some more.”

Nicole motions for Desmond to leave the table and go get the drinks. Desmond walks through the crowd and makes it to the bar. He is standing there waiting for the bartender and looking back over his shoulder towards the table where Nicole and Sincere are sitting. He turns around and notices that the owner of Image magazine Mr. Isaac Le’Fluer standing next to him.

“Bonjor Monsieur Coolwater” he says.

Desmond replies “Hello Mr. Le’Fluer”

“It is not too often that I have the pleasure of running into you.” Isaac says. “Well normally I am working and staying out of they way. I’m more of a out of sight kind of guy.” Desmond responds. Isaac smiles sarcastically and says “Well from what I have heard as of lately, you have been in as they say in your language…..a bit of shit!?!” Desmond looks over to him and says “Yeah well Eric and I have had better days, but we had a little non-verbal confrontation.”

Isaac Le”Fluer sighs. “Yes, I hear things Desmond. You are not the only one with eyes and ears around this city.” Desmond shrugs his shoulders. “Look Mr. Le’Fluer I do apologize. That situation was completely out of line and as a professional I should have handled that better."

Isaac waves over the bartender, tells him to get Desmond whatever he wants and to charge it on
his tab. "Make sure to put his drinks on my tab please."

"No, I can take care of it." Desmond declines his offer, but Mr. Le'Fluer insists. "You will do no such thing Desmond. I will take care of it. " he looks at the waiter and tells him to continue to charge his account for the drinks. "Thank you sir." Desmond says humbly.

"Listen.....there is always two sides to every story Desmond and I can tell you that both sides have flaws and faults. Beware of those around you. There are people who you work with that don't have you or the magazines best interest in mind." says Mr. Le'Fluer.

Desmond looks at Mr. Le'Fluer in bewilderment, but shakes his hand and then Mr. Le'Fluer walks away as mysteriously as he appeared. Desmond gets the drinks from the bartender on a tray and walks back to the table where Nicole and Sincere are still conversing and having a great time.

"Well hello ladies here we go. Chocolate Martini for my lady. Extra dirty martini for you Ms. Nicole. Also we have some complimentary shots from the bartender." Desmond serves the ladies. "I'm going to have to decline the shots this time you guys. I have early morning appointments and I just don't want to feel like that in the morning."

"I understand completely." Desmond says. Nicole agrees with Sincere and says "Me too honey"

Desmond and Nicole both take the shots down with no problem while Sincere stirs up her martini. As Nicole finishes her shot and begins to stir her martini, she begins to talk about the fight that Desmond got into at the Church Nightclub a few nights ago. “SO Desmond………? I heard about that fight between you and Erich Graham the other night.

Desmond looks over at Nicole with a glare for bringing it up in front of Sincere.

“Yeah…?” he says.

Nicole continues to speak oblivious to the fact that Desmond is motioning to her to stop talking about it in front of Sincere. “Yeah and word is that you 2 were fighting over that new exec at your office?”

Sincere looks over at Desmond with a curious look. Desmond looks back over at Sincere to assure her that it wasn't like that. “No, it wasn't like that at all.”

“Ok, so what was it then Desmond? I have been waiting to ask you this for days now.” Nicole asks.

Desmonds eyes are both lazer beamed in on Nicole as he answers “Well he was in my face all night long, baiting me and invading my personal space. He was feeling himself way too much because he had finally hosted an event that was somewhat successful and felt like he could come at me. I just happened to have had a long day that day, I had a few too many drinks and I let my anger get the best of me.”

“Yeah I’ve been hearing through the grapevine that she has been connecting with all your business contacts and reworking deals, sharing them with Eric Graham in turn for his connections."she says as she runs her finger around the rim of her drink glass. "Yeah it would seem something like that is transpiring, but she played him from what I hear?"

"Yeah I heard that too. After you two got into that little scuffle, she basically cut him off after that night." Nicole informs Desmond.

Sincere is sitting there during the whole conversation listening to Nicole and Desmond.

"Hmmm... Well this sounds like some daytime soap opera. She slept with him, he has your contacts, you fought him and now all we have to do is find out that someone is pregnant!?" Sincere laughs as she finishes her joke.

Nicole laughs at Sincere's comment, but Desmond doesn't laugh. He looks over at Nicole and she stops laughing. He looks over at Sincere and she gives a half sarcastic smile. "Listen.....no there is no daytime soap opera drama over here. Me and drama don't even mix well." Desmond says.

"Yeah well lately it has mixed like a well shaken vodka martini Mr. Coolwater. What do you think this chick is up too?" Nicole asks. Desmond shrugs his shoulders, takes a sip of his drink and says "Honestly, my best assumption is that she wants my job." Nicole looks at Desmond with a frustrated and curious look. "That's the best you have Desmond?" she asks.

"Yeah!!?!?" Desmond responds.

"You could never be a detective. I think that she wants more than that. I think she had and/or has some kind of inside connection inside Fly corporate offices." Nicole says to him. Desmond sits up in his seat after Nicole's revelation. "Are you being serious? I mean seriously… how?"

"I'm a woman Desmond and men are idiots!!" she replies

Desmond sits back in his seat and looks away from Nicole into the crowd. Sincere and Nicole share a smile and a high five. "She sounds like a real piece of work Desmond. You have to deal with her everyday at work?" Sincere asks.

"I don't deal with her…..I tolerate her." he says in an irritated tone. Nicole and Sincere look at each other again and in unison say "You deal Desmond!" Desmond looks at both of them and says "Whatever" and then looks away again. "No, but seriously Desmond I hear things around the city in some of my circles I frequent and its not good, matter of fact it's getting worse like people are saying that **You are not that guy** anymore."

Desmond sits up with attitude, takes a sip of his drink and tries to shake off the fact that his ego is bruised. "What? Who? I mean what circles are you frequenting Nicole? There is no way that this is talk in the town?

Nicole senses Desmonds frustration growing and tries to calm the tension, but keep it real with him as she continues. "Desmond you know that I am around the yuppies, hippies, businessmen and the rest down here. I hear it all.........look Desmond I'm not saying that you are falling off and I for damn sure will never turn my back on you, but I'm your friend and its my job to tell you when I think your slip is showing and well Desmond……… "Rumor" is that your slip is showing just a little bit.

Desmond mocks Nicole "Just a little bit…" In Nicole's voice. Nicole laughs, looks at Sincere, takes a drink, sits the empty glass down, then reaches for Desmond's face to squeeze his cheeks
and says "Calm down Mr. Bruised Ego. You will figure it out. Now let me out. I have to go to the ladies room and powder up." Desmond stands up the same time as Nicole stands up. They hug each other and as he releases her from the hug Nicole slaps Desmond on the ass and says "Tighten it up Desmond! The city is in love with you, but in the blink of an eye this fickle love could become disdain and disrespect my friend. Find your peaceful medium, balance your chi' and whatever the hell else you have to do in order to get back to the Desmond we all know and love."

Desmond sits back down next to Sincere and wipes his face as if he is wiping off the frustration. He then grabs his drink, takes a sip, looks at Sincere and smiles. Sincere smiles and says "That chick is crazy Desmond. I mean while you were gone we went from talking about you too the other girls here in the club and then that turned into what kind of girls I like?"

Desmond is sipping his drink and as Sincere is telling him that, he chokes and then starts to laugh. "She didn't?"

He says in a sarcastic kind of shock like he was unaware of what her preference was. Sincere pushes Desmond in the arm after she realizes that he knew what Nicole's preference was. "Yuu knew that she liked girls didn't you punk?"

"Well I sort of did, but wasn't really 100% sure. I mean I have only seen her with hot chicks all the time, but she doesn't dress the part though." Desmond smiles as he responds.

Sincere rolls her eyes and takes a sip of her martini. "Desmond it's obvious you don't know women like you think you do. A lesbian or any variation of a woman liking women doesn't mean they have to be butch or play certain part. Men are such pigs…" Sincere looks a little irritated, but Desmond scoots closer to her and puts his arm around her.

"Well if its any consolation……even if you were butch I would find a way to get close to you." Sincere looks back at him and smiles. "Whatever…..you can't change a lesbians mind." Desmond stares at Sincere in the eyes and says "For you……...I would try my damndest."

Sincere smiles a shy little smile and they both lean in to kiss each other. As they are kissing the music is turned down and Lyriq takes the stage and begins to introduce the next part of the show where the band will play their new single. "Hey everybody!! How's everybody doing tonight? I know I'm having a great time so I want to make sure you are here and turning it up with me."

The crowd gets loud as she is talking…. "So I'm not going to spend too much time up here. Shout out to DJ Burst in the house, keeping it live for everybody." The crowd cheers again.

"So is SHE really what all this trouble is about."

Desmond smirks and replies "She is not even worth the time or hassle, but to answer you question…..yes she is the one." Sincere looks at her again and toots her lips up. "Hmmmm…. I'm not too impressed." Desmond looks over at Sincere and smirks. Just then Lyriq announces the band and their new single.

"Up next is…. Curves. This groups going to play their new

singles……**Hold on** and **Love the Curves**." Crowd cheers and then she also announces "Also we have a special guest. A local artist by the name of Florence Sly and she is going to be painting a piece for you guys to see. Her works are going for $200 at the Champaign Art Gallery in the Denver art district. So give it up for our guest and show some support ."

Just as the band starts to play and the crowd cheers Lyriq peers thru the crowd, notices Desmond and Sincere sitting down and smiles devilishly. She makes her way from off the stage and over to their table. As Lyriq is making her way to the table Desmond says "Oh shit…...I know she is not coming over here?"

Sincere looks over in the direction Desmond was looking and says "Yes she is..." Lyriq walks up to the table looking drop dead gorgeous and then she speaks "Desmond how's it going?"

Desmond nods his head like…...what's up and then says "Hey…"

"Had I known that you were coming, I would have made sure you were on the VIP list at the front door." she says as if she really meant it. Desmond looks up at her with a blank stare knowing that she is lying. "Well you know I like to pay my way into places. Besides this is a Fly Mag and City One promotional party right?"

"Well yes it is." she answers. Desmond shakes his head in disappointment and says "Surprisingly I heard through the grapevine about this and decided to come." Sincere clears her throat as to say "Hey don't forget about me". Lyriq looks at Sincere and acknowledges her. "Well hello there. Have we met before." Lyriq asks.

Sincere cuts her eyes at Lyriq as she looks up at her and takes a sip of her drink. "No, not really. We just bumped into each other during another show that I attended with Desmond." Desmond introduces both of them. "Sincere this here is Lyriq. My co worker." Lyriq reaches her hand out like she expects someone to kiss it. Sincere shakes her hand and says "Well I've heard a lot about you."

Lyriq gives a fake smile and says "Oh really! Well I hope it was good." Sincere looks at Lyriq and responds. "No, not really." Lyriq looks over at Desmond and chuckles. "Hmmm.... That's a shocker....."

Desmond feels the tension rising and cuts the conversation short immediately. "So we are just about to leave, but good luck with your event."

"Oh Desmond don't be like that. You and I have history don't we by now?" she says. Desmond asks with a confused expression on his face. "What history?" Lyriq turns towards Sincere and starts to speak to Desmond, while continuing to look in Sincere's direction. "Hmm....... so the other night didn't exist or what?" Desmond is just taken back by Lyriq's attempt to cause problems with Sincere as they sit there. "What are you talking about?"

Lyriq smiles a devious smile at Desmond and then asks him "Geez........ you were that drunk that you don't remember?"

Desmond is stuck in between a rock and a hard place. All of his attempts to get out of the situation before Lyriq could ruin the evening he was having with Sincere has failed and he just sits there. Then he mumbles "Apparently I was" and then takes a big swallow of his drink.

Sincere looks over at Desmond in disgust. Lyriq looks over to Sincere and says “Oh don't worry about it honey. It was just an accident wasn't it Desmond.” Desmond is sitting there in shock that she would even be at the table talking about it. He then responds with “Don't you have a party to run and make sure that it’s successful?”

Lyriq looks over at Sincere. “I guess I just get caught up in the moment sometimes. Well it was a pleasure to meet you AGAIN Sincere, but I really must go…” Lyriq looks at Desmond and he is in complete and utter shock that she would mention the other night.

“See ya at the office.” he says. Lyriq laughs coy-like and walks off like she never stopped by their table. Sincere is noticeably irritated and ready to go. Desmond says playfully “Well?!?!?!.........Lets get out of here please?”

“Uh yeah I’d say so.” she responds to his comment. Desmond wants one more chance to speak to the owner of Club Beta, before they leave. “Let me go try and speak to the owner one more time. ”Sincere tries to bring him back down like **Earth to Dave**. “Newsflash Desmond…... what do you plan on getting from him?”

“Some respect!!” Desmond says. Desmond stands aside while Sincere stands up and gets herself together. Desmond finds the owner in V.I.P. chatting with some security guards. He then request to speak with the owner, but the guards stop him.

“YOU are still here little man?” The guard asks Desmond like he’s bugging them. “Look big fella I do not want to fight you, I just wanted to speak with him for a minute.” Both the guards deny Desmond entrance and reply with a “NO”.

"Look you aren't on the list and we were told that there is no space to push you or anybody else to the VIP section." the second security guard says. The first security guard just places his big hand on Desmonds right shoulder and says "Let's go buddy or we will take you out of here."

Sincere shakes her head and looks the other way like she is irritated and ready to go! Desmond notices it and decides not to fight any further. He looks at Sincere and says "Let's go!" Sincere begins to walk towards the door and Desmond follows her outside. She walks down the sidewalk in a fast pace and Desmond tries to keep up. She is very hurt and just wants to go home. Desmond grabs her arm politely.

"Sincere...? Sincere... Sincere?!?! Give me a chance to explain?"

Sincere turns around and looks at Desmond. "What Desmond? What is it that you want to explain huh?" She looks at Desmond with a hurtful stare. "It wasn't like that." he says as he tries to rub on her arm and pull her closer. Sincere pulls away softly. "What was it like Desmond? You made a fool of me in there. This is exactly why I've been single this long, because of men like you. I felt like you were different."

Desmonds shoulders drop low feeling the disappointment from Sincere. "......but I am. Just give me a chance to explain"

"No, your not Desmond. You're the same as the rest of the guys in this city." She says.

Desmond stands there with a blank stare and then tries to explain again. "Look Sincere......the truth is that yes we did hook up, but it was so spur of the moment and I don't know what came over me. I didn't mean to hurt you. I didn't mean to make you feel embarrassed. I didn't even mean for that to happen. I mean........we were drunk and one thing led to the next and it just happened. I'm sorry…"

Desmond goes to hug Sincere, but she pushes away and says "Men are always sorry. Always, always, always sorry. Sorry I hurt you baby, sorry I was so selfish, sorry it was an accident………..No, I didn't mean to get drunk and put my little weenie in her." Desmond is really feeling how hurt Sincere is and trying to get close to her but she keeps backing up.

"Sincere I just don't know what to say. I am so so sooooo sorry. I never meant to hurt you." Desmond pleads.

Sincere's eyes begin to tear up a bit as she speaks. "….but you did Desmond….you really did. I can't do this. I am a simple girl, with simple wants. I wake up in the morning and do my simple little workout, eat my simple little breakfast. Your big complexed and complicated lifestyle just doesn't fit into my simple little life."

Desmond stands there listening to her unable to say anything and then she finishes. "What can I do?" he asks.

Sincere looks him up and down and then replies "Nothing Desmond. This just isn't what I want for me...... look…. I'm sorry about your father and I hope he gets better soon, but I'm out…... don't call me anymore…"

Desmond grabs Sincere and pulls her to him in a passionate embrace and kisses her. Sincere kisses him back and then pulls away slowly, looks at him in his eyes and then walks away from Desmond. All of the lights in all the buildings seem to go out simultaneously and then turn back on forming a broken heart as the song "**I Can't Make You Love Me**" **by Tank**. The moment seems to fade out like a broken hearted movie scene with Desmond watching Sincere walk away until she is out of sight.

Chapter 42 DESMOND'S HOUSE

The alarm goes off and Desmond is laying in bed already wide awake staring at the ceiling. The radio is playing **"DEUCES" by Chris Brown.** Desmond sits up on the edge of the bed and turns off the alarm on his phone. He starts off checking his messages, but he has none for once. He throws his phone on the bed and starts to get dressed for the gym.

The radio is almost narrating his morning as he moves throughout the room, getting his gym shorts, going in and out of his closet looking for shoes and a t-shirt. He then heads to the kitchen and turns on the television, fixes a bowl of Honey Nut Cheerios and sits down to watch the morning news.

Desmond finishes his cereal, grabs his bags for the gym and work. He then heads towards the door, opens it, walks out and then slams the door. 30 minutes later Desmond is at the gym with his best friend Henry trying to make sense of it all with him.

"So you mean to tell me that you got into a fight in the club, You screwed the new chick at your job and then the relationship got even worse?" Henry asks as he gets ready to spot Desmond on his 2nd set. Desmond shakes his head and does his next set on the incline bench. "You got arrested, bailed out of jail by your boss, pops had a stroke and all this happened in the past week?" Henry continues.

Desmond looks at Henry and says "Yes!!"

"Damn man! I'm sorry bro..." Henry gives Desmond a hug right in the middle of his rep and Desmond looks at him in a weird way. Desmond puts the universal bar back on the rack, sits up and says "Yeah its been one hell of a week."

“I would say so. I mean I would have went Britney Spears crazy by now.” Henry agrees. Desmond and Henry look at each other after Henry’s statement and both shake their head. Desmond finishes his set and gets up from the incline bench.

“I am so damn close to losing it bro I don't know what to do.” Desmond unstraps his gloves. “See I told you…!?” Desmond looks at Henry with a look of curiosity. “I told you my man. I foreseen the shit before all this went down.” Desmond looks over at Henry before he walks over to the dumbell rack and says “Whatever Nostradamus”

“No, I’m being serious man. I told you all this shit was going to happen. I’m not even shocked that you stuck ya little weenie in the office chick.” Desmond looks at Henry after the little weenie comment.

“Look first of all my WEENIE ain't small…...it’s Big. Secondly if you are my real friend then you would know that hearing the old “I Told You So” speech is old and overrated.”

Henry is looking Desmond in square in the face with his lips turned up as he says “I don't care how cliche’ I may sound. I am your friend and I can tell you what I want because of that very point. You slept with the enemy. No wonder she is trying to ruin you and take your place. You already didn't like each other and then you get drunk and stick your face in the holiest of holies!!

Desmond gets defensive and says “Hey...hey...hey brother I didn't eat it!” Henry looks at Desmond and laughs and then says “Yes you did! Yes you did….if I could have taken a picture of your face as you lied to me, it would be worth a million.”

Desmond gets mad. "Whatever.....you don't know shit. You're married to a warden. Your balls are cryogenically frozen for life!" Henry looks at Desmond and replies "That may be true, but at the end of the day, I can go home and know that she is my number one. She loves me and always has my best interest in mind. She even do the super freak on my birthday and on holidays. Can you say that you have that to go home too?"

Desmond nods his head. "No"

"That's what I thought. Punk! Don't be passing judgement. I'm happy." Henry makes his point to Desmond.

Desmond feels bad and apologizes to Henry. "I'm sorry bro. It has been one hell of a week for me. Pops had a stroke, my job, getting arrested...... right now I'm like....... damn the storm is strong right now. I can't see how to paddle out of this one."

Henry smiles at Desmond and then says "Desmond just because you never learned how to lose, doesn't mean that you can't learn and then come back and win!! Sometimes you have to take a step back and analyze the situation. There is always two halves to a game and you are in the 2nd half right now. Come out swinging and fighting bro.......it's clutch time!!"

Henry hits Desmond on the ass and walks away...

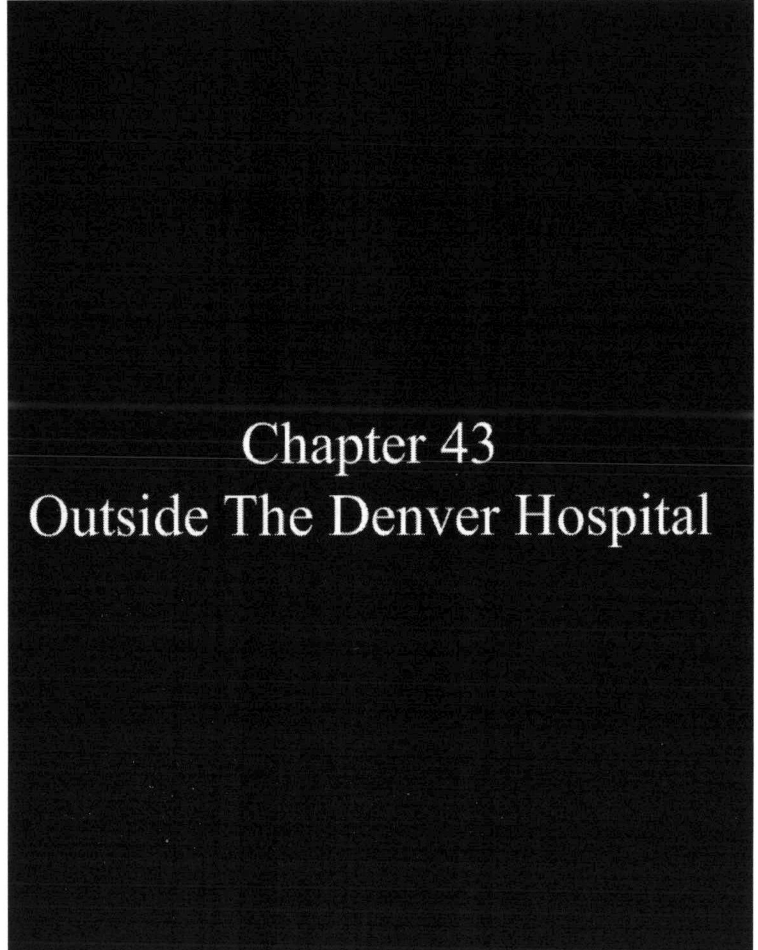
Chapter 43
Outside The Denver Hospital

Chapter 43 OUTSIDE DENVER HOSPITAL

Desmond is standing outside of the hospital with his brothers Marvin and Gerald. They're talking and joking before Desmond goes in to visit their father.

"Remember when Gerald thought he could fly and jumped off the roof?" Marvin reminisces. Desmond laughs as he recalls what Marvin is talking about. "Oh hell yeah. Remember he landed right on dads car and broke the windshield..." Desmond and Marvin laugh.

Gerald smirks and then says "Oh y'all think y'all funny....ok. Remember when Des got caught behind daddy's bar with the playboy magazine? Huh? huh?"

Marvin recalls the moment as Gerald describes it. "Oh maaaaaaaaannnnnn!!! I do remember that. Pops walked up and startled you. He was like **DESMOND WHAT ARE YOU DOING** and then you bumped your head and got a cut in the back." He and Gerald laugh at Desmond.

"Yeah man......you knocked down the whole shelf. Pops was pissed off about that one." Gerald smiles.

Desmond recalls a moment. "Marvin? Remember when pops made you stand outside in the middle of the backyard with the dictionary, while you were in your draws for getting caught cussing? Huh? Yeeeeeaaaaah you remember that don't you?" Desmond and Gerald crack up laughing.

"He still dont cuss around pops to this day..." Gerald says while laughing at Marvin. Marvin gets mad and then changes the subject quickly. Both Desmond are laughing hysterically at this point.

“Whatever fool. Anyway I am about to leave. You two can chill if you want to but I’m bouncing.” Marvin says. Desmond calms down from laughing so hard. “How is pops doing?” Marvin chills out a bit and relaxes as he answers Desmond. “He is cool......just sitting up and talking shit to people as usual.” Desmond smiles and says “Typical......”

“Yeppers..you know it.” Gerald agrees as he gives Desmond dap and a hug. “Well I’m about to go up there and chill with him for a bit. What are you guys doing tonight?” Desmond asks them.

“Man I have work tomorrow morning.” Marvin replies as he gives Desmond a hug as well. “So do I........... we don't all have the dream job where we can go in and work when we want too.” Gerald says in reference to Desmonds free fall schedule of going into work when he wants too. “Yeah school boy. Some of us have to go in when the man tell us too.” Marvin agrees with Gerald.

“Hey man I understand. I was just hoping we could hang.” Desmond says to the both of them. Marvin and Gerald walk up to Desmond. Marvin puts his hand on Desmonds shoulder and says “Look little bro. We work them regular 9 to 5’s and we are cool with that. You..... you are living your dream.”
“Everything that you have worked hard for is paying off and will continue to pay off some more. Just keep it pushing. Keep it moving! We are always going to be here.” Gerald chimes in....

“Yeah little bro. We are family. All of us. We are here for each other when we need each other. Pops loves you little bro more than you will ever understand. Hell pops would whoop us sometimes for shit that you did.” Desmond pushes Gerald away playfully.

“It’s true man. Do you remember that lamp that got broken.” Marvin says. Desmond has a confused look on his face after Marvin's question. “What? What lamp?” he asks him.

Gerald looks over at Marvin and says “...of course he doesn't remember. He was like 2 years old. Man listen you tied a string around Mr. Rogers neck and then tied him to the lamp like that lamp was going to hold him there.” Desmond looks at the both of them still confused. “Mr. Rogers?”

“Yeah don't act like you don't remember who Mr. Rogers was. He was that pug, that dog that daddy brought home with the wrinkled ugly face?” Marvin has a smile on his face as he reminds Desmond of the family dog. “Yeah you remember that dog cause you terrorized him. All the time.” Gerald says.

“All the damn time!!” Marvin repeats. Desmond starts to laugh and says “Yeah I remember Mr. Rogers.” Marvin smiles again and says “Ummm Mmmmm I know you do. So anyway you tied him to the lamp, he ran with the rope tied around his neck and the lamp fell, the light bulb broke and sparked a fire that burnt up the carpet and the drapes in the corner of the house.”

“Pops was pissed!!!! I mean he was hot!! Mom didn't even step in on that one.” Gerald stands there with his arms crossed as he chimed in. Marvin looks over at Gerald. “Shit…….I think even momma would have gotten a whoopin with us if she stepped in.” All the boys laugh as Gerald jokes around.

“Do you ever recall Desiree getting a whooping or anything?” Desmond asks. Both Marvin and Gerald look at each other and laugh. “Little bro you already know.” They both say in unison as they continue chuckling. “Desiree’s ass has never seen the belt man. Come on now…” Marvin says.

“True!” agrees Desmond. Marvin walks up to Desmond. Gives him a hug as well as Gerald and then walks to the car. Gerald follows Marvin. They are both standing next to the car. “Go up there and spend some quality time with pops. Listen to him and learn to forgive him. He loves you little bro.” Marvin yells out as they get into the car.

“Yeah little bro… he loves you. Your his baby boy even if you never did anything else in life, he will always love you. Go give him some time. Just talk and listen to him.” Gerald says.

“You might learn a little something. Ya little young Thundercat!” Marvin says. Desmond smiles. Both Marvin and Gerald get into the car and drive off. Desmond heads into the hospital.

Chapter 44 Getting MR.COOLWATER (Dad)

Desmond knocks on the door and then walks in after hearing his father yell come in. Desmond walks in and Mr. Coolwater is sitting up eating the hospital food and watchingTV. He looks up and notices that Desmond is walking in past the curtains. Grabs his napkin and wipes his face and hands.

“What's up dad?” he says.

Mr. Coolwater is shocked, but happy to see Desmond. He motions for Desmond to enter. “Son……. Come in. Come in.” Desmond walks in and sits down in a chair that is up against the wall and not close by the bed. Both men are sitting there for a moment and then Mr. Coolwater breaks the silence. “So Desmond? I feel like we never finished our conversation the other night son.” he says.

“Nah, just forget about it dad. It’s nothing.” Mr. Coolwater motions for Desmond to come here.

“Desmond come over here. Bring your chair too!” Desmond slides his chair over to the side of the bed by his father. “What's up pop?” Mr. Coolwater looks over at Desmond and begins to talk.

“Listen......there comes a time in a man's life when he is too old to be stubborn, too old to be tight lipped, too old to not change and last but not least……..too damn old to not apologize for being wrong.

Desmond is looking at his dad trying to get a word in, but Mr. Coolwater is not done. “Dad….”

Mr. Coolwater stops him again to continue speaking. "No, Desmond let me finish. Son I have worked and worked for years. Year after year after year while your mom raised you kids and thank the lord Jesus that she has done such a outstanding job. I grew up and your grandfather, my father was never emotional, never loving, he never told me that he was proud of me until he was on his deathbed and taking his last breath. I can't be like that and I won't be like that."

"Dad you aren't on your deathbed so why are you saying this stuff to me right now?" Desmond says.

Mr. Coolwater takes a bite of his Jello and says "You DAMN STRAIGHT I'm not on my deathbed. matter of fact as soon as they let me up off of this bed, I am going to put my underwear back on and walk right up out of this place and never come back." Desmond laughs.

"I said all that son because....... I know you feel like I treated you different than the rest and I want you to know how much I care for you. How proud I am of you. How I am, have been, and always will be such a fan of what you do in your life. I don't want my pride to keep me so tight lipped about how I feel about my children that I'm gasping for air at the last minute, with my last breath, trying to get out what I should have always been saying to you-your whole entire life. I love you baby boy."

Mr. Coolwater is tearing up trying to hold his composure together while he speaks. Desmond is sitting in his chair with tears rolling down his face. Mr. Coolwater sits up and wipes Desmond's face. He grabs Desmonds hand. Desmond replies "Thank you. Thank you dad for saying that. You don't know how long I have wanted and yearned for your acceptance. All I have ever wanted to do is make you proud of me."

Mr. Coolwater looks down at Desmond and says “Well done my son. Job well done…….but I have been proud of you since the day you got here. Nothing is ever going to change that.” Desmond grasps his father's hand back “Thank you. Thank you dad. Thank you.”

Mr. Coolwater smiles and shakes Desmonds hand extra hard. “The pleasure is all mine son.” he says as they both smile and share a father and son moment. The nurse comes in to check Mr. Coolwater's blood pressure and ask questions. Both men straighten up as if they weren't just having a close father and son moment.

“So when are they going to be letting you out of here?” Desmond asks as he straightens himself up in his chair and Mr. Coolwater sits back in his bed. “Hopefully soon cause this food is starting give me horrible gas.” Mr. Coolwater raises his legs up and lets out a loud rumbling, flatulent fart and the smell that follows is nose burning that even the nurse finishes up and leaves quickly. Desmond grabs his nostrils “Oh Damn.......*cough*........ damn daddy. That is some foul shhhhhhhh”

Mr. Coolwater looks at Desmond waiting for him to curse as if Desmond is still a child. Desmond is just about to cuss and he looks over at Mr. Coolwater and catches himself. Mr. Coolwater's eyes are wide open and fixed in on Desmond. He then says “Watch your mouth boy.”

Desmond stands up and tells his father that he has to leave anyway in order to make it to work. “Well dad I have to get to work, but I wanted to come and check on you first before I started my day.”

“Well thank you son. Have a great day at work.” he says. Desmond is walking towards the door, turns to his father and says “I love you pops.” Mr. Coolwater looks up at Desmond in the eyes and smiles.

“I love you too son…….I love you too!” He then lets out another bass dropping, buttock rattling fart that stinks just as bad as the first. Desmond grabs his nose again and rushes out the door. Mr. Coolwater is looking for the remote. Desmond is walking out the door just as his mother and his sister Desiree is walking up to the room. Desmond stops to speak for a moment. Desiree hugs Desmond.

“Hey little bro. You headed to work?” she asks. Desmond shakes his head and says “Yeah. I have a lot to do in the office today.”

Desiree straightens Desmonds collar and then replies “Well stop by the house if you have time to grab some dinner later. You need to stop eating out all the time.”

“I will try sis….. Love you” he says and then hugs Desiree. “Love you too little bro bye.”

Mrs. Coolwater is walking up as Desiree is done hugging Desmond bye and then stands there waiting for Mrs. Coolwater.

“Hi baby!! How are you doing?” Mrs. Coolwater asks as she hugs Desmond as well. Desmond hugs her back and says “I’m better momma. I have a lot to do today so I wanted to stop by and see dad before I went to work.”

Mrs. Coolwater smiles at him while touching his face and then asks “Did you two talk?”

Desmond looks at his mother in the eyes and replies. "Yes, mom we did and we are good. I have to go though." Desmond kisses his mom on the cheek and runs off. Mrs. Coolwater yells out "Stop by the house later if you can." Desmond yells back down the hallway "OooKkkkkkkaaaaaaayyyyy Mommmmmmmmm!"

Desiree and Mrs. Coolwater continue walking into the room to see Mr. Coolwater. They enter the room and the smell is so toxic that it overtakes Desiree first and she says

"Oh damn damn damn daddy why!?!?! SHIT!!!" Mrs. Coolwater says "Desiree watch your mouth young lady…… shit!!"

Chapter 45
Back @ Fly Magazine Offices

Chapter 45 @ FLY MAGAZINE OFFICES

Desmond has finally made it to work for the day. He is in a zone walking past everyone. He drops his bag on the floor right in front of his chair. He peers over to Mr. Elmhurst's office to see if he is in the office alone. Desmond decides to walk over there and speak to him about James getting fired. Desmond knocks on the outside door frame. Mr. Elmhurst looks up and waves Desmond in....

"Hello Desmond. How is going and what can I do for you?" he asks. Desmond enters the office and walks towards the desk. "I'm good Mr. Elmhurst. I wanted to speak to you about why James actually got fired." Mr. Elmhurst puts his pen down, takes his glasses off and sits back in order to give Desmond his full and undivided attention. "Okay let's talk." he says.

Desmond begins to speak openly about the situation, but treads lightly. "Well I just feel like every since Lyriq got here that things have just went from perfect to dysfunctional and down right cutthroat." Mr. Elmhurst looks at Desmond and motions for him to keep going. "Continue Desmond.... I'm listening?"

"Well its not much sir. She has just overtaken everything and got James fired, when I know for a fact that it wasn't that he flirted with her." Desmond says. "Oh really? And how do you know about this Desmond?" Mr. Elmhurst asks. Desmond continues defending James as he speaks with Mr. Elmhurst. "Well I don't know, but what I do know is that James seen right through her and she didn't even have to be in the room. How do you explain her connections coming together so fast in the short amount of time that she has been here? I have been in this business 5 years and nobody gets leads that fast sir?" Mr. Elmhurst sits up in his seat and crosses his fingers. "So what would you have me do?"

he asks.

Desmond sits down finally as he looks Mr. Elmhurst in the eyes intensely and says “Just watch her sir thats all I’m saying. Just watch her. Don't believe everything you see and don't believe everything Mr. Kush is telling you.”Mr. Elmhurst sits up in his seat and stretches his arms across the desk, fingers still crossed as he attentively listens to Desmonds plea. “Desmond you want me to second guess my 2nd in command here at the magazine based off of a hunch of yours?”

Desmond takes a deep breath and then says “Yes, I guess what I am asking you to do is just that sir. Don't believe everything you hear and see for a while?” Mr. Elmhurst's eyebrows are now arched with concerned and curiosity. “….and while I do that what are you going to be doing?” Desmond looks over his shoulder and then says “You can trust that I will still be working, but I need some time to do some research on her. I need time to figure out what her angle is?”

Mr. Elmhurst sits back in his seat and crosses his arms. “Alright young man I will be watching, but you be discreet and don't cause any waves around here. I need business to remain as usual.” Desmond shakes his head and says “Yes sir I understand.” Desmond gets up and leaves Mr. Elmhurst's office.

Chapter 46 IN THE BATHROOM

Desmond is in the men's bathroom stall speaking with James and concocting a scheme to call in another bomb threat to the offices in order to get Lyriq out of the building again.

"Yes I know what you went thru last time James, but come on bro I need you. Come on man..." Desmond continues to ask James. "I don't even work there anymore. Why should I even be involved?" he asks.

Desmond stands up and looks over the stall door as he answers. "Because she got you fired maybe? Because I am still here and I am your friend possibly?" Desmond says as he reminds James of the situation and why he needs his help. "Yeah and so what?" James replies sarcastically. Desmond gets frustrated as he is trying to keep his voice down in the stall. He fumbles the phone a bit as he tries to keep his balance on the toilet and remain incognito. "Ok, so I didn't want to pull this card out, but you asked for it. Remember that fat intern that I caught you boning in the mailroom a year ago?"

James replies in a calm tone. "Uh yeah?" Desmond continues. "Well.....yeah!" James is still calmly speaking to Desmond and all attitude has left his tone. "I thought you and I agreed never to bring that up?" Desmond continues blackmailing James. "Well this is the hammer and you making the call is the emergency glass that I need broken. Are you going to do it or should I post a picture on facebook of you and her in the mailroom?"

"You wouldn't!?! You don't really have a picture? Do you?" James asks with concern. "Ok, well no I don't, but I will tell a lot of people James!? James sits quiet on the other end of the phone for a moment and then he answers "Alright maaaaannnnnn damn it!"

Desmond smiles as James agrees and then says "ok cool"!

"On one condition?" James says. "Yeah alright what's that?" Desmond replies. "You give me your phone and let me erase all pictures with me in them at the end of this ordeal?" Desmond nods his head in agreement as he responds to James request. "Deal. Now go call it in now!!"

"Right now?" James asks. "Yes, right now James! I have to have that information immediately! So I need you to go somewhere and put that call in…." Desmond says.

James asks again as if he didn't understand Desmond the first time. "Now?"

Desmond gets frustrated and squeezes the phone. One of his feet almost slip into the toilet as he tries to keep his cool while huddled in the stall. "Right now James! Yes, right now as in immediately! Please! Would you…. could you please."

"Ok, give me about a half hour." James says nonchalantly. "…...and James?" Desmond says.

"What's up?" he says. "Don't do it so close to the office this time. Last time Cindy the office intern got you on camera."

James gets made instantly as he Desmond reminds him that other people seen the incident. "That bitch!!" James blirts out loudly. Desmond laughs as he looks over the stall again. "That shit was funny! YOu have to admit it."

“Fuck you! I got beat up by a mob of old ladies who had rocks in their purses.” James says in a whiny tone as he recalls the altercation.

“Yeah yeah……. just go get it done man!!” Desmond says to him as he hangs up the phone, peers over the top of the stall one more time and then steps down off of the toilet. He then opens the door, straightens his shirt and pants up and walks out of the bathroom.

Chapter 47
Breaking Into Lyriqs Desk

Chapter 47 BREAKING INTO LYRIQS DESK

Desmond is at his desk working when the alarm goes off again. Everyone is up and grabbing their stuff as they head to the exits. Desmond is moving casually, while he puts his stuff into his bag.

The office is almost cleared out as we is watching everyone move out of the office. Finally the last one is out. Desmond goes to check Mr. Elmhurst's office and he is gone as well. Desmond then goes over to Lyriq's desk to finish the work he started. As he is trying to get on her computer, he finds that her computer is locked this time, so he starts to shuffle thru Lyriq's desk and notes to see if there is a clue or something that will show him what her password and login is. He checks for a post it note that might have her info on it and something tells him to try under her keyboard.

"BINGO!! Ok, her password is "**Butterflydime@gmail.com**" and login is: **butterflydime**. Typical for her ego." he says out loud to himself.

Desmond is logged in to Lyriq's computer and heads straight back to her inbox to snoop for some more information that can help him figure out her angle. He pulls up her emails and starts reading some as he looks out for people returning from the false alarm. He comes across an email between Lyriq and Mr. Kush. He begins to read it and as he is reading it.... his jaw drops.

The email is a discussion between the two about how to close down Fly magazine by making the magazine start to show loss of accounts and revenue. It also talks about plans to destroy Mr. Elmhurst by setting him up for money laundering thru promotions and advertisement funds that are paid to the company from customers and large corporations. Desmond continues reading and decides to try and copy this information to his portable drive. He pulls it out of his pocket and sticks it in the computer port and starts to copying the emails.

Desmond is still sitting there reading through emails and not paying attention to the time. He looks up to see the clock, but instead of the clock in his view, Lyriq is standing right in front of him. “So ummmm… I think you are at the wrong desk. Don't you think? And why didn't you go outside for the alarm?” she asks. Desmond acts like he is snapping out of a daze and says “Huh? What? Why am I at your desk? I swear these days I am losing it. I was in the bathroom….. you know… umm busy doing the number# 2 and didn't hear it.”

Lyriq looks at Desmond suspiciously and says “Mmmmm Hmmmm…” Desmond sits back in her seat and starts to relax while he discreetly moves the mouse around and closes out her email inbox. Meanwhile he is talking to Lyriq and trying to keep her attention elsewhere. “Well this explains why I can't get logged into my computer. I was just sitting here trying to reset my password so I could get logged in.”

“Did you mess up my computer or settings Desmond?” she asks.

Desmond shakes his head like a guilty schoolboy who just go caught lying, but still tries to play it off. “No, I never got far anyway.” Desmond finally gets everything closed and locks the computer screen. Lyriq is standing there looking down at Desmond with her arms crossed waiting for him to move. “Well…” she says. Desmond is still sitting there acting like he doesn’t know what she is waiting for. “Well what?”

Lyriq unfold her arms and motions for him to get out of her

chair. “Move! Get out of my desk so I can get back to work.” Desmond looks around and then back at her shocked like she wasn’t talking about him. “Oh yeah! Sorry.” he says.

Desmond gets up and holds the seat for her to sit down and then he pushes her into her desk and walks away. Lyriq is looking around her desk and looking around at Desmond while he walks back to his desk. She then picks up her phone and calls Mr. Kush to let him know what happened.

Desmond looks over his shoulder at Lyriq for a split second and then he goes back to acting like he’s working..

Chapter 48
Desmond Loses It All

Chapter 48 DESMOND LOSES IT ALL

Desmond is sitting at his desk when he receives a phone call from Mr. Elmhurst asking him to come to his office. Desmond get ups and walks towards Mr. Elmhurst's office. Desmond reaches Mr. Elmhurst's office to find that Lyriq and Mr. Kush is in the office as well. Desmond knocks on the outside of the office door and waits for Mr. Elmhurst to tell him to enter.

"You wanted to see me?" he asks. Mr. Elmhurst waves for him to come into the office. "Yes, Desmond come and sit down please." Everyone is sitting down and looking at Desmond and it makes Desmond a little uneasy, so he strikes up the conversation… "So?! What can I do for everyone?

Mr. Kush sits up in his seat and then says "It has come to our attention that some security issues have arisen here in the office that is very concerning. DO you know why we called you into the office today?" Desmond sits in his seat with a blank expression on his face and says "No, I have no idea why, but I'm sure I'm going to hear about it though."

"You have no room or right to have that attitude Mr. Coolwater. You are in trouble sir." Mr. Kush says with an authoritative tone. "For what?" Desmond asks.

Mr. Elmhurst speaks up. "Well Desmond there has been complaints lodged with Human Resources about you." Desmond is taken completely by surprise by this and his look says it all. "About what? Working too much…." Desmond chuckles and then looks around to notice that no one else is laughing. He then stops chuckling. Mr. Kush continues speaking. "Desmond I think we have put up with just about enough of your shenanigans. Your constant partying on the company's dime. Your misuse of

Fly Magazine resources and your misogynistic nature that you display in the name of Fly Magazine business."

"What? That sounds asinine Mr. Kush. I have been with the Magazine since I graduated from college, if you go back and look at the numbers, which is your job, then you would see how numbers of our business would show an increase since my inception here at the magazine." Desmond says as he continues to defend himself, his integrity and his job. Mr. Elmhurst chimes in to defend Mr. Kush. Desmond looks over at Mr. Elmhurst in disbelief. "Desmond……Mr. Kush's job isn't at question here. Yours is… so be careful with this situation that you are in."

"Desmond my assessment of your job since I have been here has not been good at all. Your attitude towards woman and ego in the way you handle your job is just unacceptable." Lyriq says. Desmond continues to look at Mr. Elmhurst in shock. He then speaks up and says "What the hell is she talking about? I have done more for this magazine, no scratch that… this organization than most tenured employees have done in their entire career here. So why is my job at question right now? Why does she have any influence on whether I have my job or not?" Desmond asks.

"Desmond you have taken chances with the company's image since you have started here. I have allowed it to happen for far too long. Now you're fighting in nightclub events, getting arrested, harassing employees, sneaking around the office, going through co workers desks and computers. I can't allow this any longer." Mr. Elmhurst says.

Desmond begins to see what's happening. Mr. Elmhurst is blinded by Mr. Kush's and Lyriq's manipulation. He then tries to defend his position. “Mr. Elmhurst? Wait…(PAUSE)...let me explain. See Lyriq is…” Mr. Kush interrupts Desmond before he can get started explaining his side any further. “Desmond we have had enough of this conversation. You are hereby fired. Your desk has been packed up with all your personal effects and placed down at the security desk. Your laptop has been confiscated as well.”

Desmond looks over at Mr. Elmhurst in shock. Mr. Elmhurst looks at Desmond and then looks down at his desk at the pink slip, picks it up and hands to Desmond. Desmond sits in his seat for a moment staring at it, then gets up from his desk with the weight of the world on his shoulders, grabs the pink slip and heads towards the door. Mr. Kush then says “Umm...Desmond we will need to confiscate your corporate credit card as well.”

Desmond stops in front of the door and reaches in his pocket without turning around and pulls out the corporate card. He holds it out and Mr. Kush stands up, walks over to Desmond to retrieve the card and as he reaches for the card Desmond then lets the card drop to the floor. He looks over at Mr. Kush and then opens the door. Behind Mr. Elmhurst office door is the security ready to walk Desmond down to the security desk to pick up his box of personals.

Cool Nights

Chapter 49 MYNT CLUB WITH VINCENT

Desmond is sitting at the bar having a drink. Vincent walks up with a plate of food. “Here you go kiddo, fresh off the grill. The chef said dinner was on him so don't worry about the bill.” Desmond looks over at the plate and then slides it in front of him. “Thanks Vincent” Vincent continues cleaning the bar glasses and tidying up while he sparks up conversation with Desmond. “So… Are you going to tell me what happened or are you going to just sit there and drink yourself to sleep tonight.”

“Well I thought I would just drink myself to sleep tonight and not think about it.” Desmond replies as he continues eating and drinking.

“Well that is an option, but I can tell you from experience that-that has NEVER worked for me in the past. Take it from an old guy and you will regret it in the morning. So my advice is don't do it to yourself.”

“Duly noted” Desmond replies as he downs his drink and sits the empty glass in front of Vincent for a refill. Vincent looks at the empty glass and then says “Ok, so its going to be one of those nights huh?” Vincent pours another shot for Desmond. Desmond reaches for the shot and Vincent holds it back from him. Desmond gives Vincent an irritated look and then Vincent hands him the shot. Desmond replies “Yep”

Vincent walks towards the end of the bar as he wipes down the bar top and then walks around the bar to grab a seat next to Desmond. “Ok, so since I’ll be doing all the talking tonight then I have a story for you. It’s about a partnership between 3 men who started a promotions / marketing / advertising , etc., etc. kind of company.”

Desmond stops eating his food, wipes his mouth and then takes a sip of his shot. He sits back and looks at Vincent while he is telling his story. He then interrupts him. "Vincent is this going to be some story you tell me to pick me up or inspire me, because I've got to tell you… right now I am not feeling very inspired or motivated. The only motivation I have right now is to kill some time, kill a bottle of Fireball, a few beers and then go home."

Vincent looks at him, shakes his head and continues with his story. "So all 3 of them had special skills and they all knew their positions and how to play their part of the game of business. They got the business going and everybody started off great playing their part until one of them got greedy and thought they should get the biggest cut. Since neither partner knew how to do each others job, the one partner who got greedy started to shop around for people to hire to do what his other partners could do in order to take the whole business model for himself. When he noticed that he could get away with it, but he couldn't come up with a brand that would sell, he then got the idea to create drama between the other two partners to make them not trust each other.

As time went on both partners were divided and conquered, just as the 3rd partner had designed. The problem was that the 3rd partner wanted to steal the brand, but because they all created the "LLC and Company Brand" together, no one wanted to give exclusive rights to just one partner, so the brand died and never came to be completely."

Desmond is now listening intently. "What happened to the guy who tried to steal everything?"

Vincent takes his shot that he poured himself, stood up and walked back around the bar to finish what he was doing. "Well he decided to get out of the entertainment business. Found some business acquisition job at some government funded software company over in California's Silicon Valley."

Vincent is whipping off the bar top. Desmond sits up in his barstool with crossed fingers. "What about the other partner?" he asks. Vincent smiles. "Well he and I stayed friends after all the smoke cleared."

"I knew this story was about you." Desmond says.

Vincent walks over to where Desmond is seated and pours himself another shot along with refilling Desmonds shot glass. "How did you guess?" Desmond sips his shot and sits it down instead of downing the whole thing. "Well being that you are the owner of the Mynt Nightclub, you're still connected to the entertainment field. I'm sure you were a ladies man and probably was the one out of the 3 men who was the face of the operation."

Vincent is drying mugs off and putting them away while him and Desmond talk. "What do you mean by *Were a Ladies Man*? I'm still every bit of that man today. Watch this…" Just as Vincent is saying that a waitress walks behind him. Vincent turns to the hot waitress and says "Jody what do you think? Am I a washed up playboy?" Jody finishes what she is doing and then walks up to Vincent, grabs his face and begins to vigorously kiss him. She backs away, wipes his lips off with her well manicured fingers and then smacks him on the side of his face lightly and playfully. She then looks at Desmond, smiles and walks behind Vincent. As she is walking away Vincent looks at Desmond smiles and then snaps her butt with it. She doesn't flinch, but she turns around, winks at Vincent, blows a kiss and then walks away.

Desmond laughs with a shocked look on his face. “Ok, so I stand corrected. Whatever happened to your other partner?”

“Well he’s still here in Denver, we talk from to time. He’s a venture capitalist. Made good on some stuff that ended up being profitable sound investments.” Vincent answers. Desmond looks at Vincent and says “Mr. Peter Dash” Vincent flashes a half smile as he continues working and not looking at Desmond while he talks. “You guessed it. Peter Dash… one of Denver's biggest entrepreneurs.”

Desmond sits back in his chair polishes off his shot and then says in a somber voice.
“Well that’s a bust. I hate to let you down on this one, but I don't work for anyone right now so I have no connections to help him out.”

“Desmond sometimes when you are at the bottom, that’s the best time to look up and reevaluate what is going good for you. I can still contact anyone in this city and get the help or connections I need to succeed at whatever I want. The question is.... after everything that you have done for Fly magazine, after all the promotional parties, all the meetings, all the endorsements and everything else…… can you? Can you open up your black book and call upon your connections still? That is when you know that what you have worked so hard to do has paid off.” Desmond has finished his meal and he sitting there contentedly in his chair listening to Vincent and contemplating on how to turn his negative into a positive.

“Hey Vincent” he says. Vincent turns around from stocking his bottles to look at Desmond. “Yeah what's up?”

"I appreciate the talk. I am going to head out and go get some much needed sleep. Think about what my next move is going to be." Desmond says. "Don't sleep too long young man. There is a lot of life out here that you need to live and dwelling on what's already the past might hold you back from blessing that are right now and coming in the future." Desmond gets up and pulls some cash out to pay Vincent, but Vincent waves off the cash and says "It's on the house. Get out of here and go get some sleep."

Chapter 50
Back @ Desmonds Place

Chapter 50 BACK AT DESMONDS PLACE

Desmond is laying in the bed staring at the ceiling and trying to go to sleep, but every time he closes his eyes all he can see is the good times at Fly Magazine and working different jobs and promotional parties. His mind then stops on the thought of Sincere and all the great conversations they had. He also kept thinking about how beautiful she is and what it would be like to be in a relationship with her. It finally dawns on him that he is in love with Sincere Bouvea and that she is the one. When he finally comes to that realization he closes his eyes.

Outside the night is clear and the city of Denver, Colorado is alive. Every street is busy, people are out in droves venturing from bar to bar. Lovers are walking hand and hand through the city. The traffic is backed up on every street with cars trying to find a parking spot. As the night gives way to the early A.M. hour, the streets begin to clear like vampires looking for a mausoleum and then the sun begins to rise. The morning has come way too soon.

Desmond wakes up without his alarm blaring loud this morning. He stares at the ceiling a little bit more before he decides to get out of bed. This morning is very solemn as he goes down stairs to his kitchen and decides to make his own coffee as oppose to going out for coffee. He turns on the television and starts to make his coffee. He is listening to all the stories from the day before and the weather as breaking new comes across the television. The TV shows Mr. Elmhurst being escorted out of Fly offices in handcuffs by police. Desmond turns up the television to listen.

"Today the police make an arrest in a case that is both surprising and baffling. Fly Magazine executive and owner William

Elmhurst has been arrested and taken into custody. Elmhurst is being charged on numerous accounts, but the ones that sticks out the most is Money Laundering and Extortion. There is no bail yet set for Elmhurst. We will share more information on this as it unfolds."

Desmond is in shock and speechless. He is sitting there with his coffee trying to figure out what to do. He rushes to his computer to check his personal email account to see if he can find anything in the email between Lyriq and Mr. Kush. Desmond also decides to get dressed so he can attempt to go bail Mr. Elmhurst out of jail. After he gets dressed he calls the jail to see if there has been a bail set for William Elmhurst.

RING-RING

The jail receptionist answers. "This is Denver county jail, how can I help you?" Desmond answers "I am calling to check bail for an inmate that would have been booked this morning."

"What is the inmates name?" she asks in a dry tone. "William Elmhurst" Desmond replies.

"One moment please." She says.

Desmond waits for the receptionist to return. She picks back up the line and says "His bail is set at 100k"

"One-Hundred Thousand?!" Desmond says in a loud voice. The jail receptionist sighs as she answers him. "Yes 100k. You only have to put up 10% of that so technically all you have to come up with is 10k to bail him out." Desmonds stress goes down a notch. His tone also goes down a notch. "Oh, ok. That sounds a hell of a lot better than 100k."

“Is he not worth the 100k or what?” she asks. Desmond laughs sarcastically. “He’s questionable. Thanks for the help.”

“No problem. Have a great day.” she says. Desmond hangs up the phone and tries to figure out how to get some money together in order to bail Mr. Elmhurst out. Desmond decides to call Peter Dash for some help. He picks up his phone and begins to dial.

RING-RING

Peter Dash answers the phone. “Desmond how's it going young man?” Desmond sighs as he answers. “Well I have had better days, but I guess it could be worse like….” Peter snickers as he replies to Desmonds last statement. “….like you could be the CEO of a large magazine and get arrested for money laundering and other felonious activity?” Desmond agrees. “Yeah I guess it could be that bad.”

“So... to what do I owe the pleasure of this call for? Are you calling to tell me that you can’t help me? Peter asks. Desmond begins to explain the reason for his call. “Not quit Mr. Dash. I’m actually calling you because I have a deal and a favor to ask of you and offer you all at the same time.”

“Last time I heard that kind of proposal from someone, I ended becoming involved in a serious business venture.” he says in response to Desmond’s proposal. Desmond switches the phone to the other side of his face as he takes a sip of his coffee. “Well to be honest? This may be something very different from that, but could be very beneficial to you if everything pans out right.”

“So its a gamble huh?” he says after Desmond’s response.

Desmond stands up and paces the room as he speaks to Peter. “Definitely, chess not checkers on this one sir. Are you interested in hearing about it?” Peter dash sits on the other side quiet for a bit and then replies “Ok, you have my attention young man shoot!?”

Chapter 51 DENVER COUNTY JAIL

Peter Dash agrees to help Desmond by bailing out Mr. Elmhurst. Mr. Elmhurst is called by the guard and told he has received bail.

Mr. Elmhurst is released from jail. He is walking out of the building and checking in his vanilla envelope to see if all his stuff is in there. You can tell that he is in search of something in particular. He puts his watch on as well as his ring. He then grabs his wallet and places that back in his pocket. Mr. Elmhurst is checking each pocket while he walks towards the driver and the limo door. He finally finds his cigar in his blazer pocket, but it is smashed. Since he didn't have any other cigars he decides to light the broken one up. He reaches the limo and is still trying to light the broken cigar. Just as he gets it lit the driver opens the door to see Desmond, James and Mr. Peter Dash smoking his favorite cigars.

James steps out of the limo door smoking and smiling at Mr. Elmhurst. Mr. Elmhurst does not crack a smile back. Desmond steps out as well and introduces Peter Dash. Peter and Mr. Elmhurst shake hands. Desmond takes a puff of his cigar and hands Mr. Elmhurst a fresh cigar.

Mr. Elmhurst takes out his old smashed cigar and tosses it. He then lights up the new fresh cigar that Desmond hands him. Desmond then looks at Mr. Elmhurst and says "We need to talk…"

Mr. Elmhurst shakes his head in a yes fashion. They all get back into the limo and pull off.

All the gentlemen are sitting around the table eating lunch at Landry's Seafood Place in south Denver. Across the table from

Desmond and Mr. Elmhurst, James has a Landry's bib on, going crazy cracking and eating the crab legs like they aren't all you can eat. Peter Dash is sitting next to him as he makes the biggest mess. He has crab meat all over his face, bib and hands. Peter Dash has a look of shock and bewilderment as he keeps scooting over trying to get further away from James as he smacks and eats with his mouth open. Meanwhile Desmond and Mr. Elmhurst are sitting across the table looking on in amazement as well. After Desmond gets over his initial disgust he reaches in his bag and gives Mr. Elmhurst a folder of papers for him to look over.

"Take a look at these and tell me how you feel about these?" Desmond says. Mr. Elmhurst takes the folder and begins to shuffle through them. As he continues on through the papers he starts to get a more serious and worried expression look on his face. He looks over at Desmond and says "Where did you get this information from?"

Desmond sits back in his seat and says "This is the paperwork that got me fired sir. I knew that everything that she had the jump on so early in her employment with Fly couldn't just be a coincidence. She's not that good. So I decided to get on top of my detective thing and snoop around a bit. She caught me at her desk and put two and two together."

James is still scarfing down crab meat and yells out "….ain't as smooth as you thought you were huh? Mr. Cool fancy pants…" he chuckles as he cracks another crab leg and continues tearing down the all you can eat. Mr. Elmhurst looks at Desmond with a somber face and apologizes.

"Look Desmond.... I am sorry about that." Mr. Elmhurst says.

Desmond puts his hand on Mr. Elmhurst's shoulder. "Mr. Elmhurst you don't owe me anything. In the past couple of weeks I have really learned a lot about myself. I have been spoiled by success. I have walked, strolled and rode high on this cities back for a long time, like I was the mayor. The way I see it… it's time I actually worked for my money and notoriety."

"I think we both have taken the job and the city's love for granted then, because I hired you and gave you full reigns. I had no idea that Kush was scheming behind my back all these years. I never had a clue." Mr. Elmhurst says as he sits there.

"So what is the plan from here?" Peter Dash asks.

Desmond points at James so he could explain the plan. James pauses eating for a moment, looks up at everyone looking at him. He cracks another crab leg, dips it deep in the butter and then scarfs it down, smacking and all. He then wipes his hands with one of the many crumpled napkins he has surrounding him, sits back in his chair making the sucking sound through his teeth as he looks around and says "So this what we are going to do!?"

James begins to let all the gentlemen know about Mr. Kush and Lyriq's plan to launch their own brand of media during a Gala they are hosting at the Colorado Convention Center tomorrow night. They plan on inviting a whole list of who's-who as well as all current clients who advertise with FLy Magazine. James then goes on to explain how they are going to infiltrate the gala, expose Lyriq and Mr. Kush by showing all the emails on the big screen.

Desmond plans to confront Lyriq and have her admit to everything while James finds a way to have it broadcast over the convention centers P.A. system.

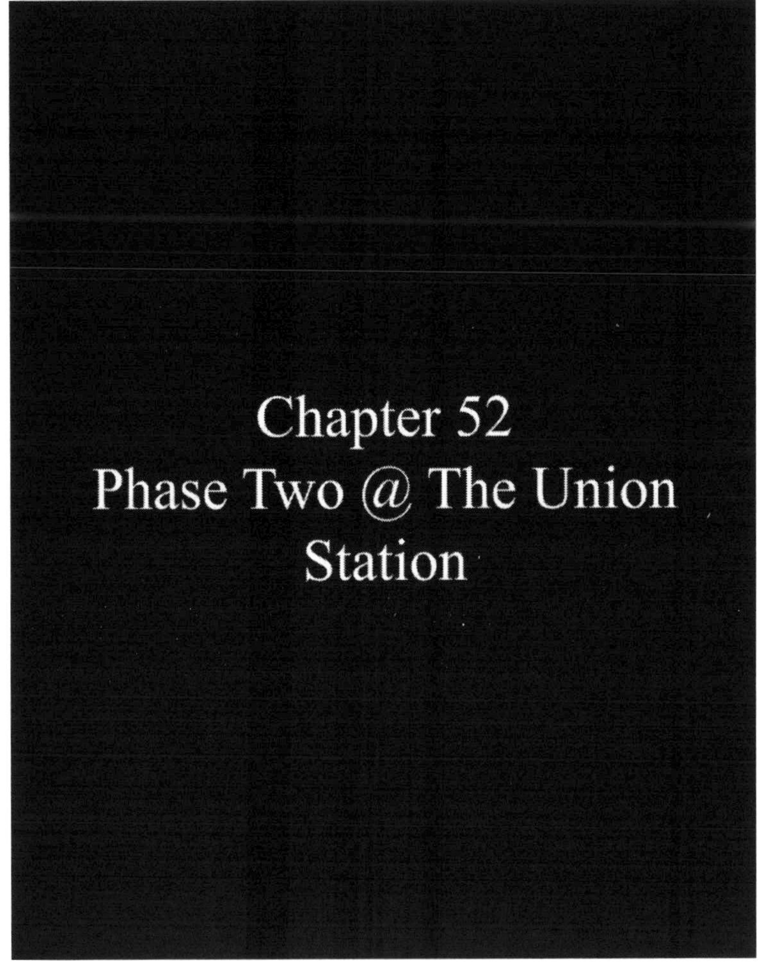
Chapter 52
Phase Two @ The Union
Station

Chapter 52 PHASE 2@ UNION STATION

Night has fallen and it's a starry night in the Mile High. Mr. Elmhurst, Desmond and James are standing next to Mr. Elmhurst's limousine, outside the Union Station train station.

James is wiring Desmond with a P.A. adaptor that will automatically be able to remote access the P.A. system inside the convention center and broadcast whatever Lyriq is talking about.

Mr. Elmhurst is smoking one of his signature cigars and dressed to impress as usual. James is dressed up as a sound guy for the gala so he can get close to the sound booth without being seen.

James begins to explain how the P.A. adaptor works. "Alright now listen? As long as you are close enough to her in order to pick up her voice then I can get it to not only record remotely to my computer here in the limo, but it I will be able to get into the gala and patch you through too the entire live system." he says.

Desmond has his hands up while James wraps wire around him and taps the wires in discreet places. "Are you sure this is going to work man?" James looks at Desmond and says "Does a bear shit in the woods and wipe his ass with a rabbit....?" Desmond looks at James with a blank look and says "That's stupid"

"Of course its going to work bro! I know my shit. I'm not just some office administrative assistant. I have other skills that I didn't list on my resume." James says as he continues to wrap wires around Desmond's body.

Mr. Elmhurst is smoking like a locomotive as he watches James work and says "......and where did you learn these life skills from James?"

James is still working on finishing the wiring job on Desmond and doesn't look up at Mr. Elmhurst, but he addresses his question calmly like he has been asked this same question before. "I learned from watching the Military station as well as I googled it too."

Desmond looks down at James with a look of shock this time. "You mean to tell me that we are trusting the entire fate of this night off of what you seen on television and then googled?" Mr. Elmhurst looks at both of them and starts to duck his head back in the limousine. Desmond grabs him to stop him from getting into the limousine and leaving them. "Come on… come on…. come on now Mr. Elmhurst don't leave."

Mr. Elmhurst backs up from Desmond and takes a puff of his cigar before he speaks "Are you serious? Desmond this isn't going to work. We don't have enough to save our asses…"

"What do you mean?" Desmond asks.

Mr. Elmhurst looks at both of them up and down before he answers. "What do you mean…. what do I mean?"

Both Desmond and James are standing there looking at Mr. Elmhurst. James is standing there with wires running from a spindle in one hand and duct tape in the other. Desmond is standing there with his shirt wide open looking like a stripper from a low budget horror movie.

"Just calm down Mr. Elmhurst. Everything is going to be just fine." Desmond tries to reassure him that the plan will work, but he doesn't believe it. Mr. Elmhurst is puffing his cigar at a faster rate now and then says "Desmond look at you two. A bunch of kids trying to take down some big money with some rank amaetuer stunts and wires."

James gets irritated and says "Who are you calling a rank amateur?"

Mr. Elmhurst puffs up his chest at James and says "You!?! This whole idea stinks like rank amateurs all over it." James stands back up after finishing Desmond's wiring, looks at Desmond and then turns back towards Mr. Elmhurst and says "I will whoop an old persons as tonight out here in this mother fucker!"

Desmond stands in between the two men. Mr. Elmhurst smiles sarcastically at James and then rolls his eyes as he looks back Desmond "I'm going to go home, take a bath, eat a steak and enjoy my freedom until they come to get me and take me back to the penitentiary."

James looks at Mr. Elmhurst with disgust and says "What grown ass man takes a bath anyway. Let him go Desmond we can do this ourselves."

Mr. Elmhurst gets into his limo, shuts the door and then rolls down the window. Desmond walks up to the window and looks at Mr. Elmhurst. "I can see why you are giving up. I mean what's the worst that can happen huh? You'll go home and the fate of Fly Magazine is decided in one night by two people that shouldn't have that kind of power right? Or maybe you're ok with that? Maybe you're ok with going back to jail and being known as the Bernie Madoff of paper media in Denver, Colorado? No, your not that kind of guy Mr. Elmhurst. Not the kind of guy to lay it down and give up. That's not what you have taught me all these years."

Mr. Elmhurst takes one more puff of his cigar and then says "Give it up kid. I know when I'm licked and this one is a no win situation. I'm going to cut my losses and prepare for the worst. Good luck kiddo…" Mr. Elmhurst reaches his hand out to shake Desmond's hand. Desmond shakes his hand back and then looks up at the driver and tell him to take him home.

James yells out "DON'T FORGET TO NOT DROP THE SOAP BOSS!!" Mr. Elmhurst's limo drives off leaving Desmond and James standing there. They both walk off and the scene fades up and into the starry night.

Chapter 53 THE BIG PAYBACK: Conv. CTR

Desmond and James are standing outside the convention center ducking and hiding behind the big giant legs of the Blue Bear statue. They are both trying to see into the party without being seen. The windows are covered with people standing around and talking. No one notices Desmond and James watching from outside. "I have never seen what this side of the party looked like before." Desmond says as him and James peer into the scene.

"Yeah!? Now you know what it feels like to be on the outside instead of always being on the inside Mr. Mayor." James says sarcastically.

Desmond looks over at James with an irritated glare. "Shut up! Lets sneak around the back and get you in with the sound crew and I will get this party started."

Both of them walk around the building casually towards the back of the building looking for a door where James can sneak in inconspicuously. They get around the back of the building finally and James finds the sound crew and waiters, then blends right in. Desmond goes through the door as well so he can get into the gala. As he walks thru the staff entrance and goes out into the convention hall where the party is happening, Desmond can see everyone who he has ever worked with as well as some new companies. While Desmond walks through the crowd, trying to remain low, but the Coors Light girls recognize him and swarm around him like bees to a hive.

"Hi Desmond! You look awesome." she says.

Desmond switches into Coolwater mode and instantly flatters her with a smooth reply. "No honey you look marvelous, very tasteful. How have you been?" The rep blushes and becomes giddy like a girl liking her first boy. The 2nd rep. is the young lady he hooked up with a week ago. She wraps her arm around his and says "I have been great, but I would be even better if we could go out and have a night together like we had a few weeks ago. That was awesome!!"

Desmond flashes a debonair smile as she talks about the other night. "It was great! I would love to hang with you and the ladies again, but I am just really busy right now."

"Well... when then Desmond?" she asks.

Desmond stands closer to her and places his arm around her shoulders as he says "I would love to but..." Just then he spy's Lyriq walking up towards the stage. "Oh come on Desmond! Please?!" the 2nd rep says.

Desmond refocus back on the group of ladies for a moment. "Ok ok ok lets work on something else so one of you give me a call this weekend and we'll set something up."

"Cool..." the rep says and then Desmond lets the ladies know that he has to go, he hugs the reps individually and then takes off through the crowd, trying to be as low key as possible. Lyriq gets on stage to announce the birth of a new magazine.

"Excuse me everyone. Excuse me....... can I get your attention." she stands there as the crowd begins to gather around the podium. Lyriq begins to speak about her rebirth from the ashes of Fly magazine. Meanwhile Desmond and James are moving amongst the crowd trying to remain inconspicuous. Desmond is listening and watching Lyriq speak, while he checks out the entire gala's set up. Video screens are showing Mr. Kush and Lyriq's new advertising partners as well as logo's from other company's.

Desmond then stops to hear Lyriq's speech. "I would first like to thank everyone for attending our ***1st Annual Media Gala*** at such short notice, but I can assure you that this evening will not be a waste of your time. Matter of fact I ask that you keep an open mind about everything that has transpired in the past week in our city's media world. I had the opportunity in a very short amount of time to see the corrupt practices of Mr. Elmhurst and some of his staff at Fly Magazine."

Desmond is standing in the crowd amazed and furious about what she is saying, but trying to maintain his composure at the same time as he listens to her speak. "I was able to identify the problems and report them to Mr. Kush. I knew I could trust him. We then were able to get the authorities alerted about the felonious activities by these people at the organization who were committing crimes like money laundering for local thugs posing as promoters and advertisers."

Desmond is doing his best to conceal his emotion, but it's hard to do as she continues. He then says "This bitch is crazy!" He then scans around the crowd looking for James and finds him across the room looking directly back at him laughing, shaking his head and moving his lips saying "CRAZY BITCH"

"We have since had these people terminated from employment at the core organization. We are now re-launching a rebirth of core media values such as truth, real fashion non-biased to gender, sports and a hardcore dedication to the scene here in Colorado. With that being said I would like to introduce Denver, Colorado's new media mogul Mr. Kenneth Kush."

Lyriq steps away from the podium and joins the crowd clapping for Mr. Kush as he walks to the podium. Lyriq then steps off the stage and disappears into the crowd.

Mr. Kush shakes Lyriq's hand and then takes the microphone. "Thank you..... thank you ... thank you! I also want to take time out to say thank you for attending this relaunch gala at such short notice. It's my pleasure to announce a rebirth of core media values. Although I had an idea that my partner William Elmhurst wasn't being 100% transparent with me, I had no idea of the scope of corruption......... that's over now. It is now time for us to move on from this in a positive direction enter our new media venture called: VMM."

The meaning of VMM shows up on the big screen above him. ".......Vision Media Magazine will be the new face of entertainment, fashion, sports and everything else in this town. My vision is to create a platform for us to expand into an internationally known publication. With the help of Ms. Moore this will be the biggest publication ever!!"

The crowd burst into a roar. "With that being said I want everyone to mingle, get to know each other because we are going to be working closely with each other to make this vision happen. Have a great night!!"

Mr. Kush walks away from the podium while the entire crowd applauds his speech. Desmond walks away from the crowd and as he is walking away he runs right into Lyriq. "So ummmm....... what are you doing here Desmond?" she says as she stands there looking as sexy and devilish as the first day they met.

Desmond keeps it cool as he replies to her. "I am a part of the

Denver elite baby. You can't deny that."

Lyriq toots her lips and smiles. "I could call security and have you removed right now."

Desmond looks at her with an ice cold demeanor and says "....but I would just appear at another event that you have no control over. You don't have control over all my contacts. Most of the city still loves me."

Lyriq nods her head. "Touche'.......... so what do you want?" Desmond paces the floor as he asks "I just want to know how you did it?" Desmond begins to walk towards a more secluded area where they can talk. Lyriq follows.

"How did I do what?" she asks

Desmond cuts his eyes at her, knowing that she is playing coy. "How did you come into Fly and get so far so fast huh?"

Desmond stops walking and folds his arms as he stares at Lyriq and waits for her to answer the question, meanwhile James is sneaking through the crowd to the sound system and the video controls. As James is moving towards the sound booth, security stops him and asks if he has an event pass.

James doesn't have a pass and security asks the other sound crew, plus waiters passing by if they recognize James as they pass and no one vouches for him. Mr. Kush walks up and recognizes James. He then orders security to grab James and escort him out, but James slips away from them and takes off running through the gala to get to the sound booth and plug in Desmond.

“He is not part of the sound crew. Detain him and call the authorities.” James takes off through the crowd trying to escape Mr. Kush and his guards. Desmond is talking to Lyriq and can see James running through the crowd. Desmond keeps Lyriq's attention while James makes his way to the sound booth. Meanwhile Lyriq is speaking to Desmond about how she took over Fly magazine so fast.

“Well, see the crazy thing is it was so easy to take over Fly magazine. The organization was so masculinity driven that it was easy to pinpoint your weakness. The company and all its employees depended upon you and you alone to bring in the sole amount of business for them.” she explains.

Desmond listens patiently as she continues. “Ahh I see!? So you played off of all the testosterone in the building.” Lyriq smiles snidely. “Exactly! Look at the big brain on Desmond! YAaaaayyy…”

Lyriq celebrates Desmond’s revelation sarcastically. James has reached the sound booth. He finds the DJ in the way so he grabs him and shoves him out of the way as he screams out “I’m sorry bro…”

They finally corner James in the sound booth with nowhere to go. Security try to take him down, but James starts to fight. He breaks away for a minute and tries to get away, but they have him cornered. He then stands up straight, fixes his waiters coat and then pulls out a mini remote and holds it up in the air. Mr. Kush thinks he has a gun and yells out “He’s got a GUN!!! Get down!!”

Mr. Kush and his entire group of guards drop to the floor. James laughs and pushes the button to activate Desmond’s wire. James then plugs in the flash drive to the computer so the emails between Lyriq and Mr. Kush start showing their emails and pictures with each other to the entire gala.

Meanwhile Desmond has Lyriq talking about the entire scheme and how she knew she could take down Fly Magazine. She also goes on to talk about how she used Eric Graham from Image Magazine for his connects. She then starts to brag about getting Desmond arrested at the party and knowing that his ego would get him arrested after fighting Eric Graham.

Desmond is smiling while talking to Lyriq. He then asks "Why did you chose Fly mag of all the places in Denver? You could have easily just went over to Image Mag and got the job without trying to destroy us?

Lyriq hunches her shoulders as she answers

"It was the thrill of the hunt Desmond. You were the highly regarded KING of the City! I wanted to show everyone how bad of a loser you were. How you really weren't as good or even great as they thought you were." she says in a smug tone.

"You sound like a 5 star hater right now. What did I ever do to you?" Desmond says. Lyriq looks Desmond up and down with a very evil yet seductive look and says "I told you it was the thrill of the hunt for me." Desmond nods his head and then asks "What purpose did Eric Graham from Image mag serve?"

Lyriq looks away at the crowd and then answers "Well Desmond if you must know. He approached me. I never intended on ever using him as a pawn in my game, but he made it easier to get under your skin, which is what my initial plan was."

Desmond is standing there listening to her break her plot down play-by-play. He then says "So he fell right into your plot without even knowing it."

Lyriq giggles before she replies. "You bet. I've got to admit though Desmond, he wasn't half the lover that you were." Lyriq starts to walk up to Desmond and he takes a step back, trying to keep his distance so she didn't notice that he was wired. "Oh no no no….. Not this time you sneaky little……" Lyriq steps back and chuckles a sexy laugh.

"Ah ah ahhhhhh Dessie. No name calling. It won't change anything now." Desmond looks her up and down "...and sleeping with you again would?" Lyriq takes another step towards him. "No, but it would be fun just one more time wouldn't it?"

Desmond smiles a suave smile and simply says "No… not this time. So I'm curious? How did you know that Eric and I would bump heads and brawl it out?" Lyriq shrugs her shoulders and continues to answer Desmond's questions. "Well I noticed the bad blood between you two from the start, when I met Eric and Mr. Le'Fluer at Club Beta. Two competitive bulls ready to clash. I figured with the size of your ego and his mixed with a little bit of alcohol and jealousy that it would all boil to a head eventually. You two were so predictable that night."

"How did you get Mr. Kush involved?" Desmond asks.

"Easy….. He chased me for a very long time before I gave in and gave the old fart some na-na. I already knew him." she brags. "I knew it. He put you in place to help him take over the mag in the first place. I knew it……" Desmond shakes his head, chuckles and looks down towards the ground a bit. "You're just putting this all together tonight aren't ya Perry Mason?" she says sarcastically.

Desmond fixes the lapels on his jacket as he answers "You damn straight."

Lyriq is laughing. Desmond begins to laugh as well. Then he pulls up his shirt revealing his chiseled six pack abs as well as the wire taped to them. As Lyriq realizes his shirt pulled up and she sees the wire taped to his stomach, her laugh subsides into anger and shock. She finally notices that the music that was once very loud and blaring, no longer cloaked her conversation with Desmond. It is now being heard by everyone at the gala.

She is mortified with her hand over her mouth as she looks around and notices everyone staring at her. She looks up at the big video screen displaying pictures of her with Mr. Kush on vacation as well as all the emails.

Desmond begins to clap and then proceeds to say "I guess James was right about you all along."

Just as Desmond is saying that James walks up, stands next to Desmond with his arms crossed and says "Yeah!! You skandalous, poisonous, two faced HOOCHIE!" Desmond looks over at James and says "Hoochie what?" They both look at each other and smile. Then they look back at Lyriq and say in unison "Skandalous Hoochie Train"

The police walk up behind Lyriq and cuff her. Desmond and James give each other dap, and a handshake with a fancy finish.

James looks back at Lyriq as the police escort her passed them and smiles at her. Lyriq looks at him and stomps on his foot with her high heels as she passes by. The police restrain her and continue walking her out.

James is jumping up and down in pain. He then goes to get Lyriq and Desmond grabs him before he can get to her.

Meanwhile, Mr. Kush is trying to sneak out of the gala through the back entrance of the convention center. He walks out the door and a security guard grabs his shoulder. Mr. Kush turns around and decks him. Knocks the guard out cold as he falls limp to the ground.

“Don't ever touch me son!” he says to the unconscious guard.

Mr. Kush then looks down at him and turns around, fixes his tuxedo lapels. He then pulls out a cigar, cuts the end. He places the cutter back in his inside pocket, pulls out a matchbox, sparks a match, sparks the end of the cigar and takes a couple of puffs. Just as he is starting to enjoy his cigar, Mr. Elmhurst comes out of nowhere and punches him, knocking him out cold, while sending the cigar flying out of his mouth.

Mr. Kush falls down, knocked out cold, leaning up against the young security guard that he knocked out earlier. Mr. Elmhurst then fixes his coat right and sparks up a fresh cigar of his own. He cuts the end, places the cutter back in his pocket, pulls out a matchbox, sparks a match, sparks the end of the cigar, takes a couple of puffs and smiles as he walks into the Gala.

Chapter 54 MORNING AT DESMONDS

Another perfect sunrise offsets the view of the mountains as the city of Denver, Colorado is up and moving…..... as usual!

The alarm goes off and Desmond opens his eyes to find himself alone. The loud sounds of the radio on the nightstand is getting on his nerves as usual, but he smiles, smacks the clock's off button and rolls out of bed to the bathroom to begin his daily grooming process.

Desmond is suited and booted in his tailor made suit heading out the door when his phone rings and he answers it "This is Desmond Coolwater……."A very smooth and professional voice on the other end speaks. It's Mr. William Dean Elmhurst. "This is your boss. I just wanted to call and tell you how thankful and proud I am of you young man. You are one of the best investments I have ever made and I should have never doubted you.

Desmond sparks a smile immediately. "Mr. Elmhurst we are good. I wouldn't be who I am today without you, so I guess we are kind of even."

Mr. Elmhurst chuckles. "Well I guess so then huh?" Desmond starts to have flashbacks of all the recent events and then says "Well I do remember a certain conversation we were going to have a few weeks ago about some kind of partnership or something?"

"I bet you do. I expect to see you in the office after the radio interview this morning superstar. We'll talk about it from there." he says.

"Now that sounds like a plan sir." Desmond hangs up the phone and heads out the door.

COOL NIGHTS

Chapter 55 KS107.5 MORNING CREW

"So Desmond you have been caught up in some real live scandal here?" Kendall asks Desmond as they all hang out in the studio. "Yes, it was some drama." Desmond replies. "Can you share it with us a bit or can you not talk about it much since it is still an open case." The whole crew looks over at Desmond.

Desmond takes a sip of his coffee before he answers "Well it is still an open case so I can't really elaborate on it, but what I can say is that everything at Fly Magazine is still cool as water."

Kathy J sits up in her chair and smiles at Desmond as she says to the ladies listening in to the morning show "Ooooh ladies we seriously just heard it hear first. So Desmond I bet you use that with all the ladies?"

Desmond laughs. "No, I'm just me. I can't help the smooth part. I get that from my father."

Larry looks at Desmond and says "So what you are saying is that someone like Kendall can never be like you?" everyone in the studio starts to laugh. "Now there you go Larry trying to start something." Desmond chuckles and then says "I didn't say that, but I will say that it has to be in you and not just on you."

"You guys Kathy J has just had an orgasm here in the studio." the fellas laugh as the studio engineer makes a female moan shoot out the speakers and over the airwaves to the city.

Kathy J laughs as she replies. "No, no, no..... shut up Larry. It was just a flutter..... the studio engineer pushes the button and another female moan blares over the speakers in the studio.

Everyone is laughing and then Kathy ask another question. "So Desmond now that everything is back to normal, what are your plans for the magazine now?"

Desmond get serious for a moment before he answers. "Kathy,

nothing is the same with the mag now a days. Everything is better. We've gotten rid of the bullshit........ can I say that on the radio?"

Kendall looks at the others and then says "Can you say what? The word bullshit… on the radio?

Desmond seems put off by it and then Larry chimes in and says it 3 times "Yeah you can see watch this... bullshit… bullshit… bullshit…" Everyone burst out in laughter as Larry continues saying bullshit on air.

Kendall attempts to bring everyone back down and get serious with the next question. "So what happened to the hot young lady you had with you last time you were here?"

Desmond sits back in his chair as he answers Kendall. "Well she was one of the bad guys… bad girls I should call her?"

Larry chimes in and says "I bet she was a bad girl huh??" Just then the studio engineer hits the button again making the female moaning sound.

Desmond smiles as Larry hints toward Desmond knowing something about her sexually. Desmond laughs with a guilty laugh and says "I wouldn't know anything about that Larry."

Larry continues to poke fun at Desmond. "Come on man. We have to live vicariously through you… Did you sleep with the enemy?"

"Nope…" Desmond smiles. Kathy J. smiles and says "Mmm Hmm… ladies he is smiling in here. Well Desmond we won't put you on blast anymore."

Desmond smiles and says "Thank you!!"

"Yeah you have just had one hell of a couple of weeks." Kendall says. "Yeah all this just happened and played out like a real life movie on you didn't it?" Larry says as he looks over at Desmond on a serious note.

"Yes, it did." Desmond takes a deep breath and a sigh as he replies. Then Larry cracks a joke as usual and says "Well at least you didn't get killed..." everyone laughs after Larry's comment. "You know how the black man always gets killed early in the story and all."

Everyone is still laughing hard as Desmond says "Thank God it didn't go down like that right."

Kathy J, Larry and Kendall all say "**YES**" at the same time. Kathy J. then puts Desmond on the spot one more time. "So Desmond what's next for the cities most eligible bachelor?"

Desmond is sitting relaxed in the chair as he answers "Tonight I am going to chill at my favorite place to eat, relax and drink. Then go home and chill for once..." Kathy J looks over at Desmond and asks "All Alone? By yourself you mean?"

Desmond looks over at Kathy J, smiles and says "That's my secret tonight Kathy."

They all laugh and then Desmond says "No, for real though... yes, I will be going home and chilling alone." Larry and Kendall both laugh as the studio engineer comes up with the sound from a game show when a person loses some money or a turn at spinning the wheel.

"Well on a serious note Desmond we are glad we finally got you on the show and I'm sure the entire city is with us when we say thank you for coming. It has been a pleasure." Kendall reaches over to shake Desmonds hand.

Desmond stands up and Kathy J says "Yes it has been a pleasure." Kathy J reaches her hand out to shake Desmonds hand he takes her hand and kisses it in true gentleman form.

Larry then says “Oh snap! Desmond just kissed Kathy’s hand and she had her 2nd orgasm you guys.” The studio engineer pushes the female moan one more time with a scream added this time. Everyone is laughing as Desmond waves bye and walks out.

Chapter 56 A NEW DAY@FLY MAGAZINE

Desmond goes about his day as planned. He meets with Peter Dash and Mr. Elmhurst. They are in a boardroom at Fly Magazine offices working on a deal to help promote Peter Dash's energy drink.

Desmond is showing images of sketches to the gentlemen so they can see how he plans to create the promo shoot with models and the energy drink logos.

The day goes like any normal busy day for Desmond as he oversees the photoshoot and interview with Chauncey Billup's. During the shoot Chauncey is sitting on a couch with Desmond as they laugh and talk candidly. In the background there is memorabilia of all the teams Chauncey played for while they talk. Chauncey shows Desmond his rings and takes pictures with him before he leaves with his agent.

Desmond is packing up his bag and getting ready to leave after a long busy day. He walks over to James office to check on him. "What's it feel like to have your own office now?"

James begins to recite Biggie Smalls line from "Juicy" as he gets up from his desk and walks towards Desmond "*It was all a dream / I used to read WORD UP magazine / Salt-N-Pepa and Heavy D up in the limousine / Hangin pictures on my wall / Every Saturday RAP ATTACK Mr. Magic, Marley Marl / I let my tape rock til my tape popped / smokin weed and bamboo / sippin on private stock...*

Desmond laughs as he rocks back and forth with James as he raps Biggie Smalls lines. Then he asks James "Man you aren't going to ever change are you?"

"Nope, why would I do something like that?" James replies as he continues to rock back and forth to the song in his head. Desmond smiles at James and says "Hell I don't know bro. I guess I wouldn't expect any less from you. You have been a damn good friend and I appreciate you bro."

James looks at Desmond straight up and says "Ditto. Don't mention it." James puts his arm around Desmond as they walk out of his office and down the hallway. As they are walking they bump into Mr. Elmhurst. "Gentleman I am not paying anyone overtime right now so get out of my building."

Mr. Elmhurst smiles as he jokes with them. Desmond looks at Mr. Elmhurst and says "Oh no, you don't have to worry about that. I am about to leave right now and go have a nice quiet steak dinner with a few drinks and then go home." Mr. Elmhurst nods his head in agreement. "That sounds awesome! I may have to copy you on that and do it too."

James takes a look at both of them and then says "Yeah… uh I don't think so. I have a date and its that night to get freaky deaky baby."

Just then Cindy McMann walks by, pinches James butt and makes him jump a bit. She turns to smiles at him and then waves at Desmond and Mr. Elmhurst. James follows her down the hallway and they leave. Both Mr. Elmhurst and Desmond look at each other and then Desmond says "He'll learn…."

Mr. Elmhurst agrees "Yes he will"

Desmond reaches his hand out to shake Mr. Elmhurst's hand before he leaves. Mr. Elmhurst shakes his hand back and then gives him a hearty big man hug.

Desmond is caught off guard, but hugs him back as he chuckles at the hug. "I'm out of here sir. Have a great night."

"You too. See ya tomorrow Mr. Coolwater." Mr. Elmhurst stands there as Desmond walks down the hallway and out the door.

Chapter 57
@ Mynt Nightclub For Happy
Hour
#WINNING

Chapter 57 HAPPY HOUR@ MYNT CLUB

Vincent and Desmond are both sitting down at the bar while a waitress serves them drinks.

Desmond finishes his dinner and the waitress picks up his plate. Vincent takes his drink and downs it with one gulp and then motions for the waitress to pour another one for him. "So you mean to tell me after all of this, you still want to work for the magazine? I mean.... you could easily open your own promotional company and go at it all by yourself kiddo?"

Desmond nods his head as he is sipping his drink and then says "I could Vince, but after hearing your story and watching Mr. Elmhurst lose his partner through all of this, I have come to the conclusion that I do want to stay part of something bigger than just me. I'm in a great place right now. People that are around me right now I can trust them and that is priceless."

"Well I guess since you put it that way I would have to agree with you then. Sounds like your learned a valuable lesson through all this." Vincent says as he sits in his chair relaxing with his legs crossed like he's sitting on a talk show couch.

"Yes I did. I learned that all that glitters ain't gold and all that shimmy's don't deserve the Jimmy if you know what I mean." Desmond takes his shot and makes an uneasy face, but manages to hold it together. He then waves at the bartender to pour another one.

Vincent smiles at Desmond's reply. "So what are you going to do now? You have experienced living in a misogynistic playground for so long how do you know that you even want to venture to the other end of the rainbow that we call love?"

Desmond gazes into his glass as he thinks "That's the thing Vince?! I don't know, but I'm curious about it." he replies.

Vincent is still sitting there as if it's an interview. "Are you going to try and call her?"

Desmond sits there in thought for a bit before he answers, sipping and swirling the straw in his drink. "I don't know Vincent. I messed up pretty bad with her. I'm better off letting her go and just being patient. There is such a thing as love finding you right?"

Just as Desmond finishes his sentence he hears woman's voice behind him say "IS THIS SEAT TAKEN? Or should I just go someplace else to have a drink?"

Vincent sees who it is and smiles. He gets up and offers his seat to the guest as he grabs his drink and walks away. Desmond recognizes the voice and smiles before he turns around to greet her. He then turns around and there is Sincere looking as beautiful as ever. Desmond is taken back by her presence, but manages to get up and usher her into her seat.

"You can have every seat in here as long as I can sit next to you." Sincere smiles. Vincent has made it back behind the bar and makes Sincere the same drink she drank when she first came in to meet Desmond the first time. He hands it to her and she accepts it.

"Thank you Vincent." she smiles as she takes the drink.

Desmond sits back down and says "So how did you know I would be here tonight."

Sincere smiles at Desmond and says "....I listen to the radio Desmond. Matter of fact I think the entire city listened to the radio this morning knowing that you were going to be on there. A local celebrity like you on the radio. Well who would miss that?"

Desmond smiles humbly. "A local celeb huh? I don't know about all that." Sincere takes a sip of her drink and hunches her shoulders a bit. "Well thats what they say anyway."

Desmond is gazing at Sincere non-stop and asks "So how have you been?"

"Just been working. I figured I would come down here and give you a second chance at a first impression?" she replies. Desmond smiles, takes a drink, but continues to look forward. Then he gives a smart-alick reply.

"Who said I wanted a second chance at that?" he says. Sincere immediately stands up and starts to walk away. Desmond quickly jumps up and grabs her and pulls her close to him. So close that it looks like they are sharing the same breathe and then he kisses her. Sincere embraces him back and Vincent and the bartender both watch and clap for them.

They both stop kissing each other, but are still embraced with their eyes closed. Sincere then says "So....... how about you and I grab that movie and chill out now?" They both open their eyes and stare into each others eyes. Desmond smiles at her and then leans in for one more short kiss and says "Yes! Lets do that."

Justin Timberlake's song " TAKE BACK THE NIGHT" starts to play on the speakers. They are still holding each other. They finally let go of each other and Desmond digs into his pocket to pay for the meal and the drinks he had with Vincent. Vincent waves him off as he is wiping off the bar top.

Desmond grabs his coat and walks with Sincere towards the door. He opens it for Sincere to walk out first. They are walking down the city street and the backdrop is of a larger than life moon that lights their way as they walk towards it. "TAKE BACK THE NIGHT" by Justin Timberlake is still playing loudly through the clubs outside speakers as they casually stroll into the night.

THE END